Readers love *Here's to You, Zeb Pike*
by JOHANNA PARKHURST

"Parkhurst has penned a brilliant coming of age story with a deep and profound moral tucked between each glorious page."
—The Novel Approach

"Well written, engaging, moving, funny, emotionally clever, endearing and with strong lessons about life. This is the kind of Young Adult story that really adds value to a young person's perspective, makes them see the world a little differently."
—The Tipsy Bibliophile

"I really hope that lots of people read this book - especially young adults. It is a great story, beautifully written and I for one would love to hear more about Dusty and his life."

—Boy Meets Boy Reviews

"…a wonderfully amazing book that has left me feeling incredibly satisfied and hungry for more."

—Greedy Bug Book Reviews

By JOHANNA PARKHURST

Every Inferno
Here's to You, Zeb Pike • Thanks a Lot, John LeClair

Published by HARMONY INK PRESS
www.harmonyinkpress.com

THANKS
A LOT, JOHN
LECLAIR

JOHANNA
PARKHURST

Harmony Ink

Published by

HARMONY INK PRESS

5032 Capital Circle SW, Suite 2, PMB# 279, Tallahassee, FL 32305-7886 USA
publisher@harmonyinkpress.com • harmonyinkpress.com

Thanks a Lot, John LeClair
© 2016 Johanna Parkhurst.

Cover Art
© 2016 Anne Cain.
annecain.art@gmail.com
Cover content is for illustrative purposes only and any person depicted on the cover is a model.

ISBN: 978-1-63477-428-4
Digital ISBN: 978-1-63477-429-1
Library of Congress Control Number: 2016906159
Published December 2016
v. 1.0

Printed in the United States of America
(∞)
This paper meets the requirements of
ANSI/NISO Z39.48-1992 (Permanence of Paper).

This book is for the readers who wondered whatever happened to Emmitt and Dusty. What can I say? I'm a sucker for peer pressure. And it's for everyone still waiting for the world to accept them as they are.

AUTHOR'S NOTE

WHEN A tertiary hockey fan starts writing a book about a character who loves hockey, two things happen. One: she becomes obsessed with power plays and the Colorado Avalanche. Two: she wants *lots* of people to read that book in order to ensure it makes any kind of sense.

So first thing first: huge thanks to Patrick Roy and the Avs. If it weren't for you, I might have had to watch hours of Wild footage in the name of research.

Seriously, though. The following readers gave me wonderful advice and loved this story enough to keep me going when I was *so over* it: Timmy Ashton, Anna Lund, Laura Rodriguez Simons, Kimi and Emi Saunders, Shantel and Sara Schonour, and Riley Stouffer. THANK YOU—there's no way this book doesn't suck without all of you. Cody Kennedy, thanks for talking me down off of writing ledge after writing ledge. Obi-Wan would be proud.

Enormous thanks also go out to Matt Mason, hockey coach extraordinaire, who gave me line-by-line feedback on every single hockey play in this book. Someone needs to let you hold the Stanley Cup for a day, sir.

Thanks as well to the fantastic students of St. Albans Town Educational Center, who love giving authors feedback on their ideas just as much as they love books.

I want to take a moment to acknowledge all the LGBTQ athletes who inspired this work, as well as organizations such as the You Can Play Project and publications like *OutSports*. The You Can Play Project works to bring true equality to the sports world, while *OutSports* is a publication that gives important voice to LGBTQ athletes and their accomplishments. Thanks to these courageous people and organizations,

I am hopeful there *will* be an out and proud NHL player by the time this book sees print.

I would be remiss if I did not thank my husband, who has probably watched more hockey in the last few years than he ever had before in his life. You're a trooper for my writing dreams, T. Love you.

And of course, thanks to John LeClair, who showed so many small-town Vermont kids like me what a small-town Vermont kid can be capable of.

Go Avs!

PROLOGUE

WHEN I was seven years old, the coolest thing that can happen to a seven-year-old happened to me.

I met my hero. Only he wasn't my hero yet.

I don't remember as much as I'd like about that day. A lot of the experience has blurred in my mind since then. I know it was snowing, as it often is in northern Vermont in March. Not hard—the kind of snow that falls quietly around you, so quietly that sometimes you forget it's there. My mother must have dropped me off at practice on her way to an early shift at the creamery, and she probably told me my father would pick me up later. Casey didn't have practice that morning, and he'd been watching TV so intently when I left the house that he didn't even wave good-bye to me.

The lights in the rink seemed unusually bright that day. Maybe that was because we had the rink all to ourselves, which was strange—normally we shared ice time with at least one other peewee team. But our team had just made the play-offs. We were skating alone that day, because there weren't any other teams left in the area to share the ice with.

Our coach that year was Coach McAlden. He was older, with white hair. I thought he yelled too much, and I remember hoping Casey didn't have him as a coach in a few years.

Our team was sitting on benches outside of the rink waiting for practice to start when Coach told us he had a surprise for us. And then an enormous man stepped out from behind him.

He was at least three inches taller than my dad, and he probably had twice as much muscle on his limbs. His hair and eyes were dark. He was younger than our coach, but not as young as my teacher, Mr. Sanfried.

"Kids," Coach McAlden told us, "this is John LeClair. He's an old friend of mine. He's from St. Albans, right down the street from here. He played in the NHL and the Olympics. Won a Stanley Cup."

My entire world shifted in that moment.

I was only seven, but people were already asking me what I wanted to be when I grew up. Asking me what I liked to do. The problem was that I liked to do everything. Math was okay, and Mr. Sanfried said I was a good writer, and I knew I could read better than most of the kids in the class. There was only one thing I liked to do more than anything else: play hockey.

I had watched plenty of NHL games at that point, and I knew there were people who played hockey for a job. People whose entire worlds were ice rinks and pads. But up until then, it had never occurred to me that playing hockey was something people like *me* did for a living. Something people from Colby, Vermont, could do for a living. People in Colby became store owners and teachers and nurses and construction workers, or they had jobs in offices in Burlington where they did things with computers all day. They didn't become hockey players.

Only maybe they did. Because St. Albans was less than twenty miles away from Colby. If someone from St. Albans could become a professional hockey player, maybe someone from Colby could too.

"Mr. LeClair was very impressed when I told him about your season," Coach McAlden told us. "He agreed to come talk to you about what it's like to be a professional hockey player. Does anyone have any questions for him?"

My hand shot into the air. And it never really came down.

At some point he signed pictures for all of us. When it was my turn, he asked me my name.

"Emmitt," I told him. "Emmitt LaPoint. Kind of like your name!"

He laughed. "Close. You asked a lot of great questions, Emmitt."

"I have lots more," I told him. "I didn't even get to ask you about other positions you played and what it was like being on the Olympic team and—"

He laughed again. "Why don't I give you my e-mail address? You can have your parents help you send me all your other questions."

I'm sure I told him I didn't need help, even though I probably did. And then I walked away, reverently staring at a signed picture of John LeClair that said *To Emmitt—keep playing hockey, and keep having fun!*

And a scrap of paper with his e-mail address.

The first thing I did when I got home was take out a notebook and start writing. I wrote pages and pages to John LeClair that day. I asked him about his family and his friends and hockey plays and teams and everything I could think of. I wrote more words that day than I'd probably written in my entire life. It was sloppy and full of misspellings and other errors, and it's still one of the best things I've ever written.

Only I never sent it.

I'm still not sure why. All I know is that when I looked back at the pages I'd written, I already knew they weren't for anyone but me. Even though the first page had John LeClair's name at the top.

After that, though, I started writing letters to John LeClair all the time. I began filling notebooks with letters, and the collection of notebooks grew over the years. It's been over nine years since I started writing to John LeClair, and I've never sent him a single letter. All of them still live under my bed, in a bin with video games for systems that aren't sold anymore and artwork I made in elementary school. For years, every horrible and wonderful thing that happened to me lived in the pages of one of those notebooks, stuck somewhere between my life and John LeClair's.

I still write in those notebooks, but not as much as I used to. Lately I've been thinking about when that changed. I think it happened last fall, at the beginning of my junior year of high school. That's when my world shifted under me again.

That's when I met Dustin Jackson Porter.

In hockey, when you score a goal and lights start flashing and sirens go off, they say you "lit the lamp." When I first saw Dusty, it was like a million goal lights went off in my brain.

And they've been going off ever since.

CHAPTER
ONE

Dear Mr. LeClair,

Thank you for visiting my team. Meeting you was so cool. I have some qestions for you.

I am wondring if you ever won a championship game when you played peewee hockey and if you did what was it like. My team is goin to win the championship we have to becuz we work very very hard even our coach says it. He yells at us sometimes tho.

I wish I could play hockey all day long the way you get to. I love hockey so much. I think about it all the time… I like watching it and playing it and I like hockey practis. Not like my frend Seth who says hockey practis is boring I never think hockey practis is boring.

I am never going to love anything more then I love hockey.

—Emmitt LaPoint, age 7

So THERE I am, staring down a player from South Burlington for a third period face-off. This isn't the biggest game of my junior year hockey season or anything. We're nowhere near the end of the season or the playoffs yet, and that's when things are going to get intense. But you'd never think this was just a normal, regular-season game from the look of the player standing in front of me right now. His eyes are wide behind his face mask, and I can practically see the stick quivering in his hands.

It's like he knows we're about to score on his team.

4

Which he probably does. Because we're in the third period now, so he's had plenty of time to watch us play. He knows how good we are, and he must know that I know where the holes in his front line are.

Still, I'm not about to get overconfident. I've been playing hockey since I was four, and if there's one lesson I've learned in all those years, it's that pride does come before the fall... or before the loss, I guess.

I make my plan. I know where I'm heading when the puck drops, where I'm going to fake, who I'm going to pass to. I take a few deep breaths and listen, letting the crowd noise motivate me for just a split second. This may be a regular-season game, but our team, the Colby Wildcats, is also undefeated right now—and we haven't been undefeated at this point in the season in sixteen years. I doubt it's been this loud in The Lewis T. Falger Sports Complex since then.

"Emmitt, you can do it!" That's Mom's voice making it over the echo of shouting and pounding. She's been yelling louder than the rest of the hockey moms since I started playing.

"Don't go left, Em! He's expecting that!" That's Casey, my little brother. He's as loud as my mother, and he always thinks he knows more about hockey than me, even though he stopped playing years ago.

It would probably surprise most people that Coach Morton, the coach I've been playing under for three seasons now, is almost completely silent by the bench. He's patting Steve Almont's shoulder and telling him something—probably explaining our game plan in more detail. Steve's a freshman who's really good, and I know Coach's hoping he'll take my spot after I graduate next spring.

Coach doesn't need to say anything to me right now. We've worked this scenario out so many times in practice, in other games. After three seasons together, he knows exactly what I'm going to do, and he isn't going to second-guess me.

Time to block out the crowd noise and work up some serious concentration.

The ref blows the whistle, and the puck drops.

I don't think anyone is less surprised than me when my stick hits the puck first. I gain possession and pass it off to Eric Perry, our left wing, before South Burlington even realizes we've moved it between them.

It's a great last period. South Burlington scores on us one more time midway through, but by then it's way too late—we're already up by four, and they can't come back from it. When the final buzzer goes off and the home crowd realizes that yes, we're still carrying an undefeated season, there's a sudden rush of people down to the bottom of the stands. Mom and Casey are standing next to the ice waiting for me, and I can see Coach Morton's wife heading right toward him, with Matt and Julia.

It's too bad there are a few key things missing from this scene. A couple of key missing people keep this from being one of those great moments in my life.

For one thing, there's the man who first taught me to skate, who first taught me the rules of hockey. He's conspicuously absent.

Then there's the person who means more to me than anything in the world right now. He's also missing. Also very conspicuously.

But worst of all? Even if he were here, I couldn't grab him and make out with him the way Steve Almont is doing with his girlfriend right now.

Because in my world, hockey players don't get to make out with their coach's nephew in public.

"EMMITT!" COACH screams. "Where's your head? I just told you to watch the high-sticking!"

Oops. Patrick O'Sheridan, the guy on the other end of my high stick, glares at me, and I shrug apologetically. I know we've got a game against Essex coming up in a few days, and I know the practices we're having right now are all crucial if we're going to keep our undefeated status and eventually win back the state championship, but I just can't seem to get it together. My mind's on Dusty lately—has been ever since he missed our last game.

At the end of practice, which is not going to go down in history as one of my better ones, I find Coach waiting for me when I come out of the locker room. Awesome. I'm already pissed off, because I just checked my phone and discovered Dusty still hasn't texted me back about hanging out after practice. At least the man standing in front of me might be able to shed some light on the whereabouts of my absentee boyfriend.

"Emmitt, what's going on? Are you all right?"

Coach pulls me off to the side of the arena hallway, away from where all the other players are coming out of the locker room, but I still don't want to have this conversation here. There's too much of a chance of us being overheard, and I'm too paranoid. "I dunno, Coach.... Can we talk in your office?"

The door's been closed for all of three seconds when I break down like a toddler who missed naptime. "Do you know what's going on with Dusty? Why's he ignoring me?"

Coach blinks at me for a few seconds and then bursts out laughing. "That's why you were so distracted at practice today? That's why you've been glaring at everyone? Because you think Dustin's ignoring you?"

My jaw drops. I can't believe he's laughing at me. Coach is one of the *very* few people on this planet who knows about Dusty and me. He's been forced to spend countless evenings eating dinner with us and giving up his big-screen TV to us—we stay in a lot because it's hard to go out with your boyfriend when you're supposed to have a girlfriend. I kind of figured Coach, of all people, would have figured out by now how much Dusty and I are into each other.

To be fair to Coach, he's almost as new at being an uncle as I am at being a boyfriend. Coach didn't even know Dusty and his younger brother and sister existed until last fall; his sister never told him about them. Then Dusty's little sister, Julia, came down with appendicitis, and the hospital realized Dusty's parents were MIA. It turned out they'd been disappearing on and off for years while Dusty took care of Matt and Julia. Since Dusty was only fourteen, no one except Dusty was excited about letting that arrangement continue. So Dusty, Matt, and Julia got shipped from Colorado Springs to Vermont, where they've lived with Coach and his wife ever since.

Where Dusty and I first met.

Coach is still laughing, and I'm getting more and more annoyed. "Well... yeah. He missed our last game, Coach! And he keeps ignoring my calls. It feels like he's avoiding me at school. What's going on?"

Coach rubs his temples like he has a headache, and I start to feel bad for him. It can't be easy raising a niece and two nephews you only recently discovered you have, and it's got to get a hell of a lot harder when one of your nephews decides to start secretly dating your star forward.

7

"Emmitt… you have to believe me when I tell you nothing's changed for Dustin. He had a huge project due in English the Monday after that game, and working on it with his group was the responsible thing to do. He's been to all your other games. As for the school thing, I think he's just making a concerted effort to make sure you two don't get found out. He knows how important that is to you. Can you fault him for that? Weren't you the one who asked him to keep your relationship a secret?"

Now I'm starting to turn red, because that comment makes me sound like a real asshole. "Yeah, you're right. I guess I'm just being paranoid." I stop to think for a few moments too long, though, and go right back to paranoid. "But then why isn't he texting me back?"

Coach groans. "Emmitt, are you listening to yourself? You sound like some lovesick teenager!" He pauses. "Jeez, you are, aren't you?"

"Am not," I mumble. I don't like the sound of that.

Coach comes over to my side of the desk and puts his hand on my shoulder. "Emmitt LaPoint, listen to me. There aren't too many teenagers—male or female—I would be happy to see my incredibly hormonal nephew dating. I get to be at least somewhat content that Dustin is dating you… and believe me when I say that's a compliment. I get that mild sense of contentment because you, LaPoint, are one of the best hockey players I've ever had the chance to coach." I start to protest, and he puts out his hand to stop me. "I don't just mean your skill at the game, Emmitt. We both know you're one of the best this school has seen in years, and we both know you still have things to work on. I mean, you are one of the best *people* I've ever had the chance to coach—you are driven, and compassionate, and intelligent, and a genuinely good person.

"And all of that means you are just driven, intelligent, compassionate, and good enough to drive yourself crazy when things aren't going exactly the way you want them to."

He's got me there. I just shrug and look at the floor.

Coach sinks into the seat next to me. "The next few weeks? Trying to stay undefeated? Getting to the state championship? They're going to be tough on you, Emmitt. Our school hasn't gone this far in a few years…. There's going to be a lot of pressure on you." He shakes his head. "You know that after our last game, the local paper started calling you the next John LeClair, right?"

I didn't know that. Someone out there compared me to *LeClair*? My ultimate hero? The guy I've been writing secret letters to since I was seven?

"It'll only get worse as it gets closer, kid. This town is becoming convinced you're our next golden boy, and a lot of eyes are going to be on you."

"Geez, Coach," I whisper. "Was this supposed to be a pep talk? 'Cause I don't think I've ever felt less peppy."

Coach chuckles. "Well, it was and it wasn't. It was supposed to be more of a warning—a warning to let Dustin be there for you and support you when he can, rather than panic over every aspect of your relationship just because you don't want to start panicking about your game."

Is that what I've been doing? Something seems a little bit off about that, but I'm not sure why.

"And to prove it, you're going to come over to our place for dinner tonight, and see that nothing's changed with my nephew. He's helping out with Matt's basketball team tonight; that's probably why he's not answering his phone."

Maybe he's right. Maybe I really have just been trying to ignore how stressful the whole hockey thing is. Either way, I'm not going to pass up a chance to see Dusty.

Plus, Coach's cooking doesn't suck.

GOING TO eat at Coach's house is a great idea. Dusty doesn't seem at all upset that I just show up without checking with him first. He thanks Coach for inviting me and gives me an inconspicuous kiss in the hallway off the kitchen. We try to be discreet around Matt and Julia. Julia's only six and Matt just recently turned nine, and they don't really understand our relationship.

When we first decided to tell our families what was going on, we sat Matt and Julia down and tried to explain the whole thing. I was reminded there are some things you just can't explain to six- and eight-year-olds.

"So, Emmitt is your boyfriend?" Julia had asked, her brows creasing with thought. "I thought boys had girlfriends."

"They do," Dusty's Aunt Beth jumped in, "and sometimes they have boyfriends."

"Does that mean you'll get married?" Julia asked.

"Jules!" Matt rolled his eyes knowingly. "They can't get married until they're thirty."

"I'd prefer they not," Coach piped in.

From there it was a *long* conversation about how people didn't really know that we were boyfriends, because it was a special secret, so they couldn't tell people about it, and no, in this case it wasn't wrong to lie, because it wasn't really lying, it just wasn't anyone else's business… sheesh. I'd rather stick needles in my eyeballs than ever have to have *that* discussion again. So now we try to keep the mushy crap away from the kids. It's easier that way. They're definitely inquisitive, and they want explanations for everything. When Mrs. Morton and Coach started calling Dusty "Dustin," which they did because they wanted to call him something different than what his loser parents used to call him, Matt and Julia didn't stop asking them questions for days. *Can we call him that too? Is that name better? What if we just call you Dust?*

Despite that whole debacle, Matt, Julia, me, and my brother Casey still all use the name Dusty. For the three of them, it's just a habit that's hard to break. For me, it's because I've been calling him Dusty since the first day I met him, and that name is special to me somehow. Dusty doesn't mind. He says it doesn't remind him of his parents at all when I call him Dusty—he says the name feels different when it's coming from me.

We're halfway through some pretty decent burgers when Mrs. Morton brings up the newspaper Coach was talking about earlier. "Emmitt, did you see the paper from yesterday? There was an article about the team, and you were all over it."

I shake my head. "Coach mentioned it."

She gets up to take the paper from off the counter, where it's open to an article about our team. And right there is a whole sidebar about me: how I made varsity my freshman year and immediately became a leader on the team, how Rick Snyder's departure from the team has really allowed me to shine and show my ability to take the team in new directions. They've even quoted a few things I'd said to them after our victory on Saturday about how it was all a "team effort" (which I maintain is totally true, no matter how lame it sounds). The whole thing is enough to make me turn beet red again.

As if the sidebar itself isn't bad enough, the small but bolded headline at the top of it asks, "Franklin County's Next John LeClair?"

"Who's John LeClair?" Dusty asks.

Coach, Mrs. Morton, and I all whip around so fast it's amazing we don't create a wind tunnel. "Oh my God," Coach stage-whispers. "Just when you thought you were raising 'em right... keeping them off drugs and all... they ask a question like that."

"Oh, forget it," Dusty mumbles. He picks a pea off his plate and throws it at Coach. "We weren't all raised in a hockey rink."

I shake my head. "Dude, people raised on Mars know who John LeClair is. I can't believe you just asked that." I duck the pea that immediately comes my way.

Mrs. Morton grins. "Dustin, John LeClair used to play high school hockey for St. Albans, which is one of Colby's rival schools. He was so good he anchored the UVM team and played in the NHL for years. He's won Stanley Cups and Olympic medals." She gets up and starts clearing the table. "Vermont's been trying to produce another great as big as LeClair since... well, since LeClair."

Dusty, who has no tact sometimes, turns to his uncle. "Was it supposed to be you?"

Coach doesn't seem perturbed at all, though. He just smiles wryly. "Some people seem to think it would have been, but no. I was considered a walk-on in college; I was lucky to get any kind of ice time there at all. I worked hard, but I have enough self-awareness to know I was never even close to LeClair's level."

Dusty's leaning over his plate now, all kinds of engaged in the conversation. "Is Emmitt really good enough to win Samuel Cups or whatever?"

"Stanley Cup," Coach and I chorus.

"No, I'm not," I add. "At least, not yet. I'll be lucky to get enough scouts looking at me to even play for a D1 college team."

Coach shakes his head and addresses Dusty. "Yes, he is. He absolutely is. And he knows darn well the scouts are looking at him, because they've been looking at him since he was thirteen."

Dusty's eyes widen. "You've had college scouts looking at you since you were in junior high?"

I squirm and glare at Coach. I *hate* talking about this subject. "Not college scouts. Some scouts from private schools with big hockey programs. And some of the more elite junior leagues were interested in me. Leagues that feed into bigger leagues." The kind of leagues that college scouts—not to mention the NHL itself—salivate over. "The high school hockey program here isn't exactly the highest level of junior hockey… it's not like playing high school hockey in Minnesota or someplace like that. So junior players who want to make it to the big leagues someday usually don't stick around here."

"Uh… so why didn't you go?" Dusty looks confused, and I can't blame him. I've never told him about any of this, never told him how close I came to leaving Vermont before I even started high school here. Never told him how close we came to never meeting at all.

I poke at my burger. "Uh, well, that was the same time that a lot of cr—" I pause when I notice Matt and Julia hanging on to my every word. "—stuff was going on with my family. I didn't want to… you know… leave. And even when that was all over, it still didn't feel right going away."

Dusty's facial expression shifts slightly, and I know right then that he gets it. Knows I couldn't bring myself to leave my family—especially Casey—after Dad had just left us. "But if they were watching you then, they must still be watching you, right?" Dusty urges. "You're still playing hockey and everything."

Yeah, that's the hope. I shrug. "But like I said, the Vermont high school hockey programs aren't as big a deal as they are in some other states. Scouts don't exactly come running out to watch our games."

"But they will for Emmitt," Coach interjects. "They've stayed in touch. They've been keeping an eye on him. They haven't forgotten his playing, and he knows it. Even if he doesn't want to admit it." He points a fork at me gently. "Don't forget, Emmitt. John LeClair went down this exact road. UVM and the NHL both wanted him straight out of Vermont high school hockey."

That's something I tell myself a lot. That it isn't impossible, that it's been done before. But Coach and I both know I took a big risk when I decided to stay in Colby a few years ago. All I've ever wanted to do is to keep playing hockey at higher and higher levels. But the hockey world takes developing its young players very seriously, and I've already missed out on some key years of that development.

"No one's asked me to commit anywhere yet," I point out. "And I'm already a junior."

"Is that bad?" Dusty asks. There's some definite anxiety in his voice.

"Emmitt's going to be just fine," Coach tells Dusty. "His junior year isn't over yet, and he knows as well as I do that people are watching this run we're making at the championship. He's got the skill and drive. But he also gets in his own head very easily, so I try not to say things like that around him too often." He makes a huge deal of looking startled to see me sitting there next to him. "Oh, Emmitt! I didn't realize you were still here."

Now it's my turn to throw a pea across the table.

Later on, after the dishes have been cleared, Dusty and I head up to his room. We're supposed to be doing our homework, but I doubt Coach or Mrs. Morton think that's what's going to happen any more than Dusty and I do.

Dusty's room is in the tower of Coach's old Victorian house, which means it has its own staircase and everything. That makes the rule that we have to keep his door open when we're alone together a lot easier to deal with; we hear the creaking of the steps long before anyone can actually get to where we are.

We start off on the bed together with our books and pencils out, but it isn't long before those are forgotten and we're lying on our sides with our tongues basically wrapped around each other's. Dusty and I were both fairly inexperienced kissers when we first met, but I like to think we've caught up quickly.

"Wow," says Dusty, lifting himself up on one elbow so he's leaning over me. "Way to make up for ditching me for your hockey team all the time."

"Hey!" He's laughing as he says it, so I'm not actually annoyed… but this does seem like a good time to bring up the fact that he hasn't been around all that often lately either. "You're the one who missed my last game, and didn't answer my text messages today, and keeps blowing me off at school." It's obvious that I've lost any anger or paranoia over this issue when I prop myself up on my own elbow and lean over to kiss him again.

Dusty's smiling when we end the kiss. "Blowing you off at school, huh? Maybe I'll just start shoving you against lockers before first period the way O'Sheridan does every morning with whoever his flavor of the month is."

I snort. "Flavor of the month? Where do you come up with stuff like this?"

"Don't be a hater because you're not up on all the hip lingo the way we cool kids are, Emmitt." I roll my eyes. "Seriously, Emmitt. I'm really sorry I missed your game Saturday. You know that, yeah?"

The right side of his mouth is still lifted in a half smile, and his features are reflected in the low light coming from the small desk lamp in the room. Dusty is a carbon copy of his uncle, right down to his blue eyes, and sometimes it's really easy to forget he only turned fifteen a month ago. "I know that, Dusty."

"Good." Dusty moves in toward me. "'Cause I do feel like maybe I've been kind of… away or something lately. This hiding thing is just rough sometimes. I mess it up a lot, I think. And some mornings I kind of wish I could shove you into a locker. You know, in a good way."

I have to laugh at that—partly because it's such classic Dusty to clarify that pushing me against a locker would be a good thing, and partly because I know exactly what he means.

"I know," I tell him. "I worry all the time that I'm messing this up. And you have no idea how much I wish I could shove you into a locker."

The grin that lights up his face before he rolls over on top of me is enough to remind me that I need to give what I have with Dusty a lot more credit.

A creak on the stairs a few minutes later has us separating like the Pope's about to walk in. Dusty grabs his math book off the floor where it's fallen, and I've got my hands on a copy of *Macbeth* so fast the Bard himself would be proud.

"Dusty?" Julia's blonde hair falls around the corner of the half-open door. "Aunt Beth says it's my bedtime. Will you read me a story? And can Emmitt help?"

Dusty's off the bed and opening up the door for her without even asking me my opinion; he doesn't need to. We've done so many co-story sessions with Julia over the last few months that I've basically memorized *Don't Let the Pigeon Drive the Bus!* at this point.

"Sounds great," Dusty tells Julia. "What are we reading tonight?"

Julia triumphantly holds up a copy of *The Pigeon Finds a Hot Dog!* It's a testament to how much I like this kid that I don't even wince.

Dusty cleans up the textbooks around us while Julia settles on the bed next to me. "Is it exciting to be in the newspaper?" she asks me. "When Matt's class had their bake sale in the newspaper, Aunt Beth hung the picture on the fridge. Is your picture on your fridge?"

I know better than to laugh at a comment like that from the highly serious Julia. "I'm sure my mom will put the picture on the fridge. It was nice being in the paper. It was even nicer because they compared me to John LeClair, and he's one of my heroes."

Julia nods, and Dusty looks up from where he's putting his laptop back on his desk. "I didn't know that."

"Yeah." I hoist Julia into my lap, and she lies back against my chest. "I met him when I was seven, and I decided I wanted to play in the NHL just like him. He even gave me his e-mail address, and I started writing letters to him."

"No kidding." Dusty comes back over to the bed and sits down. "You've sent this John LeClair dude letters?"

"Not exactly. I started writing them, but I never sent any of them." I feel weird admitting that I've been writing letters for over nine years now, but this is Dusty. If anyone's going to understand my pile of notebooks, it's him. "I, ah, guess I've been writing him letters all along—ever since I was just a little older than you, Julia. But they just sit under my bed. Sort of like a diary or something."

"Wow. You've been writing letters to this guy for that long, and now you're getting compared to him? That's crazy, Emmitt." Dusty looks impressed.

I shrug. "I'm just glad you don't think I'm a crazy person for writing all these letters I never send."

Dusty shakes his head. "No way. I… kind of write letters like that to Race sometimes. I've never sent one of 'em either." He looks pained, and I decide to let that subject drop. Race was Dusty's best friend back in Colorado Springs. Dusty still hasn't been able to figure out how to tell Race that he's dating a guy.

Julia taps at my arm. "I want to write letters like you did, Emmitt. Can you help me? Did someone help you?"

"Nope," I tell her. "I never told anyone. I just wrote them all by myself."

Julia looks horrified. "But what if you spelled something wrong?"

Dusty and I can't help but burst out laughing at that. Leave it to the six-year-old perfectionist Julia to worry about spelling errors. We both tone it down when Julia's face starts to take on this incredibly hurt look she gets sometimes. "I didn't worry about that, Julia. I just wrote the letters. Spelling and grammar and all that stuff didn't matter to me."

"Plus, Julia, this is Emmitt. I bet he could barely make a spelling mistake if he tried, even when he was your age." I glare at Dusty, but he's not *that* far off. Though I definitely made some mistakes when I was seven, I've always been weirdly good at things like spelling and grammar—probably because I've always read a ton. Even now I get the occasional teacher who thinks I plagiarized a paper because there are so few mistakes in it.

"I wish I never made mistakes," Julia tells us. "I don't like making mistakes at school. I feel dumb."

"Hey!" I say, patting her head. "You can't think like that, Jules. Making mistakes is how we learn things."

Dusty snorts. "Says the kid who never, ever makes a mistake."

I look up at him, surprised and almost a little hurt. Does he think that's true? I sure as hell don't feel that way. Especially when it comes to whatever Dusty and I are trying to build together.

Dusty must read something in my face, because he smiles. "I didn't mean it as a bad thing, Emmitt. I like that you and Julia always want to be perfect." He nudges Julia's shoulder. "But neither of you need to be perfect. Got that, Julia? Emmitt's right. You learn from mistakes. It's okay to make them." He takes the book from her and opens it. "You read the first half to us tonight, and then we'll switch."

She nods and starts sounding out words. I think about what Dusty just said.

Neither of you need to be perfect.

I wish I believed that. I wish I believed in what I said to Julia, about how making mistakes is just the way we learn.

But there's a newspaper article downstairs ready to remind me that any mistake I make isn't just going to cost me. It's going to cost a lot of other people as well.

And there's a guy sitting across from me on his bed, reading to his little sister, who I never want to screw things up with.

CHAPTER
TWO

Dear Mr. LeClair,

It's happening again, and I don't know what to do.

Today Coach had me show his nephew around school. Maybe I didn't tell you Coach had a nephew, because I didn't know. He didn't know. He just found out the guy existed. Turns out he has another niece and nephew too, but they're both in elementary school. This one's a freshman, like Casey. Anyway, they're all coming to live with Coach, but I don't know exactly why. Maybe their parents took off like Dad did.

So I was showing this guy, Dusty, around school, and it happened again. That feeling. He's hot. Skinny, but not too skinny, shorter than me, but not too short, dresses like he's half preppy and half skater. He looks a LOT like Coach—which is creepy—but his hair's a lighter brown, almost more blond, and his eyes are this color that's so bright blue I didn't think it could exist.

Yeah. So he's good-looking. And he's funny, and he's definitely smart, and I know he and Casey are going to want to hang out; they'll get along great. Halfway through the tour, all I could think about was how much I wanted to try to kiss him. Or, you know, at least go out with him.

But what was I supposed to do, ask him to the movies? Right there in the middle of the hallway?

Life sucks today. This was even worse than the first time I realized I liked Alcott. At least with Alcott, I knew he liked me before I decided I liked him. And I haven't liked anyone that way since then, I guess.

This guy, though? Dusty? I could definitely like him. More than Alcott. And he's never going to know—because there's no way he's like me.

17

I don't know what to do.

—Emmitt LaPoint, age 16

"WHAT ARE you *doing*?" I'm yelling down the rink at Eric, who just iced the puck for no reason I can figure out. Coach is already screaming, and Eric is already blaming Shaun LeRoy, who's shouting about how the whole thing is Doug Czychovi's fault. Which is kind of funny, because Dougie is the goalie and wasn't even involved in the play.

It takes all of two minutes for Coach to assemble us back at the benches for a larger version of the pep talk he gave me yesterday. The shortened version: "Lots of pressure… blah blah blah… can't let it get to us… blah blah blah… one of the best teams I've ever had the pleasure of coaching… blah blah blah…."

Not that he's wrong or anything. I just figure I've already gotten this talk, and, as successful as it might have been, I don't really need it twice. So I sort of tune him out.

I'm giving Eric a ride home later when it dawns on me that maybe I should turn on more of this "leadership" I keep getting complimented on. It's not that I think all these people who keep calling me a leader are totally wrong—I know I have a tendency to take charge of situations and people. I've been doing that for my family ever since my dad left years ago, and I've sort of been naturally doing it on our team for as long as I can remember, because our ex-captain Rick Snyder was such an asshole nobody wanted to listen to him.

It's just that I never really *thought* of myself as a leader before this week.

Still, Eric's my friend, and I'd ask him what was up even if we weren't co-captains of a team with a state championship on the line. "Eric, you okay?"

He shrugs. "Fine, Emmitt."

Yeah, right. "Um… you sure? You seemed a little out of it at practice today."

"Like you always have perfect practices," he snaps.

"Uh… yeah. That's true." His anger catches me a little off guard. I mean, Eric and I have been friends since I made varsity when I was just a freshman. He's a year older, so he sort of showed me the ropes.

"Not that you'd know it from the newspaper or anything."

Oh. So that's what this is about. Suddenly the puzzle pieces snap into place. Eric is the one looking to play college hockey next year. He's the one who needs sidebar articles in the paper; I'm only a junior. "Dude, you know I didn't ask them to write that, don't you? I don't even know where they got half of that."

He shakes his head and scoffs. "Emmitt, you're not that great at being humble, okay? Stop trying."

Personally, I think I kind of rock at humility… but that's too ironic for me to think about, so I shut up.

We get to Eric's house, and he sighs before he opens the door to the truck. "It's not you, okay? Not really. Just kind of hard to be the senior in the junior golden boy's shadow." On that note he closes the door hard and starts pulling his gear out of the back of the truck.

Leaving me pretty damn humbled, I guess.

THE NEXT day, I find Dusty before our lunch period and ask if he wants to go to Burger King with me. This is actually pretty risky for several reasons. I'm a junior on the high honor roll (and usually much more humble about that fact), so I can go off-campus for lunch, but Dusty is a lowly freshman and technically can't. Plus Coach flips out if we eat fast food. He says it's poison for athletes.

I don't care, though. I need to get away from the school crowd for a while. Dusty and I usually eat at this huge table with a bunch of hockey players and friends of Dusty and Casey's from their skateboarding club, and I don't feel like seeing any of those people today. Especially Eric. It's bad enough I'm going to have a two-hour practice with him tonight after school.

"Emmitt, are *you* trying to get me to break a rule?" Dusty's mouth is twitching; this usually works the other way. I didn't get my golden-boy reputation by being constantly rebellious.

I sigh. "Yeah. We can invite Casey if you want. I just need some space from this place for a minute."

I must look or sound desperate, because Dusty instantly agrees.

I meet him at the side door by the gym, where we're less likely to get caught. We've almost made it out when I hear a noise from behind me.

"Emmitt!"

All I want to do is ignore the high-pitched voice and keep walking, but Dusty's already turned around, so it would be rude if I didn't. I stop and glance back over my shoulder.

It's Dawn Pikadoy, my lab partner in physics class. She's surrounded by a group of giggling girls.

"Skipping out?" she teases, sidling up to me and away from her group.

"Nah. I'm on honors—I have off-campus privileges."

"Sweet! Me too. Where are you guys going?"

Crap. "Uh… we're not sure yet. We were just going to drive around and maybe do some Burger King."

One of Dawn's giggling lackeys has started chatting up Dusty— who is she? Why does she know him? This trip suddenly has *epic fail* written all over it.

"That's cool. Maybe next time. Listen, Emmitt…." She starts playing with her fingernail polish, and I start to get nervous.

I'm sure most teenage guys have trouble talking to girls. I have trouble with the fact that I *don't* have trouble talking to girls. Because I've never found girls all that attractive, I've never worried about what they think of me. This makes me look really confident around girls, which seems to encourage them.

Vicious cycle, but it's kind of worked to my advantage—I've always had a date for a dance, or a party, and I didn't let anyone get attached. The whole thing sort of makes me look like a player, but I've always preferred that to the whole school knowing I'm actually into guys.

"Umm…." Dawn's fidgeting, and I know what's coming. She's about to ask me to the Winter Ball, which is the week after the state championship. At least I'm prepared when she finally blurts it out.

Dusty's not. His eyes narrow, and I realize this is the first time we'll have to deal with a situation like this.

"Geez, Dawn, that's really nice. It is. I just… I kind of don't want to commit to going to that yet, you know? If we lose the game or don't make it to the championship, I'll probably still be holed up in my room crying."

That gets some chuckles from her group, but it only seems to egg Dawn on. "Well... if that happens, we could always hang out together that night, and I could cheer you up."

Some people just can't take rejection gracefully.

I put her off with some lines about seeing how things go, and I finally get Dusty out the door without Dawn and her crew a few minutes later. Sadly, they've taken up most of our lunch period. Now we'll have to go through the drive-through.

The car is quiet. "This whole secrecy thing kind of sucks, sometimes, you know?" Dusty finally says. "Do you ever think about us... you know... telling people?"

"Sure." I say it quickly, because it's true. I think about it all the time. I think about taking Dusty with me to the Winter Ball, and Junior Prom, and us going out to the movies together without worrying what people think.... I think about not having to hide out in our houses all the time. I think about making out with him after hockey games. "But I still don't think I can, Dusty. There's just so much on the line, you know? All I've ever wanted is to play hockey. Hopefully even NHL hockey someday. Who knows if all that will still happen if people find out?" I shake my head. "You see what it's like, Dusty. There aren't exactly gay college hockey and NHL players hanging out all over the place."

"I know. I just thought.... Sometimes I think it would be really nice if everyone just *knew.* Casey's really cool about it."

"Casey's my *brother*," I point out. "That doesn't count."

"If it wasn't for hockey, Emmitt, do you think you'd be willing to try? Telling people, I mean?"

I'm a little surprised he's taking the conversation this far. Last I checked, Dusty was just as nervous about telling people as I am. "Dusty, I thought you were okay with us keeping this on the DL."

"I was...." He sighs. "I am. I just don't like the idea of you going out with that chick."

I grab his hand and hold it against the cool seat of the truck. "No worries there, Porter. I'm not going anywhere with her."

He gives me one of his amazing grins, and Eric and Dawn both seem to melt away.

CHAPTER
THREE

Dear Mr. LeClair,

Hi. Are you having a good week? I hope you are. I'm having a terrible week. My mom and dad have been fighting all the time again.

I thought they were stopping and they were going to get along again. But they're not. Last night Dad came home late from work, and Mom was yelling at him about how he never thinks of anyone but himself, and Dad said to Casey and me, "Do you both think that's true? Do you think I don't care about you?"

"Don't bring them into this!" Mom shouted back.

It was awful.

I think they were fighting about money. They fight about that lots. We never seem to have enough. We always have food in the house and everything, but there's always something there isn't enough money for, and then they fight about it. That makes me feel really bad, because I know hockey is expensive. Last month I told Mom I would quit if that would make her and Dad stop fighting.

She hugged me. "Emmitt," she said, "playing hockey makes you happy, and I don't ever want you to quit unless it's not making you happy anymore. I don't want you to worry about this anymore, okay? I promise I will be honest with you if Daddy and I need you to quit playing."

My mom is the best. I'm going to get a job this summer anyway, though, so I can try to pay for some of my own stuff next year. I bet I can get a paper route. And at least next time O'Sher makes fun of me because my pads are old, I won't feel embarrassed. I will be proud because I know my parents work hard to get this stuff for me.

Anyway, I don't know exactly what Mom and Dad were fighting about tonight, but I bet it was money again. Casey came into my room with me, and we both put on our headphones and listened to music together until we fell asleep. Casey didn't want me to see it, but I think he was crying.

They're going to get divorced, right? I think that's going to happen. And then what will happen? Will Casey and I have to live in different houses or something? I never want to live without my brother.

I hate this week.

—Emmitt LaPoint, age 12

MAYBE I need to start skipping lunch with the crew every day, because practice that afternoon goes great. Eric is back on his game, and the whole team seems to have synced up together again. Coach is happy, I'm happy, everybody's happy. I've decided not to second-guess the whole thing too much, but it does make me wonder if Eric and the other seniors on the team would rather see less of me these days. I'm not sure I can blame them.

I arrive home to find Casey glued to some skateboarding video game. "'Sup?" he calls as I walk by him.

"Nothing much. Practice was good."

"I heard Dawn asked you out."

I roll my eyes. Casey and Dusty were tight even before Dusty and I were together, and my world has gotten awfully small since I started dating my brother's best friend—no secrets left here. "Yeah. I felt bad about that. Thought Dusty was going to gouge her eyes out."

"Think he wanted to." That's how Casey likes to talk to me, in sentence fragments.

"It's all good, though." That's how I usually talk to him, in half thoughts. My mom jokes that Casey and I adopted our own language years ago for the sole purpose of leaving her out of our conversations.

"Ma coming home?" I call from the kitchen.

"Working. Eat yet?"

"Nah. You?"

"Nah."

"Burgers?"

"With barbeque sauce."

I start cooking, and he keeps playing. This is a typical night for us, and I don't mind it at all. It feels comfortable. Our family's financial situation has never exactly been perfect, and things have only gotten tighter since my parents' divorce. Mom's been working overtime at the dairy co-op in Colby basically since the day my dad walked out, and I've been cooking for me and Casey basically since the day after that. Good thing I learned, too, or we would live on macaroni and cheese.

Eventually Casey wanders over to the kitchen area, just in time to pull some salad out of the fridge, and we eat while we watch some bad reruns on TV. It's a chill night, all in all.

Until Casey turns on the laptop we share to start his homework—which is really code for *get on Facebook and write to girls*. Next thing I know, he's smacking me on the arm. "Look. Now."

I haven't heard Casey sound this shell-shocked since he found out learning to skateboard was actually going to require practice on his part—it didn't require much—so I turn off the TV and look over his shoulder.

My dad took off when I was thirteen and Case was about eleven. He lives in Ohio now, where he has a whole new family we've never met. We haven't seen him since I was in junior high. Not once. He has never invited us to visit him. He has never visited us. He calls us every few months. If that.

And he's never e-mailed us. Not once. So I'm more than a little shell-shocked myself to see this e-mail blinking away on the computer screen.

To: clapoint@colbyhs.edu, elapoint@colbyhs.edu
From: alex.lapoint@westinggroup.com

Subject: Looking forward to seeing you both

Hi boys,

Sorry it's been awhile since I've been in touch—work's been busy, and little Gina's been quite a terror now that she's walking! Honestly, it reminds me of when Casey learned to walk; I thought we'd never be able to keep up with him.

I wanted to reach out because I heard how well things are going with Emmitt's hockey team this year. I know I haven't been around much over the past few years, but I would really like to be there to see a game or two during the rest of this season—especially if you make it all the way to the state championship AND get the undefeated season! I've decided to fly in for the game next week and stay with your Uncle Dave for a few days. That way I'll get to spend some time with both of you.

Looking forward to seeing you soon!

Love,
Dad

Casey and I stare at the computer until I finally lean over and close it.

Casey swears.

I reach over and open it up.

Casey swears again.

I reach over and close it.

And then we both do our homework and go to bed without mentioning it again.

We manage to not talk about the e-mail until the ride to school the next morning. Mom is still asleep when we leave, and I have no idea if she even knows Dad is about to show up in Colby next week.

"What a prick," Casey finally says as we pull into the high school parking lot.

"Yup."

"Coming back just to show you off, you know."

"I know. He was always into our athletic stuff—I should've known, I guess."

Casey shrugs. "Wonder if he's still pissed that I don't play anymore."

I shrug back. "Probably." When Casey told Dad—over the phone, of course—that he'd quit hockey, Dad laced into him about how Casey was ruining his entire future. Which of course just made Casey even more unlikely to ever pick up hockey again.

"Wonder how he got the news?"

"Probably Uncle Dave."

Most of my dad's family still lives around here, but we haven't had a lot to do with them since Dad left. He and Mom didn't end things on good terms, and his family definitely blames her.

"Probably."

"Emmitt…." Casey looks at me hesitantly. "Are you going to see him? Catch up? All that crap?"

One of the biggest things Dusty and I first bonded over is how seriously we both take our roles as big brothers. Nobody ever got how protective I am of Casey… until Dusty. He gets it. He gets it completely. He gets that I'm the best male role model Casey's had in recent years, that I've had to be the person looking out for Casey and taking care of him ever since Dad left. Dusty gets that I have to take that seriously, because our mom is doing the best she can, and she needs someone else to pick up the slack.

I wish Dusty were here right now. He'd tell me what to say.

"Can I use a lifeline?" I joke.

Casey stares out the window, and I realize that was probably the wrong answer. "I mean, I think I kind of have to, Case. I mean, he's coming to my game."

"So?"

"Yeah, I know."

"I don't want to see him, Emmitt."

I've been Casey's protector for so long—since long before Dad left. Since he started walking, since his first day of kindergarten, since he stopped playing hockey and started wearing shirts with weird slogans and took up skateboarding, a sport I have never, ever gotten and probably never will. Most of the time he doesn't need my protection, but when he does, I think I'll always have this feeling that I'd rather die than let him down. So even though I've got no idea how I'm going to keep Dad from seeing him for an entire week, I say, "So you won't."

AT LEAST the small world I live in ensures that I don't have to relay crappy news too many times. By the time I see Dusty at lunch, Casey's already filled him in. We're back at the lunch table today, mostly because there's no way

I'm going to leave Casey alone right now, and I can't figure out how to sneak him *and* Dusty out without getting them both caught.

"Your dad's coming back, huh?"

Dusty's eyes are filled with sympathy, and it feels good to know that he, at least, does get it. His dad was a much bigger letdown than mine ever was. Dusty's pretty sure his dad was dealing drugs most of the time he was growing up, and when Julia got appendicitis and Dusty begged his dad to get his shit together so social services wouldn't send Dusty, Matt, and Julia to Vermont, his dad basically blew him off. "Yup," I tell him. "Gotta show off how athletic we LaPoints are, you know. What a prick. He hasn't even seen me skate since I was in, like, junior high."

Eric overhears. "Dude, your dad is coming back? I thought you guys didn't talk to him."

I reach over him for the ketchup. "We don't. Not much, anyway. But now he wants to show back up and see us again because he heard the team is undefeated."

Eric shakes his head. "Man, that's screwed-up." He punches me on the shoulder, and I start to wonder if maybe one decent thing will come out of my father's crazy selfish behavior.

Patrick O'Sheridan ruins that pretty quickly. "Like he could miss this! The next John LeClair—with a perfect GPA and everything—is his kid. You'd show up too!" He shakes his hamburger at me. I just roll my eyes.

"I don't have a perfect GPA, Pat." It's close, but it's not perfect. I actually got a B+ in World History last year. Either way, O'Sher's ruined the moment Eric and I just had, and Eric is back to scowling at his mashed potatoes.

Patrick isn't done, though. "Better start dating Dawn soon, Emmitt, so you can show off a hot girlfriend too!" The other hockey guys at the table start hooting, and Doug goes off about how easy Dawn is.

Dusty concentrates on his cheeseburger.

Mom's actually home for dinner that night, all excited to hear about our days at school and gossip about one of her coworkers, and I decide it's time to find out if she knows about the e-mail.

"So Carla's son—you guys probably know him, I think he's in your grade, Casey, his name's Scott—well, he decided he wanted to get a *nose ring*. And of course he didn't tell her; kid's completely out of control. So when she came home and found him with it, you won't believe what she did. She—"

That's it. I can't let Mom babble on about Carla's stupid kids much longer. I mean, I do know Scott, and he's a total dick. "Mom, Dad e-mailed us. He's coming to visit," I blurt out.

Casey almost spits out his Chicken Helper. "Geez, Emmitt, lead with something, will ya?"

Mom's just looking at me, blinking. "What? Did you say your father is coming to visit?"

I nod. "He, uh, heard about our hockey season. Says he's coming to our next game. Actually, do you know how he got our e-mail addresses?"

My mom looks a lot like me. She's got the same darker blonde hair, the same green eyes, and her face is shaped the same. So I've always known what I look like when I'm pissed off.

And I'm seeing it right now.

She gives us a tight smile and shakes her head. "I gave him your e-mail addresses. I thought maybe staying in touch would be… easier that way."

My mom's a class act. She never talks crap about my dad, no matter how much right she has to. The fact that she didn't just say "I gave him your e-mail addresses because he never remembers to call and it was pissing me off" is just one more testament to how amazing she is.

Casey leans over and pats her arm. "Ma, you okay? I mean, I don't even want to see him. Emmitt can just write him back and tell him to forget it." He pats her again, totally avoiding my eyes.

Mom frowns. "Don't be silly, Casey. He's your dad. Of course you should both see him if you want to." She gets up and starts putting dishes in the sink.

"Why would we want to see him?" Casey pokes at what's left of his food. "Ma, the guy's an asshole."

Mom looks up sharply from where she's rinsing dishes. "Casey, don't talk about your father that way. And don't swear."

"Why can't I talk about him that way? After he took off like that and married that other chick?" Casey practically throws his fork down onto his plate. "I don't even like talking to him on the phone when he calls."

It wasn't always that way, and Mom and I both know it. When Dad first left, Casey would run to the phone every time Dad called. He'd ask Mom every day when Dad was going to call again. Then the calls got further and further apart and shorter and shorter in length. At some point Casey started asking Mom to tell Dad he was busy when he called, or he'd answer all Dad's questions in monosyllables and hand the phone to me as fast as he could.

"Do you want to see your dad, Emmitt?" Mom asks me quietly over the sound of the running water.

I can't help it. I hesitate.

The thing is, I don't *want* to see him. Not really. But he is my dad. It's been a long time since he was at one of my hockey games, and the only reason he's come back to see one is because my team is doing so well. "I don't know. I mean, I don't, not really, but…." I don't know how to explain it, so I stop trying.

Mom just shakes her head. "Listen, boys, you know I think it's important that you both keep a relationship with your father. If he's making the effort to come back and see you, I think you should meet that effort. But," she adds as Casey starts to protest, "you're both in high school now, and you can make your own decisions. If you don't want to see him, I'm certainly not going to make you."

"Good," Casey tells us, "because I don't want anything to do with that assh—that guy. All those years of practically nothing, and now he decides to show up. He just wants to brag about Emmitt. All the guys at lunch said so too!" Mom and I both know what he's thinking: that Dad hasn't ever bothered to come back to visit because of something Casey's accomplished.

Things are looking like they could get out of hand here. "Casey, calm down. You don't have to see him, I promise. I'll make sure you don't. And…." I take a little bit of a breath. "Mom, I'm not sure I want to either. Especially after what he did to you."

Mom turns off the water and turns around to face us. "Boys, I appreciate how much you both care about me. I always have, and I always will. But I don't need the two of you to stand up for me. My marriage to your father was a mess long before he left and met that other woman; we all know it. He's not entirely at fault here, and you both need to remember that."

Casey's still scowling, though, and I know why. It's never *felt*, somehow, like my parents carry equal fault in the divorce. Maybe because Dad's the one who left and moved to Ohio, or maybe because he got married so quickly after things were over with my mom.

I'm not sure exactly why I feel like he still owes our family something. All I know is that's how it feels for me, and I'm fairly certain that's how it feels for Casey.

When dinner's over, I call Dusty. He'll get it… whatever *it* is. Somehow I know he will.

"Man," he says when I tell him about my mom's reaction at dinner. "So he really didn't tell her he was writing to you guys, huh? Or that he was coming?"

"Nope. That's my dad—does whatever the fuck he feels like."

"Huh. He's got balls, I guess." Dusty sounds almost impressed. "Emmitt? Can I ask you something? You never talk about what your dad was like when you were growing up. Was he always a dick? When you were little and stuff?"

There's this picture on my desk that was taken when Casey and I were young, probably four and six. Mom and Dad took us skating that day at the local rink, and in the picture we're all posed together. We look happy. It's hard to remember sometimes that there are a lot of pictures like that somewhere in this house, buried in albums and on old computer drives.

"No," I tell Dusty. "He was a good guy. He taught me and Casey to skate, you know. And my mom, actually. He signed us up for hockey; I probably never would have played if it wasn't for him. He tried to come to every game Casey and I had, for all the sports we played. But the older I got, the more I'd hear him and my mom fighting. And there were always money problems, and they fought about that and other stuff, and eventually he started working more and coming to fewer of our games… but sometimes that happened with Mom too, so I'm not sure how much I noticed. And then one day he was gone. Just like that."

"No shit," Dusty says softly. "It was kind of the same way with my dad. He was great when I was little. The older I got, the more he disappeared. Sometimes I think the worst part about it is that Matt and Julia never got to see much of the good side of him."

I think about Casey's reactions at dinner tonight. He's not that much younger than me, but he's just enough younger that our dad's leaving hit him a lot harder than it did me. "I know exactly what you mean," I tell Dusty.

"So, what are you going to do? Are you going to see him?"

"I meant what I told Mom. I don't know. At all."

"But you want to."

I knew he'd say the right thing. Dusty usually knows what I'm thinking before I know myself; it's been that way since the first time we kissed. Maybe before that.

"Yeah. I guess maybe I do."

"Emmitt...." Dusty pauses for a second before he goes on. "Listen, you can't be upset with yourself for wanting to see your dad. It doesn't make you love your mom any less or whatever. Hell, Emmitt, if my dad suddenly showed up, and I wanted to see him, I hope Jack wouldn't think it meant he's not my uncle anymore or that I don't care about him."

"Would you?" I asked. "Want to see him, I mean?"

Dusty doesn't answer right away. Since his dad basically abandoned him, Matt, and Julia when Julia was dying of appendicitis, I almost feel like if Dusty says yes, I'm justified in wanting to see my dad. At least my dad still tries to call us once in a while.

Finally Dusty answers. "I don't know, Emmitt. But I can't say for sure that I wouldn't."

I STARE at the blinking cursor on my computer screen for a while that night, but I finally figure out what to e-mail back.

To: alex.lapoint@westinggroup.com
From: elapoint@colbyhs.edu

Subject: Re: Looking forward to seeing you both

Hi,

I thought I'd let you know that I got your message. I guess I'll see you at the game on Wednesday.

I want to make sure you know in advance that Casey won't be there. He's not really interested in seeing you right now. I'm busy, so I'm not sure how much time I'll have, but we can probably talk for a few minutes after the game.

Anyway, have a safe trip. I'll see you soon.

Emmitt

THE DAY before our next game rolls around, and Casey and I haven't talked much about my dad since I sent that e-mail. I've had insanely long practices for days, and Casey keeps holding skateboarding club meetings.

The meetings are a total nod to how Casey handles stress. It's the middle of winter, so there's not much skateboarding to be done in the snow, and all the club can do is watch videos and talk about the petition they recently made to the town council asking for a new skate park. Casey just needs something to do this week rather than sit around and think about our dad coming, so he keeps calling meetings. Dusty's a good best friend, so he keeps going.

After practice I find a text from Dusty asking if Casey and I want to come over for dinner. With Dad coming tomorrow, the tension in our tiny house is going to be about as thick as butter. I text back that I'll check with Casey, and then I head home to shower and change.

When I get there, I discover Casey is researching chinchillas. "They make great pets, Emmitt!" he tells me, showing off a picture of something that appears to be a cross between a kitten and a rat.

The boy doesn't handle stress well. I text Dusty that we'll be over soon, and we take off.

Dusty must have clued Mrs. Morton in on what will be going on the next day, because she very politely doesn't mention anything about our father and keeps the dinner conversation on topics like school and Julia's upcoming talent show. Nine-year-old Matt is sort of in awe of Casey—he tends to follow him around whenever Casey goes over there with me—so he spends most of the meal telling Casey every single thing that's been going on in his life since the last time they saw each other.

It's actually kind of perfect. Casey is completely distracted. Dusty and I hold hands under the table.

We're nearly through dessert when Dusty's cell phone starts ringing. He keeps declining the calls, but whoever it is keeps calling. Coach finally just tells Dusty to take it in the other room; he and Mrs. Morton have a weird thing about answering the phone at the dinner table. I don't think too much about the phone calls. Their mom still calls them once in a while, so it's probably her.

Only this time Dusty doesn't call for Matt and Julia to talk to her after he's done. In fact, by the time dessert is over, he still hasn't come back. Matt is still chattering at Casey about his last basketball game, so I help Mrs. Morton clean up and then head off to see what happened to Dusty.

He's coming through the hall toward the kitchen, but his eyes aren't on anything in front of him. Instead, they're focused on the floor, and they're as narrowed as they were the day Dawn asked me out. Like he's pissed off at something.

"Dusty? You okay?"

He glances up. His hard eyes soften… and then do something I've rarely seen them do when he's looking at me. They harden again.

"Fine. You and Casey leaving?"

What the hell happened to him? Just a minute ago he was holding my hand and nudging my knee under the table. "Um, I was going to see if you wanted to watch a movie or something. You know, keep Casey occupied with me."

"Oh, sure. If you want." But his eyes are still hard, and I'm starting to get worried.

"Dusty, what's up? Did I do something wrong?"

He blinks and suddenly shakes his head, and it's like a dog shaking off the flea that's been bugging him for hours. His eyes relax, and his mouth turns up in a hint of a smile.

"Not you. Just… bad phone call."

"Was it your mom?"

"Yeah. Yeah, it was."

Something's wrong. I don't think Dusty's ever lied to me before, but I'm damn sure he's lying to me now… or not telling me something important.

33

I'm not as upset about that as I probably should be, though. I get not wanting to talk about things. It was a real relief for me when Casey told Dusty about our dad coming back before I had to. Not because I didn't want Dusty to know, but just because I didn't feel like telling anyone about it. If that phone call had anything to do with his family, I bet he feels the same way right now.

His mom's always jerking him around. She's a real trip—she showed up in Vermont last fall, right after Dusty, Matt, and Julia had gotten settled here, claiming she'd fixed up her life and wanted them back. Then she took off again in the middle of the night without telling anyone. Dusty caught her.

I wouldn't be surprised if Dusty looked that way every time he got off the phone with his mom. And I can't exactly blame him for not wanting to talk about her.

So I don't push it. We watch *Charlie and the Chocolate Factory* with Casey and Matt and Julia. Julia falls asleep on my lap and Matt falls asleep on Dusty's. Dusty walks us out, and kisses me good night, and Casey pretends to be grossed out. Casey and I drive home and don't talk about the fact that our father is coming to town tomorrow.

The only thing I can say for sure is that there's a whole lot of pretending and ignoring going on.

CHAPTER FOUR

DEAR MR. LeClair,

You won't BELIEVE what happened yesterday.

For one thing, Dad called. That was crazy enough. He hasn't called since Casey's birthday, and I was starting to think he'd forgotten our number or something.

The conversation started out okay. Mostly just me telling him about how freshman year is going. How hockey tryouts are coming up. I'm hoping I'll make the varsity team as a freshman, but I guess that almost never happens. Then Dad said of course I'd make varsity, and he bugged me again about how I shouldn't even be playing in Colby anyway, how I should have taken that scholarship to Deerfield Academy or considered going to play for that midget team in Michigan. He pisses me off so much sometimes. Doesn't he get that he's pretty much the reason I'm playing in Vermont? He decided to leave, so I decided to stay. I mean, I can't explain that to him, though. He'd never get it. He'd just say something like, "You have to do what's best for you, Emmitt."

Asshole.

Then he said he had something to tell me. And you won't believe it, because it's psycho. He's getting married again! He already met some other woman out there in Ohio. I guess they work together. And she's pregnant, and they're all happy about it, so they're getting married.

I'm going to have a sister. I guess. Will she even be my sister? Like Casey is my brother? It's not like we're even going to Dad's wedding or anything. They're getting married at some courthouse in Ohio, and he didn't even ask us to come. Not that I would have wanted to.

I wonder what Dad will be like with this new kid. I wonder if he'll love her more than me and Casey, since he'll be around her all the time. The truth is that I'm not sure how much my Dad loves Casey and me right now. He says he does. He ends every phone call with, "I love you, son."

But if he still loved us the same way he used to, wouldn't he try to visit once in a while? Or call us more often? He used to be this awesome dad. When we were little, he'd bring us hot chocolate at the end of hockey practices, and he'd have us hold it to warm up our hands while he unlaced our skates and helped us take off our pads. We'd tell him what we worked on in practice, and he'd rub our feet to warm them up.

Casey wasn't home when Dad called. Dad asked if I could tell him the news. I don't want to, but I guess I have to.

I wish I didn't always end up doing whatever my dad wants me to do.

—Emmitt LaPoint, age 14

WHEN I get up the next morning, Mom is in the kitchen making coffee. She pours me a cup before I can even sit down. "Game today?" she asks.

"Yeah."

"So your Dad's going." She says it quietly, like she hasn't just pointed out the elephant in the room.

"Yeah, I guess. I told Casey he shouldn't come to the game. He's not ready to see Dad yet. Maybe soon, but not yet."

She pulls bread out of the toaster and starts buttering slices. "You know something, Emmitt? You might be a great hockey player, but I know you're an even better brother."

Then I know I have to talk to my father. It's the only way I can protect Casey from him.

It's another Wednesday night game, and since JV plays first, our game doesn't even start until 7:30. At least this one's away—all the way in Essex—so it isn't all that weird Casey doesn't come. Dusty doesn't come either. He wanted to, especially with my dad being there, but I asked him to hang out with Casey and keep him distracted. Mom usually works on my away-game nights so she can get home-game nights off, and I don't want Casey to be alone.

We're finishing up the team huddle right before the opening face-off, and Coach is reminding us about defensive lapses we've had, when I see my dad. He's sitting in the stands, leaning forward eagerly, as though we're playing the final minutes of some nail-biting game. He's grinning.

I tune Coach out for a moment to study Dad in my peripheral vision; I don't want to give him the satisfaction of thinking I care that he's there. He's gained a little weight. He's always looked thicker and stockier than me, like Casey, but he had muscle to back it up. Now he's got a little pudge around the middle that I'm pretty sure he didn't have three years ago. He's got the same brown hair and eyes, but he's balding a little on top these days. It's tough to tell because he's sitting down, but I bet he's only got a few inches on me in terms of height now.

I remember when he used to tower over me.

I tune back in to Coach in time to hear him say, "Okay, let's get out there."

The rest of the team skates off, but Coach gestures for me to stay. "Yeah?"

He's writing something on his clipboard as he talks to me. "That your dad in the stands?"

I blink in surprise. "How did you know that?"

He grins wryly. "I live with Dustin. And I made an inference. Speaking of which, I'm inferring right now that this is freaking you out a little bit."

"Uh, no. I mean, I knew I'd see him today, but…." I take a deep breath. "It's just been a long time."

Coach nods and sets his clipboard down on the bench. "Hmmm. Listen, Emmitt, here's the thing." He straightens up and shrugs. "Just play, okay?" And then he walks away.

It turns out to be some of the best advice he's ever given me.

I'd sort of forgotten that after Dad left, I used hockey as a straight-up escape. I'd forget that the rest of the world was going on around me, that Mom was crying all the time, that Casey was getting in trouble at school and yelling at home a lot. Hockey was where I could be in control and make things work my way. Hockey was where nothing else mattered out there as long as I could skate.

Coach's words trigger something, and suddenly I know that's what I need to do: I need to use this game to escape. And just play.

Eric and I are on fire. Essex is really good—they've only lost two games all season—but they can barely keep up with the two of us. It's like we're completely in sync all night. He reads where I'm going with the puck on every play, and we end up drilling them 5-2.

Since we're in the Essex arena, there isn't an astounding amount of applause when the final buzzer sounds. The families and friends who've made the trip from Colby head down the stands toward the benches, and Dad, who has Uncle Dave with him, is suddenly only a few feet away from me.

Screw that. I decide to take back some control, and I pull off my helmet as I skate over to them and step onto the padded rubber mats in the seating area.

"Emmitt!" Dad throws his arms around me, pads and all. "You guys look great! You startin' to feel the pressure?"

That's my dad—not exactly a calming presence. "Yeah, I guess. A little, I mean. I'm trying not to pay too much attention, you know?"

Now Uncle Dave goes in for the hug. "Great to see you, kid. Good for you. Don't pay it any attention."

Dad looks around. "Is Casey here? Where is he?"

I shake my head. "He didn't come. I messaged you and said he wasn't coming."

His eyes widen in shock. "What do you mean, he didn't come? You couldn't talk him into it?"

He just doesn't get it. Doesn't want to, I guess. I was trying to soften the blow, but I'd forgotten that subtlety doesn't really work with my father. "Dad, of course I didn't 'talk him into it.' I told you in the e-mail that Casey doesn't want to see you," I blurt out.

"Why?" Dad looks genuinely hurt. "I thought by now he'd be feeling better about me. I mean, I know he hasn't been my biggest fan the past few years, and he doesn't say much when I call, but he is a teenager…."

I don't really feel like trying to explain something I think Dad should be able to understand pretty easily, so I just shrug. "Listen, I have to go change. Bus is going to leave soon."

Dad puts his hand up like he's pausing me. "Get changed, yeah. But then let Dave and I drive you home. I want to catch up."

I smile thinly. "Yeah, Dad. Sounds good."

I CHANGE quickly and tell Coach I'm heading home with my father. He eyes me warily. "You sure, Emmitt? We could tell him I need you to ride with the team."

"Nah." I shake my head. "It's okay. This is something I gotta do."

The first few minutes in the car are awkward. Uncle Dave and I don't see each other much more than I see Dad, so none of us have anything to talk about once we get past the how-are-you-doing-in-school stuff. Finally Dad leans around from the front seat and asks me something I knew was coming: "How's the truck running?"

I knew this was coming because my truck is one thing in my life Dad's been a part of in the last three and a half years. Of course he would bring it up.

When I first learned to drive, Mom was ecstatic; she'd been giving up tons of overtime opportunities to cart Casey and me around after Dad left. The problem was that we still only had one car.

Mom and I couldn't bring ourselves to ask Dad for help, but he ended up getting involved anyway. My Grandma Iris, who hates my mom but still sees Casey and me once in a while, found out some friend of hers was selling his old truck dirt cheap and told my dad she thought he should buy it for Casey and me.

To Casey's and my shock, he did. To this day I'm pretty sure it was the ultimate divorce-guilt gift, but I've never really cared that much. It's a '99 Chevy, nothing special. I've learned how to do basic maintenance on it, and Casey and I pay for the insurance and gas with our summer lawn jobs.

"Yeah, it's running okay." I could tell him the shocks need to be replaced, and maybe he'd help pay for it. I don't. If I've learned one thing from my mom, it's pride.

"Glad to see it's worked out for you. I wanted to make sure you and Casey had a way of getting around on your own. Hopefully it's helped with all the hockey practices I'm sure you've been having lately."

Am I supposed to thank him for the one thing he's done for me since junior high? Apparently. "Um… yeah… thanks."

Conversation dies again until we're on the interstate.

We eventually end up talking about exactly what you'd expect: Dad tells me all about his life and asks me a few questions, and I mumble some answers. Real excitement. He tells me a little about the half sister I've never met. I guess Gina looks a lot like me and acts a lot like Casey. Whoop-de-do.

I wonder if I'll ever meet this elusive sister. I decide to ask. "Why didn't you bring her with you?"

"Ah, well… she's still young, you know… not quite up for the trip yet." He quickly changes the subject.

We're almost back to the house before Dad brings up Casey again. He turns around all the way in the seat to look at me, so I know he's about to go for The Serious Moment.

"So, I'd very much like to see Casey while I'm here."

I stare out the window at passing traffic. "Dad, I'm not even getting into that right now. He doesn't want to see you. Maybe someday, but not right now. You walked away from us, remember? So he gets to decide."

Dad starts to get frustrated. "Emmitt, I know you remember things a certain way, but—"

"Yeah, Dad," I almost snarl. "I remember that you left and that you haven't shown up a whole lot since. The truck is great," I add, looking at him again, "but I don't think it means Casey's going to forget about all the other stuff you missed." *Or me either*, I add silently.

Dad frowns. "Emmitt, he just needs to understand. I'll come to the house with you. I'll explain everything to him. He'll be fine."

Now *I'm* pissed. "Understand?" I hiss. Uncle Dave's eyes are glued to the road; he's doing an impressive job of pretending this conversation isn't happening right in front of him. "Understand what, Dad? That you didn't care enough to stay around here after you and Mom split? That you call maybe once a month? That Mom's been working double shifts ever since you left? That Casey and I work our asses off at school, and hockey and skateboarding, and have to do all the housework too because she has to work that much to keep us going financially? Because you've got another family to support, don't you, Dad? And they have to come first."

I rip my eyes away from him and go back to staring out the window. "You know, Dad, you're right about one thing," I tell him, still keeping my voice low. "Case doesn't understand. But you know what else? Neither do I."

"Emmitt," Dad says quietly, "I know you're angry at me, and I don't blame you. But I'm here now, kid. And I want to help you. Emmitt, you've got the world knocking at your door right now—college scouts, newspapers. Everything's going right for you. You've got the grades and the smarts to back it all up too. We both know playing in Colby isn't going to get you where you want to go. You need to be playing for something bigger. Listen, I got in touch with the US National Team Development scouts. I told them what you're doing for Vermont high school hockey right now. They're interested, Emmitt, and if they decide they want you, D1 colleges are going to be knocking down your door. Not to mention the NHL."

The US National Team Development Program is *huge*. It's USA Hockey's junior program, and making that team is every American teenage hockey player's dream. It seems unlikely they'd be interested in me now—the NTDP is everything I thought I gave up a few years ago when I didn't leave home.

It's also based in Ann Arbor, Michigan.

It just figures that the man who basically kept me from going down that kind of road in the first place is now sitting here telling me he wants to get it back for me. I couldn't keep the scowl off my face if I tried. "Dad, I'm going to get D1 hockey—and the NHL—on my own. I don't need you. I've gotten this far without you, and I can go the rest of the way."

He just shakes his head, almost… maybe sadly? "Emmitt, I know you think that. But who knows what's going to happen in the future? Your team might not be as good your senior year, and you might not pull off an undefeated season. People might not keep paying attention to your talent. Emmitt, you need to maximize what you have *right now*, and I want to help you do that. I know you don't want to leave Casey and your mother, but this is about your future."

"Gee, Dad," I choke out, "funny how only one of us has absolutely no problem leaving Casey and Mom behind."

His face colors, and he can't seem to look at me after that.

We finish the rest of the trip in silence, and I've got the car door open before the thing has even come to a complete stop. "Bye, Dad. Bye, Uncle Dave," I say. "Thanks for coming." I wonder if I sound like a zombie to anyone besides myself.

I think I hear Dad calling after me, but it's like I'm on the ice or something—I don't hear a thing that's being yelled up in the stands.

It's late by the time I get home, so Mrs. Morton has already picked Dusty up, and Casey is asleep. I get to go to bed without having to explain a thing to anyone.

But all good things must come to an end, right? When I get up the next morning, Casey and Mom are eating cereal together in the kitchen. Definitely waiting for me. Definitely ready to ask me how things went the night before.

Mom pats me on the shoulder and gets up to pour herself more coffee. "I heard you won last night."

"Yeah." I sink onto a stool and grab the box and bowl Casey passes me. "We slaughtered 'em."

Casey nods. "Great job, man. Does that mean you're in the playoffs?"

Casey already knows our record has guaranteed us a spot in the playoffs, so I'm not sure why he's asking the question. Except I am sure, and it's because he's stalling. He's not quite ready to ask what he really wants to know.

"I mean, we won't know who we face in the first round until after we play our last game against Rice next week. But we'll definitely be in the quarterfinals the game after that."

Casey just nods and asks Mom if she needs him to do the laundry when he gets home.

Mom finally pops the bubble. "Did you see your father?"

Casey stares deeply into his Cocoa Puffs. I take a long time finishing my mouthful.

"Ah, yeah," I finally say. "Uncle Dave too. They gave me a ride home."

"Oh," Mom says. She concentrates on her toast.

Most. Awkward. Breakfast. Ever.

"He wants to help me out with all this hockey stuff," I finally add. "Wants me to try and get into the NTDP."

Casey looks up, shocked. "Wouldn't you have to, like, move to Michigan to be in that program?"

"Yeah." I keep my eyes on my cereal. "He's still an asshole."

"Don't swear at the breakfast table, Emmitt," Mom murmurs.

Casey scoffs. "*That's* what's upsetting you about this conversation?" She leans over and cuffs him lightly on the back of the head as she gets up to take her dishes to the sink. "Just because your father's visiting doesn't mean I'm letting you forget all your manners. Emmitt, what did you tell your father?"

Casey's staring at me intently, waiting for an answer to that question. I shrug. "I didn't tell him sh—anything. I just reminded him that I don't need his help."

"Good job, Emmitt." Casey takes a huge bite of cereal. "Fway to fshow fhim," he says with his mouth full.

"Ma, Casey's talking with his mouth full again," I call out, only half joking. It grosses me out when he does that.

She comes back over to the table and sits down. "Emmitt," she says, "I know you two are both unhappy with your father... but you might want to consider letting him help you."

Casey's eyes widen in surprise, and I can feel mine do the same. "What are you talking about?"

She smiles and brushes some hair off my forehead like I'm still a little kid. "Honey, we both know you could be playing for better hockey programs right now. Coach Morton is wonderful, and there's nothing wrong with your high school team, but trying to play for one of those elite leagues may not be such a terrible idea. I know you didn't want to leave home when you were younger, but you're sixteen now. Maybe it's time."

Casey finally swallows his huge bite. "Ma," he says shortly, "are you actually saying that Emmitt should let that douche bag help him? That he should move to Michigan right now?"

Mom frowns. "Casey, don't say that word," she scolds. "Listen, I will never want either of you to leave. But Emmitt's a junior; he'd be leaving for college soon anyway. And Emmitt, I will always want you to have whatever opportunities the world can give you. You both have every right to be upset with how your father's acted since the divorce. But I need you both to remember that he's always loved you very much, and once upon a time you worshipped him. If he wants to help either of you out—ever—I'm going to encourage you to take that help. If he can get you into an important hockey league and support us financially with making that kind of move happen, I don't think you should turn that offer down." She gestures to the driveway outside the front window. "We didn't turn down that truck, now, did we?"

Good point.

Casey scowls. "I think I'm going to start walking to school again," he says.

CHAPTER
FIVE

DEAR MR. LeClair,

I heard you're having a golf tournament in St. Albans this spring. I'd come, but I don't know how to play golf. I hope you have fun, though. I hope you raise a lot of money to cure cancer.

Tonight was our Valentine's Day dance. I wasn't going to go, because dances are stupid. Everyone just stands around talking. But my friend Mitch wanted to go, because he has a crush on this girl named Mel. So I went with him.

It sucked. Mel didn't talk to Mitch, and the music wasn't very good. And we all just stood around talking like we always do. The suckiest part was when this girl June asked me to dance. I don't like dancing, and I don't like June. Mitch thinks she's hot, and he doesn't get why I don't like her. He says she has great boobs.

That makes me worried. I don't get what he's talking about. I don't think June's that pretty. She's nice, I guess. And we talk about video games sometimes. But I can't even imagine kissing her or anything.

I'm getting worried, Mr. LeClair, because a lot of the guys I hang out with now talk about wanting to kiss girls in our class. And I don't want to kiss any of them. That just sounds gross.

I'm sort of scared about it. I haven't told anyone this, but there is someone I want to kiss. Only it's not a girl. It's Mitch.

I think I might be gay. But gay guys can't be hockey players, right? I've never heard of a gay hockey player. Ever. So I guess I can't be gay.

Because all I want to be is a hockey player.

—Emmitt LaPoint, age 11

I DROP my books off at our usual lunch table that afternoon and head off to get the classic cafeteria chicken burger. You know the kind: limp, sitting on a paper-thin bun. They're the most edible thing our cafeteria serves, so most days I just smother one in ketchup and pile up the fries next to it. Coach says the cafeteria's chicken burgers are just one step up from fast food and we should all be eating salads for lunch, but I don't see him trying to pick through the yellow lettuce at the salad station.

Back at the lunch table, Casey and Dusty are debating whether or not it's worth having another skate club meeting this week. "I'm just saying, Casey, there's nothing to do," Dusty's telling him. "We've got all the petitions and crap lined up for the skate park. And everyone's sick of watching skating videos. Let's just take the week off."

Casey waves half a sandwich at him. "Dude, what's wrong with you? Where's your passion? I *never* get sick of watching skating videos. I could watch 'em all day long."

"And he has," I say drily as I sit down next to Dusty. "Trust me."

Dusty looks over at me and smiles. There's this lightness in his eyes when he sees me, like his smile is relaxed and excited at the same time. I bet my face looks the same way right now. I haven't seen him since yesterday, and all I want to do is lean over and kiss him hello. Since I can't, I settle for passing him a fry.

He takes it, and we lock eyes for a moment when our hands touch.

He pulls away quickly.

Life sucks sometimes.

I pull myself out of that tunnel of thought and back to the lunch table, where the hockey team and Casey's skating friends are settling around us. "Casey, stop being a dictator and cancel the meeting this week. Not everyone's as obsessed with skateboarding as you are."

Casey glares at me. "Says the guy who rollerblades everywhere in the summer to keep his form up."

O'Sheridan looks up from his own chicken burger. "Shit, no wonder you're better than the rest of us."

I squirm uncomfortably. "Casey, stop exaggerating. I don't rollerblade everywhere." And I don't. Just to any place under three miles away.

Lucas Doherty, who's sitting with his girlfriend, Piper, weighs in. "Casey, let's cancel the meeting this week. That's Valentine's Day, remember? Piper and I are going to John's Seafood."

There are catcalls from around the table, because John's is the fanciest restaurant in Colby. "How'd you score that?" asks O'Sher.

Some days I'm really proud of how Casey and I have brought the skateboarding and hockey crowds together at our high school. Without us, the hockey guys here would probably all make fun of the skateboarding crowd and call them emo druggies, and the skateboarders would all think the hockey players were just stupid jocks. But Casey and I have always been a package deal, and we bring our friends with us, so a lot of our friends hang out with each other now. Luke and O'Sher party together a lot.

"My dad knows the manager," Piper tells him. "C'mon, Casey. I like skateboarding videos too, but they can wait a week. None of us will forget what a half-pipe looks like, I promise."

"You're supposed to be on my side," Casey tells her. "I thought you had commitment, Piper." She rolls her eyes.

Valentine's Day. I've been so caught up with all the hockey stuff happening and my dad coming back that I basically forgot about it. I don't think Dusty has, though, judging from the way he's staring at the ketchup pile on his tray and avoiding looking at me.

Shit. Who's in charge of Valentine's Day in a relationship, anyway? I've never been in a relationship—not for real—so I've never had to worry about it before. I always thought the dude was in charge when it's a guy-girl relationship, but it sounds like Piper took care of things for her and Luke. And how do you ever know who's in charge when it's two guys? I don't care about Valentine's Day, so how am I supposed to know if Dusty does?

"Uh," I finally ask, "what's everyone else doing for Valentine's Day?"

Dusty's eyebrows go up slightly.

Everyone chimes in with plans. Movies, dinner, nothing. Same old stuff they always do with their girlfriends or boyfriends, just with fancier restaurants and more chocolate involved. I relax a little. I can do that.

47

Except I *can't*. If I take Dusty out somewhere in Colby on Valentine's Day, that's going to raise all kinds of red flags. Pun not intended.

"You know," Piper tells us, "if any of you don't have plans, you should go to this concert my cousin's band is playing in Burlington. They're called Abnormal Anyway, and they're pretty good. It's at Higher Ground."

Now *that's* a good idea. We don't have our last game of the season until the following weekend, and Valentine's Day falls on Friday night. Dusty and I could go, stay out late, eat in Burlington. Nobody's going to think it's a big deal if two friends who like music go to a concert on Valentine's Day, and we're not going to run into that many people in Burlington anyway.

"What's their music like?" Dusty asks, and I know he's thinking the same thing.

Piper drones on about how they're like a bunch of bands I've never heard of, and I'm already making plans in my head. There's this little restaurant my parents used to take us to in Burlington that's not fancy but still has great food. No one's going to see us there. I've got the whole date planned out in my head before I've even finished my chicken burger.

Dusty and I are walking to class after lunch when I casually bring it up. "So," I tell him as we stop at my locker together, "we're going to that show on Friday together, right?"

"As long as you don't already have plans with Dawn," he says, smirking.

I pull out my physics book. "Don't even joke about that, dude," I tell him. I glance around. The hallway's emptying out; no one's going to hear me right now. "Seriously. Will you go out with me for Valentine's Day?"

He wants to kiss me. I can always tell with him: he gets this look in his eye like someone just handed him a hundred-dollar bill or a brand-new skateboard. He steps back slightly, probably to avoid that temptation. "I think I might be able to free up my schedule," he tells me. Then he slides down the locker and sits on the floor. "Hang out for a minute. We've got time before class."

We don't have a lot of time, but I'm not in that much of a hurry to rush off to physics and see Dawn. I sit down next to him.

"How was seeing your dad last night? You didn't text me when you got in, so I figured it went okay. Did it?"

He's got such an earnest look on his face. Half-worried, half-caring. Sometimes I think the most amazing thing about Dusty is his ability to care so much about other people. With the hand the world dealt him, you'd think he'd be this selfish and closed-off asshole. But he's the exact opposite. He always puts everyone else before himself, even when he shouldn't.

Sometimes I try to imagine what life was like for him back in Colorado Springs, when he was just a kid himself and trying to secretly raise Matt and Julia every time his parents disappeared. He must have been so lonely and terrified all the time.

The whole situation sure puts my measly problems into perspective. And yet here's Dusty, worrying about how I'm feeling right now.

All I want to do is hug him, but that's not happening. So I settle for lightly bumping shoulders with him. "I dunno. It went... fine. He was pissed Casey didn't come, and I had to remind him that Casey doesn't have to see him if he doesn't want to. He wants to help me get scouted by the National Development Team. He thinks I need to be playing in a bigger league right away."

Dusty's face takes on just a hint of panic at the words "bigger league," but he hides it fairly well. "Wow. Where's the National Development Team?"

"Uh... Michigan." Dusty's face drops just enough that I quickly follow up with, "I'm not going to listen to him. I don't need him or his advice. I want to play for Colby."

Dusty doesn't look like that statement makes him feel any better. "I want that too... but is playing here going to get you all the other stuff you want? College hockey or the NHL?"

I shrug. "Coach thinks it can, right? It worked for LeClair. Look, this is just what my dad does. He shows up when it's convenient because he wants something. Right now he just wants the chance to see his son play junior hockey for the national team."

"Shit." Dusty snorts. "Is he that selfish?"

We're not sitting that far from one of Colby's many trophy cases. I watch the light glint off the gold of a gymnastics award someone at this school won years ago. "I never used to think so. But the way he took off like that... that was pretty fucking selfish, don't you think?"

Dusty nods. "Yeah. True. Hey, listen." He bumps my shoulder back, then glances around to make sure none of the people left in the hallway are paying attention to us. No one is. "Try to remember this: whatever happens, you get to be selfish sometimes too, Emmitt. You can do what's best for you right now and not worry about what that means for anyone else. Take your dad's help and think about joining that team if you want. Don't do it if you don't want to. Do whatever you need to do." His mouth tilts up into a smile. "Wherever you go, I'll still be here."

I smile back, wondering how I got so lucky.

And if he's ever going to get tired of how selfish I am where he's concerned.

FAST-FORWARD TO Friday, when I'm chomping at the bit for our date. Dusty and I used to go into Burlington to get some time to ourselves when we first started dating, but we haven't gone much since hockey season started. I've been geared up all day for tonight.

I ring the Morton/Porter doorbell, and Coach answers. He's got pink and red heart stickers all over his face.

"Don't say it," he growls. "This holiday is bad enough on its own. It's even worse with a first-grader in the house."

"Emmitt!" Julia runs up behind Coach; she's covered in even more stickers than he is. She hands me one of my own. "Happy Valentine's Day!"

"Thanks, Julia." I unzip my coat and carefully place the sticker on my sweater.

She throws her hands on her hips. "It goes on your forehead," she says.

Dusty comes up behind them as he's pulling on his coat. "Yeah, Emmitt," he says knowingly. "Don't you understand anything?" He leans over and gives me a little peck on the cheek, which surprises me. Dusty's still a little weird about doing stuff like that around his family, but Coach just smiles at us.

I move the sticker, and Julia nods approvingly.

"Have fun tonight, guys," Coach tells us. "You both know the rules, right? No drinking. No drugs. If you need a ride, call us. No cops, please."

"That was one time," Dusty and I remind him together. Coach is never going to let that incident go, and I guess I can't blame him. Rick

Snyder, our team's ex-captain, crashed a party Dusty and I were at and started a huge fight. Dusty and I both ended up at the police station. I wish I could say that was the worst night of my life, but it's actually the opposite.

That night was the first time Dusty and I kissed.

"No cops," Coach says again. "Both of you, just be careful. Emmitt, people are paying a lot of attention to you right now. You need to remember that."

Yeah, I've got plenty of reminders of *that* right now.

"And Dusty, if anything happens to you, Beth will probably make me move out."

Dusty rolls his eyes and gives Coach a hug.

Julia asks for hugs before we leave, and Coach gets us out of the house before Matt notices I'm there and begs us to watch *Transformers* with him. I spend a lot of time appreciating Coach Morton, but this moment's topping the list.

In the truck, Dusty cranks up the Led Zeppelin album I put in before I left. I've always liked Zeppelin because my mom used to listen to them a lot, and it turns out Dusty *loves* them. We have some similar tastes in music, so I'm hoping we'll both like this concert. Not that I was listening when Piper was telling us about the band.

"Hey," Dusty says as we're pulling onto the highway, "what did Jack mean about a lot of people paying attention to you right now? Have more reporters been up in your business or something?"

"Not exactly," I tell him. "He was just reminding me that scouts and reporters are watching our team right now. Colby hasn't gone undefeated in a while, so that's sort of a big deal. Coach is just trying to help me make sure I don't screw it up."

Dusty rolls his eyes. "Emmitt, you don't screw shit up," he says knowingly.

"Yeah?" I lean over and rest my right hand gently on his leg. "Sometimes I think I'm screwing this up." I can't believe something that sappy—or honest—just came out of my mouth, but there's no going back now.

Dusty puts his hand over mine. "Me too," he says softly.

That relaxes me a little, knowing Dusty worries about us the same way I do. "Dude, what could you possibly be doing wrong? I'm the one who won't let us tell anyone what's going on, so we have to go out secretly on Valentine's Day and sneak off to Burlington and pretend to be two friends going to a concert. You're the one who just goes along with it. You're amazing, Dusty. You never screw anything up with us. You always make it better. That comment you made the other day, about how it would be okay if I was selfish with my dad? I'm always the selfish one when it comes to you and me. Or that's how it feels."

"Not always," Dusty says softly. "I missed that home game of yours, remember?"

"You were studying, weren't you?" My voice sounds small.

"Yeah. Of course." But he definitely seems hesitant as he says it.

There's something going on that he's not telling me. Something to do with that phone call he got the last night I was at his house, I'm sure. But I don't want to ruin this date, and honestly? I trust Dusty. More than I've trusted anyone. He's going to tell me what's going on. Eventually.

So I don't push it. "Then don't worry about it," I tell him. "So what's this band going to be like? Honestly, I wasn't paying attention to Piper when she was talking about them."

Dusty wraps his fingers around mine and starts telling me about how they're a little like Mumford and Sons, but harder, and his eyes are lit up again.

I can't wait for him to see what I've got waiting for us in Burlington.

The restaurant is this little place that looks out over Lake Champlain, and it's called The Champlain Cookery. It's got fewer than twenty tables, because it's actually an old house that's been converted into a restaurant. It's not as fancy as a lot of the places on Church Street, and not as well-known, but I remember how much my parents used to love the food here. This was always where they'd take us when our family went into Burlington together.

We walk in, and I head to the server station. Dusty's lagging behind me, probably wondering if he's dressed nicely enough for this place. He doesn't have to worry. We're both in polos and jeans, and that's just fine here.

"Two for LaPoint," I tell the guy. He nods and starts leading us to our table.

"You made reservations?" Dusty hisses in my ear. He's looking around us frantically, and I can practically hear him worrying—that people will see, that they'll assume things. I punch his shoulder lightly.

"Of course I did," I tell him. "It's Valentine's Day. And don't worry. I've got this under control."

We head around the corner and arrive at our table, and Dusty's eyes widen.

I picked this place for another specific reason. Because it's an old house, a lot of the tables are in tiny areas with walls separating them from the other tables. I asked them to give us a table in a space of its own, and they came through. We're tucked away in what probably used to be a hallway, and you have to come all the way around a corner to see us. We've got our own space, and nobody but the servers are likely to even notice we're here.

We sit down, and the waiter hands us menus. "Can I get you both something to drink?"

"Coke, please," I say, suddenly feeling grown-up. I don't think I've ever been to a restaurant this nice without my mother.

"Yeah, me too," says Dusty.

The waiter leaves, and Dusty's just staring at me, wide-eyed.

"What?" I finally ask, grinning.

"How'd you do this?" Dusty asks, glancing around us. "This is so… private."

I shrug. "My parents used to take Casey and me here when we were little. I remembered what the place looks like. It wasn't that big of a deal, Dusty." Even as I say it, we both know I'm lying. I do think it's a big deal—that I thought of this place, that I called and got us a table here.

That I found a way for us to be out in public and still have a real Valentine's Day.

Dusty shakes his head. "This is crazy."

"What's so crazy?" I'm honestly curious. What's so crazy about me wanting to go out on Valentine's Day with my boyfriend?

He shakes his head again. "Emmitt, I've liked you since basically the first day I saw you. Remember when you took me on that tour of Colby? I couldn't stop staring at you. You were such a fucking preppy, in those khakis you like to wear, but they looked great on you, and I wished

I could ask you to the movies or something. I kept thinking how shitty it was that I'd never get to do something like that with you. How there was no way you felt the same way I did." He waves around us. "And now…."

"Here we are." I smile. "I know what you mean."

The waiter comes back with our Cokes, and we get our shit together long enough to order. We both get burgers, because we're boring like that, and because I told Dusty they're amazing here, which they are. Then we're alone again, waiting for the burgers.

"I got you something," I tell him, and Dusty turns red.

"Emmitt, I didn't get you anything," he says. "I didn't know if we were doing that, and I don't have much money right now—I had to get Jules and Matt some little things for Valentine's Day, and dinner tonight and the tickets…."

I shake my head. "It's not big, Dusty." I hand him the small wrapped package I've pulled out of my coat pocket. Thank goodness Casey's a wrapping genius, because I'm not even sure how he got the corners to look like that. "And I've got dinner tonight. All that lawn mowing this past summer finally pays off."

Dusty's still blushing, but he pulls off the wrapping paper and opens the small box in front of him. And stares.

"I know it's not big or anything," I tell him, "but I wanted you to have it. It's the first one I ever got."

He lifts his gift slowly out of the box, the gold coloring of metal glittering slightly in the light. "It's… are you sure, Emmitt? Are you sure you want to give this to me?"

I was worried, actually, about giving it to him. I didn't spend any money on it, and the skateboarding DVDs I got him for Christmas were definitely harder to find. It isn't exactly the typical Valentine's Day gift. But I thought it would mean a lot to Dusty, and that he would know how much it means to me.

The lettering on the medal hits the light and flashes at me: FIRST PLACE: PEEWEE I TOURNAMENT.

"I was seven," I tell him. "The first championship my team ever won. I scored two goals. That medal's been on my bookshelf ever since. Yeah, I want you to have it."

He holds on to the medal a little bit tighter. "I can't believe I didn't get you anything," he says softly.

"Hey." I push the medal down and grab for his hand, reflexively looking around to make sure nobody's about to come around the corner. "I gave this to you because I wanted to. Because I want you to always have something to hang on to from me—you know, when I'm gone and you're still in Colby." Dusty winces a little; we don't talk much about what's coming a year down the road. "You don't owe me anything, Dusty. I'm lucky just to have you here with me. No matter what."

Dusty glances over at the corner of the wall behind us and gets out of his chair. He steps around the table and leans down. "Thank you, Emmitt," he says softly, and then he pushes his mouth against mine.

It's the first time I ever stepped onto the ice. The first time I ever looked at Casey. The last Christmas my family spent together before my father left. Just like it is every time Dusty kisses me.

We're like that for a long moment before he pulls away and goes back to his seat.

Thank you, Dusty.

CHAPTER
SIX

Dear Mr. LeClair,

Today was so cool! Mom and Dad took me and Casey to a hockey game at UVM. Your name was everywere cuz you went to school there. Dad said your one of the best hockey players who ever played there!

It was a good game. UVM won by one goal. They had some good plays.

Someday I'm gonna go to collage at UVM just like you did. I'm going to play hockey and get a degree and I will still be able to see Casey anytime I want cuz Burlington is not that far away from Colby. That is important cuz Casey is my best friend.

Maybe someday you will even be at a game at UVM and you will see me play. That would be the coolest thing ever.

—Emmitt LaPoint, age 9

DINNER'S EXCELLENT, and the show is good too. They're not going to be my favorite band or anything just yet, but they've got potential. Dusty and I have a great time just standing there, bumping into each other as people rave and thrash around us in the darkness. No one's paying attention to what we do. At some point I even slip my hand into Dusty's back pocket for an entire song. It feels reckless and dangerous, and by the end of the song I can tell he's as turned on as I am.

After the show we drive back down to the waterfront and park in an out-of-the way parking lot. Dusty and I don't get a lot of chances to be completely alone, so we're taking advantage of this one. We make out for a while. We've still got plenty to practice in that area.

We've fooled around a little since we started dating, but not too much. Privacy's hard to come by, after all. We go a little further tonight, testing some new boundaries. We're careful, and we only go as far as we're both comfortable with. The best thing about being with Dusty is that I never worry about being honest with him if we're going outside my comfort zone, and I always know he'll tell me if we go too far outside his. I feel bad for people who don't have that in their relationship—it would be so shitty if I couldn't be honest with Dusty when we were right in the middle of being so close.

That part of the night is great, and I'm basically as happy as it's possible to be as we're driving home. We drive by the UVM campus, and I notice Dusty's eyes are on the dorms there.

"You still want to go to UVM someday, right?" I know he's thinking about what I said the other day about junior hockey and Michigan and my father.

I shrug. "I've always wanted to play for UVM. Who knows if they'll be interested, though."

Dusty doesn't say anything.

"Dusty," I tell him. "I still want UVM. I want to play where LeClair played, and I want to be just a few miles away from you. From Casey and Mom."

Dusty frowns. "But you'd have a better chance of that if you got a spot on this national team your dad was talking about, right?"

My boyfriend's got to be one of the most selfless people on the planet.

"Probably," I tell him. "But I have a chance now, staying exactly where I am."

"I guess," he says. He plays with the radio and shrugs. "I just... I wouldn't want you to give up some great opportunity because of me, you know? Not ever."

I don't know what to say to that. So I just grab his hand and lace our fingers together. We sit like that for four exits of the interstate.

SATURDAY MORNING hockey practice is a good distraction from thinking about that subject too much more. Coach Morton is all over us—passing drills, shooting drills, speed drills. Halfway through I'm ready to collapse. I fall onto the bench and drain a bottle of Gatorade. Coach Morton comes over and pats me on the shoulder.

"Maybe you shouldn't have stayed out quite so late last night, LaPoint," he says, grinning.

I groan. It's going to be a *long* morning.

Dusty and Casey are in the stands, supposedly doing homework. Every now and then I look up to watch them. They spend most of their time on their phones—Casey's been stalking Maria Vornage on Snapchat—but once in a while it looks like some actual homework might be happening.

I'm taking a break in the middle of our final scrimmage when I look up to see them having an intense conversation. They're not exactly yelling, but it doesn't look like they're planning a skate club meeting either. Casey's waving his arms around excitedly, and *serious* is plastered all over his face. Dusty's shaking his head rapidly back and forth, and he doesn't look happy.

There's basically only two things they can be talking about: whatever Dusty's keeping from me right now, or Dad.

Practice ends, and Eric falls onto the bench next to me. "I need food," he says. "Wanna hit the diner?"

I shouldn't. I'm low on cash after last night. But if Eric's going to act like we're buddies again for a few minutes, I'm taking him up on it. "Sure," I tell him. "I bet Casey and Dusty will come too."

Less than an hour later, Eric and I are stretched out across the booths in Ella's Diner, groaning.

"That was brutal," Eric moans.

"Brutal," I agree.

Casey raises an eyebrow. "You two are such wusses. You never see skateboarders whining about a few hours of practice."

Eric chokes on his orange juice. "Yeah, right. Because you could do skating drills for a few hours and not look like this."

I shake my head. "You don't want to bet him on that," I tell Eric. "Casey can probably do hockey drills three times as long as us before he even breaks a sweat." Sadly, I know this from experience. My brother's natural athletic prowess includes some scary endurance.

Eric looks at Casey warily, and Casey just nods. "You're all pussies."

Dusty's not even trying to hide that he's laughing at us.

"Hey, Eric." Mel Everitt walks up to our table, and Eric brightens. He leans over to give her a fist bump.

"Hey, Mel. Didn't see you here. Want to sit?" He pulls back his long legs so Mel can fit onto the bench seat.

This is interesting. I wasn't even aware Eric knows who Melinda Everitt is, let alone talks to her. Mel's a junior like me. She's also one of the few black kids in our whitewashed school, and her grades are even better than mine.

And she just happens to be the president of the Gay-Straight Alliance, a club lots of kids won't even admit they know exists.

A club I basically pretend I don't know exists. Mel has a lot more balls than I do, that's for sure.

"You guys know each other?" Dusty asks the question for me.

"Mel's my lab partner in Anatomy and Physiology," Eric tells us. "She's the reason I have an A right now." He slaps Mel's back.

"We have a deal," Mel tells us. "I get him an A, and he starts coming to GSA meetings as soon as hockey's over. Having a hockey player there is going to be great for our rep."

All our eyes must widen, because Eric starts laughing. "Chill out, guys. It's the Gay *Straight* Alliance, remember? I'm still straight."

Next to me Dusty's whole body seems to relax.

Mel grins. "What about you three? Casey, we'll support the skate club if you and Dusty join us. And Emmitt, it looks great on college applications."

Casey's looking at me closely. "Yeah, Emmitt, it does," he says.

"Are you gay?" Dusty blurts out. I assume he's talking to Mel. We all stare at him. "What?" he asks. "Are you not supposed to ask that?"

Mel laughs. "It's fine," she says. "I'm pansexual, which lots of people think is just bisexual. It's not the same thing, though." She glances around at our confused expressions. "Seriously? Not one of you knows what pansexual means?"

"*I* know," says Eric. "It means she doesn't care about gender or biology or whatever. She's just into people." He is way too proud of himself.

"Aww, look who's learning." Mel pats his arm. "Mr. Newly Enlightened over here apparently listens to me once in a while. Anyway, there are lots of different orientations in the club. We're just about keeping Colby safe and happy for everyone, you know? We sponsored that antibullying campaign back in December, and we're going to do some stuff for the spring dance and prom to encourage people of all orientations to attend. You know, stuff like that."

Eric takes a bite of his pancakes. "You should come with me, Emmitt," he says.

My heart starts pounding almost as hard as it was during drills. Has he guessed something? "It sounds cool," I say, slowly. Carefully. "Just have to see how busy things get after hockey." Next to me, Dusty has tensed up again.

"Maybe I'll start going," Dusty says. "Since skate club's slow right now. Casey, you'd come with me, right?"

Casey nods slowly from around his bite of sandwich. "Sure, man. I'll go with you."

Mel beams. "Excellent! I promise we'll support the skate club in any way we can. Eric, call me later and I'll talk you through the homework for this weekend."

"Thanks." Eric gives her another fist bump, and Mel gets up to leave.

"She's cool," Eric says as Mel is walking away. "I've invited her to join us for lunch a few times, but she won't. I guess O'Sher's a complete dick to her—used to write 'fag' on her locker all the time. And some of the other hockey guys always follow his lead. You know who I'm talking about."

Dusty's eyes narrow.

"That's shitty," I say. Just call me Captain Obvious. "Should we say something to Patrick?"

"Already did," says Eric. "He just told me he was joking around and that he wouldn't do it anymore if her 'sensitive little pussy' couldn't handle it. He can be such an ass."

Casey frowns. "Makes me sorry I called you both pussies a few minutes ago. I'll pick a better pejorative next time. I swear."

We all stare at him. "Did you just use the word *pejorative?*" I finally ask.

"I've been studying for the PSATs," Casey says innocently.

Which basically proves I will never stop being surprised by my brother.

CASEY AND I are doing our homework the next afternoon when the doorbell rings. Mom's pulling overtime at the co-op, so Casey gets up to answer it.

"What are you doing here?" I hear him snarl, and I'm not too surprised by what I see when I look up.

Dad's standing in the doorway.

"Hi, boys," he says. "Can I come in?"

Casey's face is so dark it's amazing the lighting level in the room hasn't dropped. "No," he says shortly.

I sigh and head over to the door. "Dad, you should have called first."

"To see my own sons?" He looks genuinely hurt, but Casey just scowls harder.

"Oh, you still think of us that way? I thought you had a new kid to replace us with."

Dad's mouth drops open. "Casey, is that what you think I—"

Casey storms off before Dad can finish speaking, and his bedroom door slams shut.

I sigh again. "C'mon in, Dad," I tell him. "I'll get you some coffee. But you can't stay long, okay?"

Dad's frowning, and he hasn't moved out of the doorway. "He hates me, doesn't he?" His voice sounds hollow and broken.

"He's not giving you any father-of-the-year awards." I pull down a mug and start microwaving some of the coffee I made that morning.

Dad finally closes the door and steps into the entryway. He looks around. "The place hasn't changed much."

I pull the mug out of the microwave and take out sugar and cream. "Yeah, well, we're not exactly swimming in money to remodel."

Dad slips off his shoes and comes over. I gesture for him to sit down at the table, and I bring the mug and coffee supplies over to him.

61

Times like this are when I appreciate the completely open floor plan of our house. Since the living room and kitchen don't have any walls between them, it will be easy to see if Casey decides to come out of the bedroom, which is off the living room.

"What are you doing here, Dad?" I ask.

He sips the coffee and coughs slightly. "Your mom still likes Folgers, I see."

I snort. "Are you seriously insulting our coffee? Up the child support and we'll switch to Starbucks."

He has the decency to blush at that, at least. "I guess I deserve that." He holds the mug a little tighter. "Emmitt, for what it's worth, I certainly haven't replaced you and Casey with Gina. I love her, but I love you and Casey just as much."

"You've got a funny way of showing it." I cross my arms.

He rubs at his forehead. "You have to understand—it isn't easy not seeing you and Casey. But my life is in Ohio now. I call as often as I can, son. I do. And if I thought you and Casey wanted to come spend holidays and summers with us, I'd invite you. But is that what the two of you really would have wanted all these years? To leave your mother alone on Christmas and come spend it with me and your stepmother?"

He's got a point.

"Maybe not," I tell him. "But it still wouldn't kill you to invite us. I've never even met this stepmother. For all I know, you made her up."

He sighs. "I know. I thought about bringing her along on this trip… and Gina. But I've never exactly figured out how to do this, not well. I'm doing the best I can."

I'm thinking that his best is about as weak as fathering can get—until I think about Dusty, and then I immediately retract that thought. Our dad has always called. And made sure we were fed and taken care of.

"Anyway," Dad says, "I didn't come here to fight. I came because I heard back from someone from the NTDP. They did more research on you, and they'd like to meet you."

"Seriously?" I can feel my eyes widen.

"Look, I know you weren't planning on leaving home until graduation, but you know what an amazing chance this is. To be honest, when I reached out to them I didn't expect them to be quite this interested.

But it seems like someone remembered you from a few years ago, and here we are. This is a once-in-a-lifetime opportunity, Emmitt."

I know that.

"You'll have your choice of almost any college if you do well there. Maybe even the NHL."

I know that too.

"Anyway," Dad says, "one of their scouts is going to be in the upstate New York area this week watching games. He agreed to make a side trip and come have dinner with us. Tuesday."

My mouth must drop open. "Seriously? This week? He's never even seen me play."

"I guess he looked up some of your video. And when I told them about your GPA, they were especially interested in talking to you right away. They like discipline, and your record shows you have it." He nods over to where my schoolbooks are still out and open on the living room table next to Casey's. "I know you've got a lot going on right now, but keep up your grades, okay? That's the big key to your package right now: you're not just an amazing player, you're got the brains too."

No pressure at all.

Dad glances back at Casey's bedroom door. "How do I get him to see me while I'm here?" he asks. His voice is smaller than I've ever heard it.

It's an interesting question. I think about why I'm talking to him right now… why I even let him in the door. I think about Dusty's dad. "Don't give up," I finally tell him.

Dad looks up, startled. "Oh," he says.

I'm not sure either one of us knows what that means. But if anyone needs to figure it out, it's him.

"So." Dad drains the last of his coffee. "You in? Tuesday?"

I wish it were easy to say no. To blow him off and go back to just hoping for some college scouts to love what I'm doing in Colby.

But then I think about what Mom and Dusty both said, about me not giving up opportunities just because of who they're coming from and what I'm afraid of losing. Can I pass up the chance to talk to someone from the National Team Development Program?

"Sure," I tell him. "Why not?"

CHAPTER
SEVEN

Dear Mr. LeClair,

Today was my first day of high school.

It went okay. Colby High is huge compared to our junior high, but I got around okay. I know a bunch of guys from summer hockey camps, so that helped. All of my teachers are decent, and the work looks like it's going to be easy. That's good, 'cause I hear the hockey coaches here are slave drivers.

During lunch a bunch of clubs had booths out in the cafeteria, and people from every club were standing around trying to recruit us to join. They had a skateboarding club, so Casey will like that. Speaking of Casey, did I tell you how weird he's been acting? When he dropped hockey and learned to skateboard after Dad left, I thought that was weird. Then, today, he came out of his room wearing black eyeliner. He's been wearing a lot of black clothes lately, but this was the first time he put on makeup to go with them. I didn't know what to say.

Mom just smiled at him and told him he had some eyeliner on his cheek. Then she helped him clean it up. "Tomorrow I can show you how to apply it so that you don't get it all over yourself," she told him.

My mom is seriously the coolest person alive. She's handled everything Casey's done since Dad left like it doesn't faze her at all. When he snuck out in the middle of the night this summer to go skateboarding with some of his friends (and do hell knows what else), she just texted him one thing: Be safe. I'll be waiting up when you get back, and then we'll talk. I'll always love you no matter what.

Casey hasn't snuck out since.

I don't think it's that big of a deal if Casey wants to start wearing eyeliner and stuff. He'll give it up when he gets sick of it, the way he gave up gymnastics when we were little.

Here at Colby, the kids who dress all Goth like that definitely DO NOT sit with the hockey players. The cafeteria here looks like it's been divided by wardrobe or something. But if Casey's still dressing in black when he gets to Colby in two years, I don't care what anyone says. I'll always sit with my little brother. Even if his eyeliner does look completely ridiculous. Which it does.

I saw a few clubs I might want to join, if I have time. I'm going to sign up for weight training to keep in shape for hockey tryouts. I'll probably apply for the National Honor Society next year when I'm eligible. And I might even join Mathletes if I have time.

There's this other club I want to join: the Gay-Straight Alliance. I'm not sure exactly what they do, but I think they try to get gay and straight people to work together and get along or something? Mostly I just want to join because I never knew there could be a club where you talked about being gay. I can't join, though. There's no way. If I join, everyone will think I might be gay. And then what if I don't make the hockey team?

I thought about talking to my mom about all this. I know I could. She's been so cool about everything that's going on with Casey, and she's always listened to me whenever I needed to talk about anything. I could tell her that I'm worried about joining the GSA and why I think I might want to join, and I know she'd understand. I know she'd be there for me.

But I also know that then I'd have to think about actually joining the GSA. And that might screw up hockey. And I have to play hockey. I have to. I can't take the chance.

So I guess I'm joining Mathletes.

—Emmitt LaPoint, age 14

MONDAY'S A blur of school and hockey practice. Dusty and Casey spend lunchtime holed up in the library together, and when I ask Dusty why, he gives me some vague answer about a math project.

"Math?" I ask him. "I thought your math teacher never gave you anything but tests."

Dusty concentrates hard on his locker as he's opening it. "Not always," he mumbles. "Listen, I'm going to be late for science. Did you want something?"

"Whoa." Why is he trying to get rid of me? "Dusty, man, did I do something to piss you off? If I did, I'm sorry, but you gotta tell me what."

His shoulders slump. "You didn't do anything. Sorry I'm being an ass. Just have to do this other… thing after school today that I don't want to do. For math," he adds hastily.

He's acting weird again, and it's gotta have something to do with whatever he hasn't been telling me for weeks. But then the bell rings, and I can't be late for AP History. The last kid who tried that wrote extra essays for two weeks.

I QUIZ Casey after practice that night. After all, what good is having a brother who's best friends with your boyfriend if you can't pump him for information? But Casey's not cracking.

"Dusty's fine," he tells me. "We were just doing math stuff together, that's all. Mrs. Roberts is on him right now."

"You sure?" I ask. "He's been weird lately. And you two have been all weird together sometimes. Like you're hiding something."

We're sitting in the living room, half watching a hockey game. Casey's paying more attention to his Facebook account than the TV, though. "Listen," he tells me, "I'm not getting in the middle of whatever spat you two are having. If you want to talk to Dusty about shit like this, talk to him. Not me. Now what are you making me for dinner?"

I eye him suspiciously. Something is *definitely* going on. Casey's never this secretive with me.

"Does he want to break up?" I ask Casey. "Is this because of what happened with Dawn? Is he pissed off because I still want to keep things a secret? Or is he—"

Casey groans and puts his phone down. "Shit. E, he's not breaking up with you, okay? Although if you want my honest opinion, you need to seriously think about what you're doing to him with this whole closet romance thing."

"*Closet romance?* Have you been watching rom-coms again?" But now he's got me thinking. "So he is upset because I still don't wanna tell people."

Casey shakes his head. "You always want everything to be so black and white, Emmitt. Dusty would do anything for you; you have to know that. He'd take this secret to the grave if you asked him. But that doesn't mean it's easy for him or anything. Think about what this is like for him. You're this guy that half the girls in our school drool over and half the guys want to be, and he's just this kid who hangs around you all the time, watching all that shit."

I guess I've never thought about it like that before.

"And… well, let's just say that sometimes keeping the Emmitt LaPoint secret is harder for Dusty than it is for Emmitt LaPoint."

I jerk my head up from where I've been basically staring at the floor. "What's that mean?"

He frowns for a moment like he wants to say more, but then he stops and shakes his head. "Nothing. It just means… what I said before, okay? You need to talk to Dusty, man. You need to make him talk to you. 'Cause he's never gonna tell you on his own how hard this is getting for him."

That sounds like Dusty. Always putting other people first.

"Anyway, you didn't answer me. What are we having for dinner?" Casey goes back to staring at his phone.

I groan. "I'm too tired to move. Practice was rough today."

"Hot dogs and macaroni it is," he says, standing up. "I got it." He heads to the kitchen, and I can hear him turning on the tap to boil water. "So you're going to that dinner with Jackass tomorrow, huh?" he calls over to me as he's working.

Now I groan inwardly. Just what I want to talk about. "Yeah, I guess so."

"What a fuckwad. Coming back out of nowhere and just expecting us to be happy to see him. Like he hasn't been hiding us from his new family all this time."

I get up painfully off the couch and limp into the kitchen to sit down at the table. "Actually, I don't think he's been hiding us. I think…

maybe he was just trying to respect Mom, let her have us to herself. Or something." I shake my head. "I don't really understand him. But he wants to help, and the NTDP is a big deal. So yeah, I'm going."

"Wow. You mean you actually might move to Michigan?" Casey's voice is quieter now.

"No," I tell him quickly. "I'm just talking to the guy. They probably talk to lots of people who never make the team. It's not that big a deal."

Casey seems to accept that, and he doesn't even burn the macaroni and cheese.

CASEY'S NOT the only one who's got the dinner on his mind. "How are you feeling about tonight?" Dusty asks me as we're walking back to our lockers after lunch the next day.

"Actually, I feel okay about it," I tell him. "Maybe it helps that making a team like that is such a long shot, you know? Takes some of the pressure off."

Dusty nods and spins the combination on his lock. "Just… don't forget what I said in the car on Valentine's Day, okay? I don't want you to think you can't go to Michigan because of me. I want you… to go wherever you want." Dusty stares intently into his locker the entire time he's saying the words.

"I want to stay in Vermont. I want to go to UVM," I tell him. "I always have. I mean, am I going to listen to what this guy has to say? Hell, yeah. This is the squad that builds future NHL players and Olympians. But whatever he says or doesn't say, it's not going to change things for us."

Dusty leaves for class with a small smile, and I leave hoping I just made a promise I can keep.

On the way to dinner that night, Dad talks so fast I'm a little worried he's going to work himself into a heart attack. "Don't forget to tell him about all your hockey awards and how you were team MVP the last two years. And make sure you mention your GPA once or twice. And what other sports and clubs are you in right now?"

This is already exhausting. "Track in the spring and weight-training club. I'm in the National Honor Society, and I'm a Mathlete. Oh… and I'm thinking of joining the GSA after hockey's over. Casey's joining."

"GSA?" Dad looks curious.

"Gay-Straight Alliance."

Dad shakes his head. "Emmitt, I think that's a big mistake. Now, don't get me wrong; I'm as open-minded as anyone. But hockey teams don't want to worry about whether they're going to have to deal with some Michael Sam drama on their teams. And it's not like you're gay anyway, son. Pick another club to join, okay?"

I open my mouth to tell him all the things wrong with what he just said. For one thing, Sam got drafted to the NFL, didn't he? For another, all kinds of college hockey teams have been making these YouTube videos saying they're fine with having gay players on their teams. They're part of this thing called the You Can Play project.

I looked a bunch of them up after Dusty and I kissed the first time, and I've been watching a lot of them lately.

But I don't feel like trying to explain all that to Dad, and I sure don't feel like answering a bunch of questions about why I want to join the club so badly. I'm the one who won't tell anyone in school that I have a boyfriend, so maybe Dad's got a point. And it's not like those hockey players are coming out themselves or anything. So I just nod.

Dinner goes... well, fine. I'm nervous, but I don't think I screw up anything too badly. The scout's name is Jason Lewis, and he's from Maine.

"I remember you from when you were younger," he tells me. "I used to coach in the Deerfield Academy hockey program. We wanted you badly, and we were disappointed when you turned down our scholarship offer. You've just been playing local hockey since then? Here in Colby?"

"Yeah," I tell him. "It's a long story, but my family was going through some stuff, and I wasn't ready to leave them just yet. But I've been lucky enough to play for a killer high school program with a great coach."

"I watched some of your video from the playoffs last year. You scored seven points in one game?"

I sort of blush and beam at the same time; I can't help it. That game's basically the pinnacle of my hockey career so far. "He had four goals and three assists," Dad breaks in. "They slaughtered the other team nine to two."

I stare. How the hell does he know that?

"That is impressive," Coach Lewis says, "for any hockey division or league."

Yeah, it felt that way. Until I hurt my wrist and we got knocked out of the semifinals. "Like I said, I've been lucky. I have a coach who's pushed me and pushed our team. I really look up to Coach Morton."

Dad looks uncomfortable and starts asking Coach Lewis questions about how many NTDP players get drafted in the NHL.

At the end of the dinner, Coach Lewis shakes my hand and tells me he's decided to come watch my game this coming weekend. "I'd like to see you play live," he says. "And this is a big one, right? I hear this game is for the undefeated record."

"Sure is," I tell him. I haven't thought much about that in the past few days. Other things to think about, I guess. But in some ways, this game is almost as big as any of the playoff games that will come after it. It's been a lot of years since Colby had an undefeated season.

"Good luck, son," Coach Lewis says. "Though if your record says anything, you won't need it."

Dad can't stop talking about how well the dinner went as he's driving me back to my house. "He loved you!" he crows. "Emmitt, you had that man eating out of your hand. Especially when you were telling him about those games last year against...." He goes on, and I stop listening.

Playing for the NTDP would be amazing. In a lot of ways. I've lived in Vermont all my life, and playing for that team would mean traveling to parts of the country and world I've never even imagined visiting. Meeting people I've never even imagined meeting.

We get back to the house, and Dad hands me an envelope. "Hey, this is for you and Casey," he tells me. "Can you give it to him for me?"

I raise my eyebrows and open the envelope. Inside are two vouchers for plane tickets to Columbus, Ohio. Round trip. Open-ended.

"What the hell, Dad?" I ask. I'm not angry. Just surprised.

"I have to head back after your game on Saturday," Dad says. "Running out of time off. I may or may not be able to come back for the championships." I almost interrupt to remind him that the championship isn't a guarantee, but I decide not to. "So I'm not sure when I'll be back to see you boys again. But

I don't want things to stay the way they are between us, and I don't want you to think I'm hiding from you anymore. So this is the open invitation: come visit anytime you want. Doesn't matter when; you're always going to be welcome." He leans over and gives me a hug. If he notices I don't hug him back, he doesn't say anything. "I love you, son."

If he notices I don't respond, he doesn't say anything about that either.

THE NEXT day's Wednesday, and now we're only three days from the last game of the season. Talking with Dad and the scout last night has made me incredibly aware of that fact, and I'm feeling the pressure to make our next few practices count. I tell Dusty I'm going to do my homework in the library over lunch so I can finish it and get in some extra workouts that night, and he looks disappointed. "I'll come with you," he says.

I try not to look put off by that idea. "Dusty, if you come, I won't concentrate," I tell him. "I won't get anything done."

"I can be quiet," he insists.

"Man, it doesn't matter how quiet you are. When you're around, you're what I pay attention to."

After that he's definitely not as upset about eating lunch without me.

Wednesday evening's gone to hockey practice and extra workouts and more homework. It's like our teachers don't even know I'm coming up on one of the most important hockey games of my life. I fall asleep early and miss four calls from Dusty.

When I get up for breakfast the next morning, Casey and Mom are talking about Dad's airline tickets. Again. That's basically all they've talked about since I brought them home on Tuesday.

"I'm just saying," Mom tells him, "that it might be worth going." Again.

"I'm just saying," responds Casey, "like hell." Again.

I rub my eyes and go for the cereal.

"Your phone was ringing forever after you fell asleep," Casey tells me. "Learn how to put that thing on vibrate, man."

"Emmitt, who was calling you?" Mom asks.

I shrug. "Just Dusty."

Casey coughs. "*Just* Dusty? That's a crappy thing to say."

"I didn't mean it like that," I tell him. "I just mean that Dusty always calls me. I'll see him this morning at school."

"Make sure you do that," Casey tells me as he puts his dish in the sink.

"Make sure you do that?" Mom repeats. "Is something going on with Dusty?" Which is exactly what I'm wondering.

"Course not," Casey says airily. "Just wouldn't want Golden Boy over here to forget us little people in between all of his important meetings with national scouts."

"He's such a drama queen," I say to Mom.

She just raises an eyebrow. There's definitely a lot she's not saying to me right now. Good. I'd rather not hear it.

But just in case Casey's making one of his rare good points, the first thing I do at school that day is find Dusty. He's in the library staring at a math problem.

So maybe all this moodiness lately really is about math.

"You called me a bunch last night," I tell him. "Everything okay?"

Dusty looks up. "You didn't answer," he says. "Everything okay?"

That's not an answer. "I'm fine. I just fell asleep. What's up with you?"

He smiles, but it's forced. Not his usual smile at all. "I thought… that I needed your help with something. Math," he adds, gesturing to his paper. "But I figured it out. Everything's good."

Like hell it is.

"You sure?" I ask.

"I'm sure." He gives me another half-baked smile.

"You coming to practice today?" He hasn't come the last few days, and it would be nice to see him there. Even if he's just doing his homework in the stands.

"Maybe," he says. "Could you give me a ride home afterward? We haven't hung out, just the two of us, in a while. You know, outside of school."

He's right. It's probably been since Valentine's Day. But I hesitate anyway. Because the game's coming up on Saturday, and I've got a few tests the next day to study for…. Taking Dusty home is going to end up taking hours I don't have right now. Not if I'm going to ace those tests.

Dusty must see the look on my face, because he starts shaking his head. "Don't worry about it, Emmitt," he says. "I know you're busy right now. I should probably just go home and get ahead on all this math stuff anyway." He goes back to doing the problem.

"Hey." I lean down and stare at him across the table. "I promise we'll hang out after the game on Saturday. Just the two of us. Okay?"

He looks up. Smiles slightly, and there's a little more light behind this one. "I'd like that," he says.

Me too. I start to get up to leave.

"I'm going to my first GSA meeting next week," Dusty tells me casually. His eyes are back on his paper. "You going to come once the season's over?"

The amount of time I take to answer has to be all the answer he needs.

"I'm not sure yet," I tell him. "Dad seems worried that it might turn some scouts off if I do. Don't want to screw things up with any of them," I add hastily.

Dusty just nods. "Nope," he says, slowly. "You don't."

He doesn't say anything else when I get up to leave.

But the rest of that day holds itself together pretty well. Dusty and I eat lunch together, and laugh at some jokes together, and everything seems to be okay between us. I walk him to the bus stop before I leave for practice, and we do that thing where we look at each other like we want to kiss good-bye, even though we know we can't. Things feel good. The way they've felt so many times before.

So Thursday ends up being just fine.

Friday is when everything falls apart.

CHAPTER
EIGHT

Dear Mr. LeClair,

My dad left on Saturday.
Like, left. The state. For good.
Casey wouldn't come out of his room to say good-bye. He's barely come out since Mom and Dad told us they're getting divorced, and he's been getting in a lot of trouble at school. I'm worried about him.

I thought maybe Casey screwing up at school would make Dad stay, but it didn't. He told me that he knew this was hard, but it was the best thing for all of us. I still don't believe him. Maybe the divorce is best, but why does he need to move to Ohio? Is he trying to get away from us? I don't get it.

He said he'd call us all the time, but I don't think he will. I love Dad, but he's not the best at remembering to do things he said he was going to do. He's always forgetting to do the grocery shopping and stuff. It isn't his fault, I guess. He just gets distracted easily. Kind of like Casey.

He's been staying at Uncle Dave's since he and Mom separated, so he came over to say good-bye to me and Casey. But Case wouldn't leave his room.

He told me he loved me and that he would always love me. "I need you to take care of Casey and your mom," he told me. "You're the strong one, Emmitt. You always have been." I guess that was nice of him to say. And it made me feel kind of glad that I decided not to take that scholarship to play hockey for that high school in Massachusetts. But I don't want to be the strong one. I just want my dad to stay in my house.

Tonight Casey and I got home from school and the house was empty. Usually if Mom gets home late, Dad makes dinner, and the other way around. Mom told me that Casey and I were going to have to make dinner tonight, and she left macaroni and cheese and hot dogs.

I've made both of those things plenty of times. But when it was dinnertime, I just stared at the stove. Like I wasn't sure how to boil water or something. Then Casey started crying. He tried to pretend he wasn't, but I could hear him sniffling from the couch.

I didn't know how to make him feel better. But I remembered what my dad said about me being the strong one. So I made hot dogs and macaroni and cheese and cut the hot dogs into the macaroni, just the way Casey likes it. I brought it over to the couch and I gave it to him. "It's gonna be okay," I told him.

I don't know if he believed me. I don't know if I believed me. At least there's hockey practice tomorrow. Hockey practice always makes me feel better.

—Emmitt LaPoint, age 13

ON FRIDAY, Dusty isn't at school.

Casey claims to have no idea where he is. "Maybe he's sick," he tells me. I text Dusty over and over, but he doesn't answer. Casey tries texting him too, and I make him show me his phone to prove Dusty's not replying to him either.

Maybe I am getting just a little paranoid.

Then I get to AP History and find out I got a B- on a quiz we took the day before. For anyone else, a B- in this ridiculously hard class might be okay. For me? It's basically a stab in the heart. I've never gotten anything lower than a B+.

Mrs. Adwidzyc just pats my arm and tells me it's not the end of the world. "Your average is still quite impressive," she claims.

Then lunch comes, and I try to go to Coach's office to ask him if Dusty's okay, but he's not there—and he's got a sub. One of the other teachers assures me Coach is coming to practice later, though. "He took a personal day to deal with some family issues," she tells me.

Family issues? The last time Coach Morton took a day off to deal with family issues, Dusty had tried to run away to Colorado Springs.

For the rest of day, I can't let go of the sinking feeling that something's wrong. The day Dusty tried to run away last fall was the first time since my dad left that I'd felt truly hopeless. Alone. I'd just told Dusty I didn't think we could be together—that I couldn't be a hockey player with a boyfriend.

And then Dusty disappeared. Took off, just like that. I was convinced it was my fault, and it kind of was. It took me a while to realize Dusty ran away for a lot of reasons, not just because of me. But I was definitely part of the problem.

I'm a mess the rest of the day, and Casey's not much better. "Dude, everything's fine," he keeps telling me. "Matt and Julia are probably just sick or something, and he's busy taking care of them." But neither of us believe it.

We're twenty minutes into practice, doing drills for Coach Riley, before Coach Morton even shows up. He's pissed off about something; that's clear from his first whistle. He screams at every player who misses a pass or a play like they just brought Hitler back from the dead.

At the end of practice, he gathers us together. "I know I was hard on all of you tonight," he tells us. "But it's important we all remember what a big day tomorrow is. Sure, we're in the playoffs this year; that deal is done. But tomorrow you boys get to mark your places in history. You have a chance to prove to this community that you're some of the best Colby has ever seen. Let's show this town what this team is made of!"

Okay, decent pep talk. Maybe he's fine, and this practice has just been a reminder that we need to keep our heads in the game.

I find Coach in his office before I go to change, and I shut the door behind me. "Hey, is everything okay?" I ask him. "You and Dusty weren't at school today, and he's not texting me back."

Coach rubs his hands tiredly over his face. "Emmitt, you should change and go home. Big game tomorrow."

I laugh out loud. "What the hell is that supposed to mean? Did something happen?"

Coach shakes his head. "Dusty hasn't texted you back because I took his phone away." He sighs. "Emmitt, last night Beth and I discovered

Dusty has stolen over $300 from us. We keep a stash of cash on hand in the house for emergencies. Dusty knows where it is. Last night we found most of it was missing."

I'm instantly defensive. "That doesn't mean Dusty took it! Maybe Matt or Julia grabbed it."

Coach shakes his head again. "He admitted it, Emmitt. What's killing us, though, is that he won't tell us why. He keeps saying it's something he has to take care of himself and we can't help him. He's not talking to us; he barely left his room all day."

"What?" I can't even imagine how shocked I must sound. "Why would he need all that money? Was he trying to run away again?"

Coach shrugs. "I've wondered that too. I don't know what to do, Emmitt. I thought cutting off his means of communication with you and Casey might get him to talk to us, but that seems to be backfiring. I hate to ask you this the night before a game like tomorrow's, but if you want to come over for a few minutes after you change.... See if he'll talk to you...."

"Of course I'll come over." I'm up before Coach can say anything else. "He has to talk to me. He has to."

Coach smiles, but it's weak.

Dusty's house is unusually subdued when I get there. Usually I open that door to laughter or screaming or lots and lots of voices. But tonight all I hear is the sound of the TV from the living room. Coach is sitting in the kitchen with Mrs. Morton, drinking tea.

"Thanks for coming over, Emmitt," she tells me softly. "You don't have any idea what's going on?"

I shake my head adamantly. I still have a feeling Casey does, but I haven't even tried to push him for more information yet. I want to hear what Dusty says first.

I hike the two flights of stairs it takes to get to Dusty's room. "Dusty? It's Emmitt," I call through the closed door.

No answer.

"Are you okay?"

No answer.

Whatever. He's not getting away from me that quickly. "Dusty, I'm coming in," I tell him, and I shove the door open.

He's sitting on his bed, reading. Or maybe just pretending to read. *The Perks of Being a Wallflower*—a book I recommended to him a while ago.

"What's going on?" I ask him.

He shakes his head. "Emmitt, I don't wanna talk right now," he tells me.

"Dusty, *please*. What's going on? Why did you need all that money? Were you trying to take off again?"

He's biting his lip behind the book, and his next words sound shaky. "What if I was?"

What the hell? "It'd be a stupid idea, that's what! Are you trying to get away from me? From us?"

Dusty makes a snorting sound. "You can't run away from something that doesn't exist, Emmitt."

He might as well have just punched me in the stomach. "Excuse me?"

He shakes his head again, never taking his eyes off the page. "This isn't real, Emmitt. Not to anyone but us and our families. We're never gonna go to GSA meetings together or have a real date that isn't behind a wall somewhere or kiss in public or any of that shit. Not without messing up all your chances."

I don't know what to say. I thought he was okay with… this. With us. "Why didn't you say something like this sooner?" I finally ask.

He shrugs. "I thought it would be fine. But I'm getting sick of it, okay? I'm tired of being your dirty secret or whatever." He finally looks up, and the look in his eyes—I haven't seen that look since that time we got arrested together.

Which was also the first night we kissed.

"Emmitt, you have your secrets, and I have mine. I needed some money, so I took it. Let it go, okay?"

"I'm not gonna let it go. And you're not my dirty secret!" I probably sound like I'm about to cry or something, because I feel like I am. It's like I can't keep track of what's happening in this conversation. Like it's spinning around me and I'm just standing there, watching it go.

"Yes I am, Emmitt. You're always going to be the golden boy, and you're always going to have to be perfect for the people around you. And me—I'm never going to be perfect enough for you. For this." He heaves himself off the bed and goes over to his dresser, where he takes something out of a wooden box.

He barely turns around before I know what it is. The medal.

No. Nonononononononononono.

"Dusty, don't do this," I whisper. My voice is cracking and not stable at all, but I'm not going to cry. I'm going to fix this. "We can figure this out. We can tell everyone. It's fine. I'll still get to play hockey. We can go on dates and be like all the other couples and join the GSA and do whatever you want to do. Please don't end this." I know I sound like I'm begging, because I am. And I don't care.

I'd tell him anything to keep him from handing that medal back to me.

"No," he says, and now his voice sounds like it's cracking. "You deserve all the success you've worked for, Emmitt. I don't want to get in the way of any of that. I'm not... I'm not like you, Emmitt. You just get stuff... *right*. I get it wrong, no matter what I try to do. I thought I had this right, but I don't. I haven't had any of it right." He pushes the medal at me. "It's over, Emmitt. It probably should have been over a long time ago."

"It's *not* over." My voice is past cracking now, and my face is wet. Maybe I'm finally crying. Who cares? That's the least of my worries. "Dusty, you don't just get to decide this."

He takes one of my hands and pulls it toward him. Opens it up from the fist it's making. Presses the medal into it. "Yeah," he says. "I do." Then he leans over and kisses me gently. Lightly. "Go home, Emmitt. Get it all. The perfect season and the perfect GPA and the national team and whatever else you want. You deserve it all. You don't need me, Emmitt."

He's wrong. He has no idea how wrong he is. But every word I want to say is caught in my throat, and all I can do is stand there and stare, trying to pull in breaths that don't sound like mine at all. Eventually Dusty leaves the room; I can hear him padding softly down the stairs.

And I'm standing alone in his room.

Part of me wants to stay, to wait him out. He can't avoid his room forever. He'll have to come back sometime, and then we can talk about this. I can make sure he knows how wrong he is.

Then I look over at his bulletin board.

There used to be a picture there, of Dusty and me. Mrs. Morton took it at Thanksgiving right after we told my mom we were dating. She was so happy for us—didn't give one shit. She just hugged us both hard and told Dusty he was welcome at our house anytime. In the picture Dusty and I are sitting on the Mortons' couch, grinning at each other and laughing. Dusty printed off that picture and hung it up the next day.

The picture's gone.

I guess we are too.

I head down the stairs slowly, like I'm afraid I'll fall and break the rest of me if I walk too quickly. When I get into the kitchen, only Coach is there.

He takes one look at me and opens his arms. "Emmitt, come here."

I walk into him like a zombie, and he wraps me up in his arms. "I don't know what I did wrong," I whisper. "I don't know why he doesn't want me anymore."

Coach doesn't answer. Just holds on to me.

His sweater smells a lot like Dusty.

I WAKE up the next morning feeling like I drank *way* too much the night before. Which I didn't, even though I wanted to.

After I stopped snotting into Coach's sweater, he told me he didn't know why Dusty was breaking up with me either—but there was nothing either of us could do just then, except let Dusty be alone. So he sent me home, telling me to get as much rest as I could before the game the next day. "It'll work out, Emmitt," he told me. "Somehow. However it's all supposed to work out."

I wanted to go home and drink all the vodka in our freezer, but even in my sorry state I knew that wasn't a very good idea. So instead I spent most of the night tossing and turning, waking up every time I fell asleep for longer than ten minutes.

I've definitely been better rested for games before.

Casey was out at a party when I got home, and I didn't feel like texting him the news, so he probably still doesn't know Dusty and I are over. I'm not exactly excited about telling him, but I'd also like to get it over with… so I head out to the kitchen, where he's eating cereal and messing around with his phone.

"Hey," I say.

"Hey," he says, looking up. "Happened to you? Today's the game."
Thanks, Captain Obvious. "Rough night. You talk to Dusty?"

"Nah, still not answering. You?"

"Ah, yeah. He… broke up with me."

Casey's head shoots up. "The fuck? Why?"

I shrug. "No idea. He got caught stealing from Coach and Mrs. Morton… won't tell 'em why. I went over to talk to him, and he ended it. Said I'm too perfect for him and some other shit." Some of which was completely true, but I don't feel like getting into that right now.

Casey narrows his eyes. "That dickhead. He—" He stops and shakes his head. "Emmitt, don't worry about it. I got this. You're not staying broken up."

Now I know for *sure* Casey knows something I don't. "What's going on? What haven't you guys been telling me?"

Casey waves me off. "Nothing important. Just friend stuff. I've got this."

"Casey, tell me what the hell is going on right now."

Casey stands up. "No. I told you. It's a friend thing, Emmitt. Respect that. And don't worry about it. He's getting back together with you as soon as I talk to him." Casey puts his dish in the sink and points a finger at me. "Big game today. Go. I'm on it. See you at the game."

If my stomach weren't flipping over out of anger and frustration and about a zillion other emotions, the whole thing would be a little bit funny. Usually I'm the one telling Casey I'll take care of all of his problems.

It's kind of nice to have someone else taking care of me for once. Especially the one person out there Dusty might listen to.

"Sure thing, boss," I tell him.

"Emmitt?"

"What?"

"Eat something. You look like crap."

CHAPTER
NINE

DEAR MR. LeClair,

Do you like the locker room at your hockey rink? I don't think I like mine very much. I just decided that today. I used to like it. It used to be fun. Everyone would goof around and laugh together, and it was like we all got to hang out before practice. It was one of my favorite parts of the day.

But the locker room isn't as much fun as it used to be. Now guys like Patrick O'Sheridan and James Efferty are always throwing stuff, and people are calling other guys names. They say they're just joking, but last week they called Luis Henner "brown dick." I thought Henny was going to cry.

Like "brown dick" is even funny. What a stupid name to call someone.

I told Patrick to stop it, and he told me to stop being a faggot. Then I got really mad, and I told him I'd beat him up if he ever called me or Henny a name again. Patrick just laughed at me and told me to chill out, but I think he might have been a little scared. He's bigger than me, but he's also fatter. I could at least get him on the ground if I had to.

After practice Luis thanked me for standing up for him. I told him he didn't need to. Patrick's a jerk. "Thanks anyway," Luis said. "No one else stands up for me."

I guess he's right. People call Luis names a lot, now that I think about it. Now I wonder if that's because he's the only kid on our team who isn't white. We've been playing hockey together since we were six, and he's always been the only kid who isn't white.

Before, I never used to think about what it must be like to feel different from everyone else. Now I feel different all the time.

Thanks a Lot, John LeClair

Especially when Patrick calls me faggot.

—Emmitt LaPoint, age 12

So here I am. Center ice of the biggest game of the season. Probably the biggest of my high school career, and possibly the biggest of my life, if that scout from the national team shows up. I'm also newly single with less than four hours of sleep to my name.

At least there's plenty of noise in the rink to keep me awake. We're at home, and all of Colby seems to have come to this game. Dad's out there somewhere; I saw him come in with Uncle Dave. Mom and Casey are front row together. When I went by to bump fists with Casey, he just nodded at me and said, "I got this."

I wish I knew exactly what that meant.

Matt and Julia and Mrs. Morton are all here too. They came over to give Coach hugs a few minutes ago. But Dusty's nowhere in sight.

There's not much time for me to think about that, though. Because the buzzer goes off, the puck drops, and we're playing for the perfect season.

It's clear from my first pass that I should have gotten more sleep last night. I completely overshoot Eric, who glares at me while the other team steals the puck. When one of the Rice players checks me a little too hard, I grab for his uniform and end up getting called for holding. I almost *never* get called for holding. I also manage to get called for high-sticking and tripping at other points in the game. I look sloppy and undisciplined, and I know it.

Coach calls for a line change at some point. "What's going on with you?" He's leaning down, and our faces are even closer than they were last night. "Emmitt, I know you're not in the best place today, but you've *got to be here*," he tells me. "Not wherever you are right now."

I nod at him. I want to come back. I want to get so into the game that I can forget everything. Forget what Dusty said to me last night. Forget that he's missing my last game of the season. Forget that he doesn't want to be with me anymore.

But when I hit the ice a few minutes later, it's all still there.

Dusty's in front of the defenseman who gets the puck away from me with some stickhandling.

He's in front of the goaltender who blocks every shot I send his way.

He's on the side of me when I try to send a drop pass to O'Sher and completely miscalculate where he is.

And the more I screw up, the more frustrated I get. And the more frustrated I get, the more I lose my temper. By the end of the second period, I've amassed more penalties than I probably have in our last three games combined.

The only good news is that the rest of the team still has their heads on straight, so we're tied with Rice. It's a miracle I don't deserve to be a part of.

We're in the final minute of the period when their left winger goes after me, hoping to get the puck away, and I finally have a few seconds of decent enough stickhandling to keep it and send it to Luis Henner. "Faggot," the guy snarls as he heads after the puck.

Everything goes red, and all I see is Dusty, in that helmet, saying that to me over and over.

Faggot. Faggot. Faggot.

I rip after the guy, grab his pads from behind, and throw him to the ice. He hits it hard, and I start throwing punches so fast and so furious I'm not even sure they're coming from my hands. Behind me I can hear whistles and yelling, and then a few different people are pulling me up off the guy.

"Hey!" Eric spins me around and shakes me. "What's wrong with you, LaPoint? Get it the fuck together!"

"Game misconduct!" calls the referee.

I've been playing hockey since I was four years old. In all those years I've gotten called for almost every penalty there is at one point or another. But I've never, ever gotten called for game misconduct. I've never been thrown out of a game before.

Until now.

I'M SITTING in the locker room. Alone. Listening to the cheers from the rink while the game goes on without me.

84

I'm following the score on my phone every few minutes. We're still tied, but I'm not sure how long that will last. There's a lot of muffled groans coming through the walls, so Rice has probably taken more control of the game since I was escorted off the ice.

The door opens behind me, but I don't look up to see who's come in. It doesn't matter much anyway.

"You okay?"

Dad. Great. He's standing in front of me.

I look up. "What are you doing here?"

He snorts. "My son just got thrown out of a hockey game for fighting. My son who—despite playing hockey—never fights with anybody."

"If you were around more, you'd know that isn't true. I got arrested for fighting at a party last year. So did Casey. They just didn't press charges."

"Oh." He looks startled. "Your mother failed to mention that." There's cheering from the rink, and Dad gestures toward it. "You should still be out there. What the hell just happened, Emmitt? That scout saw all that."

I'm still in my pads—I haven't quite been able to bring myself to take them off, like there's some chance of someone coming back here and telling me they made a terrible mistake and of course I can still play—so I just give an awkward shrug under the padding. "Took my eyes off the prize, I guess."

"Is that supposed to be funny?" Now he sounds annoyed. "What's going on with you?"

He wants to be part of my life? He wants to know what's going on with me? What's *really* going on? Fine. I can do that. I chuck my phone down on the bench next to me. "You want to know what's going on? Here's the deal, Dad. I've been dating someone for four months. A guy. As in, not a girl. And he's Coach's nephew. And last night he broke up with me, probably because I said we couldn't tell anyone we were dating, so for four months he's had to keep it a secret. All so the team and the scouts wouldn't find out and I wouldn't ruin all the *chances* I'm supposed to have right now. Only now I messed up my chance to be with him. So I guess no matter what, I was always screwed."

Dad closes his eyes and rubs his forehead. "Emmitt, are you being serious right now? Are you telling me that—"

"I'm gay, Dad. I wanted to join the GSA because I'm the G part. And that asshole from Rice I just got into it with called me a faggot, and I lost it. Probably because I am a faggot, and maybe that's what faggots do. They start fights in ice rinks. So I may as well tell the world."

Dad's just standing there, staring at me. "Does your mom know?" he finally asks, and his voice sounds all strangled. "Casey?"

"They know," I tell him. "They don't care."

Dad takes a deep breath and sits down beside me. "Emmitt," he tells me, "you're my son, and I'll always love you. No matter who you want to be."

"It's not who I *want to be*, Dad. It's who I am." I sort of growl that.

It's an important point, but he waves it off. "Whatever. Emmitt, I'll love you no matter what. But you've got the whole world stretched in front of you right now. Success that millions of people dream of is waiting for you right outside that door. Son, you did the right thing keeping this to yourself. You're going to have to find a way to keep doing it. Later on you'll be able to do things differently—I really do believe that—but right now everything you've worked for is hanging by threads. Emmitt, I think you need to let this kid go and keep this secret. That's the best thing for you."

He's shaking his head slowly, like he's sad to have to say it or something, but it has to be said. And somehow, I'm angrier now than I ever have been. Angrier than the night he and mom told me they were getting divorced. Angrier than the day he drove away. Angrier than the day he called to say he was getting married again.

Maybe it's because up until now it's been my choice to keep this secret. He's the first person who's ever told me out loud that I have to.

I stand up and start pulling my pads off. Time to face the facts. No one's coming to rescue me from this locker room and put me back in that game. No one's coming to give me back my perfect season.

"You know what, Dad? It's *not* the best thing for me. It might be the easiest thing, but it's not the best thing. I know because I've tried it, and it's not the best thing for me at all. Just like you taking off to Ohio and never visiting us might have been the easiest thing for you, but it wasn't the best thing for us." I punctuate that last sentence by throwing my pads into my gear bag. "Just like me and Casey going to Ohio would probably be the best thing to do, but it isn't the easiest. Go home, Dad. Just go home, okay?" I grab my bag and my phone and head for the door, just in time to hear the goal buzzer go off and the crowd groan and boo.

Rice must have scored.

Looks like everyone's perfect season is about to come to an end.

I GO home and head straight for my bed. The world is shit, and I don't feel like being in it anymore.

I don't study for the big quiz I have coming up in science on Monday. I don't check the game score on my phone. I don't even look at my phone, which is buzzing away with texts and calls.

I pull out my ancient, beat-up copy of *The Perks of Being a Wallflower.* The book Dusty was reading when he ended things.

Perks is about secrets. The secrets we keep from ourselves and others. The fact that secrets always have a way of coming out in the end, no matter how much we try to hide them. The first time I read it was right after Alcott Moreau and I kissed at a summer hockey camp. That book helped me believe I wasn't the only one with secrets, and that I'd survive mine. It might be hard, but I'd survive.

Then Dusty came along, and it seemed like maybe there was going to be more than just surviving, and I started to believe that. Hope for that. Hope for something bigger than just perfect seasons and perfect GPAs and championships.

I throw the book against the wall. Even great literature lets you down sometimes.

There's a knock on the door. "Emmitt?"

Mom.

"Are you okay?" She waits a few minutes, but I don't answer. "Casey told me what happened, honey. Emmitt, I'm so sorry." She opens the door just a crack. "Sweetie, please answer me. I want to make sure you're okay."

I bury my head in the pillow. "We lost, didn't we?"

She comes in and sits down next to me on the bed. She combs her fingers through my hair, the way she used to do when I was little and feeling sick. "Yes. I'm sorry."

I shrug. "Doesn't matter anyway."

"Of course it matters." She sits up farther on the bed and pulls me toward her until I'm resting my head on her shoulder. She keeps combing her fingers through my hair as she kisses my forehead. "I wish there was something I could say that would make you feel better. You have no idea how much I wish for that right now," she says softly.

I wish for the same thing.

Casey peeks his head into the doorway. "Emmitt, I'm fixing this. I promise. Just give me some time."

I look up long enough to smile at him and shake my head. "Thanks, Casey. But you can't fix a perfect season once you've lost a game."

He frowns. "That's not what I meant. I meant—"

"It doesn't matter, Casey." I bury my head back into Mom's shoulder. "None of it matters anymore."

Then I sleep. Finally.

CHAPTER
TEN

Dear Mr. LeClair,

Were you ever bad at something? Probably not. I bet you are good at everything.

I want to be good at everything. My teachers say I am smart and my hockey and soccer coach are always saying I have lots of talent. I think that means I work hard? Or maybe that is something different.

But today I was not very good at science. I got a D on my quiz. Mom and Dad are going to be disapointed. They worry about Casey's grades all the time and they wont want to have to worry about mine too.

I'm not sure what happened. I studied. I guess maybe not enough. We have had lots of practices lately and I'm tired lots. I forgot to do some of the extra exersises Mr. Zidecky told us to do.

I have to get my quiz signed by Mom or Dad. How do I tell them? I have never gotten a D before.

—Emmitt LaPoint, age 9

Sunday's a lost day. I spend most of it sleeping. Some of it rereading books I've already read. A lot of it wondering.

Stupid shit. Things like:

Do straight guys feel like this when they break up with girls?

Shouldn't I be pissed off at Dusty or something? Why aren't I mad?

Should I try calling him?

Should I call Eric and apologize for screwing the team over?
Will any team ever want me to play for them now?
What's that scout from the national team telling people about me?
What's Dusty doing right now?

Eventually I give up trying to figure anything out and go back to sleep.

I'm up at four in the morning on Monday, so I go to school way early and work out in the weight room. It doesn't help much, but at least it takes my mind off things for an hour or so. I'm leaving the gym's locker room when I almost walk right into Dusty.

Dusty's got brown hair and blue eyes, and his darker hair always seems to make his eyes look brighter than they probably are. In that moment they widen so much all I see is blue, and I have to step back to keep myself from grabbing him and walking into it.

Dusty takes his own step back before he turns and goes in the other direction.

It's my own fault. I completely forgot that a lot of freshman lockers are out here in east buttfuck by the gymnasium. I slam my fist into the wall, which doesn't do anything except hurt my hand and draw a lot of strange stares from people around me.

This day's off to a great start.

My walk down to the juniors' lockers comes with a mixed reception. People who hate Rice (they're one of our biggest sports rivals), want to congratulate me for trying to take that guy out in the game. People who actually get hockey want to know why I got myself thrown out.

Doug Czychovi meets me at my locker. "Dude, are you okay? You didn't answer any of my calls yesterday. What the hell happened to you on Saturday, man? You looked like a different player or something. That was some crazy stuff."

I just shake my head. "Dougie, I'm sorry. I screwed up. I wasn't… feeling well. I didn't sleep much the night before. I should've said something, I guess."

"That's you not feeling well?" Dougie chokes on a laugh. "When I don't feel well, I cough a lot. You start fights with the goons from Rice."

"Umm… everyone gets over the flu differently, I guess."

Dougie shakes his head. "I guess. You okay now?"

Not really. "Better. I hope."

"Cool." He hesitates. "Listen… did Eric call you?"

He might have. I let my phone die sometime on Saturday night, and I haven't checked it since. "I don't know. Why?"

Doug tries to shrug nonchalantly, but he doesn't really pull it off. "Maybe give him some time to cool off. He was kind of pissed you got yourself kicked out like that. Even if you weren't on your A-game, we definitely fell apart once you were out."

Great. More people who don't want anything to do with me.

Doug pats me on the shoulder. "I'm just glad you're gonna be back for the quarterfinals. That's what really matters anyway: the state championship. Screw this perfect season bullshit. No one cares about that if you win the championship."

Neither of us believe him, but I nod anyway.

The morning's a wash. A few teachers pull me aside to ask if I'm okay. All of Colby was at the game on Saturday, so all of Colby watched me have that meltdown.

Then we have a pop quiz in physics. I look at the paper and realize I know maybe half the answers.

So I answer the ones I know and leave the rest blank.

Mr. Porwitz picks up my paper and does a double take. I didn't actually think people did that except in cartoons, but I guess they do.

After that encounter I probably shouldn't be too surprised by what happens in my next period, which is AP history. We're right in the middle of a Vietnam War video—definitely puts my measly problems in perspective—when Coach interrupts class. "Could I see Emmitt for a minute?" he asks.

I step out with him into the hallway. "Mr. Porwitz told you about my pop quiz," I say before he can state the obvious.

He smiles. "There's the intelligence we all know and love."

I want to smile back. Only Coach still looks like the older version of Dusty—blue eyes and all. So now I'm staring at them again.

"C'mon, Emmitt," he says. "Let's take a walk."

We go down to his classroom, which is empty. He grabs a chair from one of the student desks and sets it next to his desk, gesturing for me to sit down. "You did a nice job of ignoring all my calls yesterday."

I shrug. "I was asleep."

"Well, that's good. On Saturday you looked like you needed it." His eyes narrow. "You eat anything?"

Mom tried to get some food into me yesterday, but I wasn't exactly hungry. "A little. I guess." Come to think of it, I should be a lot hungrier than I am right now. Especially since I worked out this morning.

"Emmitt, listen. Don't come to practice tonight."

"What?" My head snaps up. "Am I off the team or something? Coach, I know I screwed up, but—"

"You're not off the team. Far from it. But we've got quarterfinals this weekend. I need your head back in the game. And the odds don't look good for my nephew getting his own head out of his butt and talking to you…. He's just as much of a basket case as you are, and he still won't tell me and Beth why he took that money." He shakes his head. "Listen. Take tonight to get yourself together. Sleep some more. Eat. Please, eat. Figure out how to be Emmitt again. The Emmitt who actually studies for quizzes and plays clean hockey and doesn't start fights with people for no reason. I was hoping Dusty would figure out his crap, but I'm not sure when that's going to happen, Emmitt. You may have to do this by yourself."

I swallow. "What if I don't want to be that guy anymore, Coach? What if I don't want to get the grades and play the perfect games anymore? What if I don't want to be the golden boy? What if I don't care about any of that anymore?"

"Emmitt." Coach smiles. "You think success is some trophy you put on your shelf? Some number you graduate high school with? Success isn't something you hold up for other people to look at. It's a life that's filled with happiness. Hope. Meaning. Things like that. *That's* what the goal is. You end up with any of those things, and it won't matter how many trophies and numbers you have to show off."

I don't answer.

"You don't believe me." He leans forward over his desk. "There are a lot of people in this world—hell, in this town—who think I'm a failure. Because I never made it to the big time. Because I coach a high school team and I didn't play in the Frozen Four or the NHL. But you know what? I've had either happiness or hope or meaning in my life every single day since I finished high school. I wouldn't trade my life for anything—even a career in the NHL."

I think about that. "So you're saying it doesn't matter if I fail my next science quiz?" I finally ask.

Coach laughs. "He's back! From wherever he was Saturday and Sunday and wherever he's been all day today." He claps me on the back. "Don't worry so much, Emmitt, about being the golden boy. I know who you are, and so do you. Getting As on quizzes and playing good hockey are the things that make you happy. There might be other things you want to start doing besides getting As and playing hockey. Doesn't mean you have to give those first two things up."

I'm not sure whether that's right or not. So all I say is, "I'll take practice off tonight." I stand up. "Hey, Coach?"

"Yes?"

"I'm sorry I ruined our perfect season."

Coach cocks his head at me. "Emmitt, there was a whole team on the ice Saturday. And several coaches. We took or gave up that perfect season together. That game was never all on your shoulders, and I'm sorry if I ever made things seem otherwise."

"No." Now I shake my head. "You never did, Coach."

"Good. Because I don't need the perfect season trophy on my mantel to call myself a successful coach."

I groan. "You just crossed into after-school-special territory, Coach."

He pretends to look surprised. "But I haven't even pulled out my 'don't do drugs' talk yet!"

I laugh and head back to class. I can get through the rest of the day now, I think.

I might be ready for the rest of the day, but I'm not quite ready for lunch with the hockey crowd yet. So I sneak Casey off campus and take him to Burger King. We sit in the parking lot in the cold cab, eating Whoppers and fries and talking about Dusty.

"He's not talking to me," Casey says. "I'm trying, Emmitt, I swear. I can fix this, I know I can—if he'll just talk to me. But he's ignoring me. He even walked away from me in the hallway this morning, told me to leave him the hell alone."

That doesn't sound like Dusty at all. But then again, none of this does.

"But you know why he stole the money." I point my Coke at Casey.

Casey shrugs in response. "Doesn't really matter if I know or not. The money doesn't actually have anything to do with why he broke up with you."

"You said you haven't talked to him!" There's a lot of accusation in my voice.

Casey rolls his eyes. "I haven't. But I don't have to be in the National Honor Society to get why he broke up with you. He's sick of you acting like this is 1996 or something and refusing to tell anyone you're as queer as ABC Family."

That's a lot of references in one sentence. "Why 1996? And why ABC Family?"

"Clinton signed the Defense of Marriage Act in 1996. Duh. And I dunno if ABC Family's all *that* queer, but the last time I was at Maria's house, she made me watch this show on that channel where they were talking about lesbian bed death. So I just figured…."

That almost beats his use of *pejorative.*

"Okay," I say. "So I've been acting like an asshole. I want to fix it. I don't care what the hockey team or the scouts or Dad or anyone else says. How do I fix it?"

"Dad?" Casey's eyes narrow. "What's he got to do with this?"

So then I have to tell Casey what went down in the locker room, and *that* doesn't end well. Casey's practically snarling by the time I'm done. "I'm so glad he went back to Ohio."

"I didn't realize he did." I guess that answers all my unasked questions about the scout. If Dad went back to Ohio without even talking to me, the scout must have decided he wasn't interested. I can't say I blame him.

Casey shrugs. "Mom told me. On Sunday, when you were in your bed coma. Now I'm definitely not going out there to meet Family Numero Dos."

I don't exactly want to go either, but I'm also not interested in talking about Dad right now. "Focus, Casey. How do I convince Dusty I don't care who knows about us anymore? That I just want us to be together?"

"Easy. Tell people. But Emmitt, you've been making Dusty hide this thing for a while now, so you've got a lot to make up for. I think you're going to have to go for a grand gesture if you want him back."

"A grand gesture?" I'm lost.

"Sure. You know—that big moment that shows him how much you care. That moment he won't see coming." I have zero idea what he's talking about. "You know!" Casey adds. "Um… like that moment in *The Mighty Ducks* when the coach comes back and apologizes for being a jerk to the whole team, and they all do the Flying V to show him they forgive him."

"Which *Mighty Ducks*? That happens in all of them. And which one is the grand gesture? The apology or the V?"

Casey throws up his hand. "Both! Don't worry about it. Listen, you need this grand gesture, Emmitt. And I know exactly what you need to do. Ask him to the spring dance."

"Oh." My eyes probably go crazy wide. "That is… that's big. That's telling everyone."

"Yup. Which is the point. But he's not talking to you, so you need to find a better way to ask him than texting him or e-mailing or something. You're going to go old school here, Emmitt. Leave a note in his locker. All apologetic and begging him to forgive you or whatever. Asking him to the dance. You still know his combination, right?"

"Yeah. If he didn't change it."

"I bet he didn't. Listen, you need to do it tonight, Emmitt. Five o'clock."

That's awfully specific. "Five o'clock? Why then?"

Casey hesitates for just a second. "Because that's when everyone's gone but the school's still open for people who are finishing up with clubs and stuff. It's the best time."

He's got a point, I guess. "Okay. Will you help me write the letter?"

"No." Casey bites off a huge chunk of Whopper.

"No?" I fire up the truck. We're going to be late for sixth period if we don't head back now. "I thought you wanted to help me fix this."

"I do. But Emmitt, if this is gonna be a grand gesture, it's gotta be totally from you. Dusty can't think I had anything to do with it."

Another good point. My brother's got more than just PSAT vocabulary and vague pop culture references going for him.

CHAPTER
ELEVEN

Dear Mr. LeClair,

THE WEIRDEST THING JUST HAPPENED TO ME.

First of all, I'm at hockey camp right now. Did you ever go to hockey camps? I bet you went to a lot of them. I go every summer. It's the best part of summer, you know? Playing hockey all day long. So great.

Anyway, hockey camp's always full of lots of interesting people. At the beginning of camp this year I met this guy named Alcott, who lives all the way down in Bennington. He's funny, and smart, and his playing style is a lot like mine. We've been hanging out a lot. He's a year older than me, so he can drive. After practices are over, sometimes we'll go out for burgers or whatever with the guys and then drive around and talk. We've talked about a lot of things so far. My dad leaving, his uncle dying of cancer. Which one of our teams is going to take state next year. (Honestly, it probably won't be either one. Rice has the best team right now.) Why Vin Diesel is the shit. Just random stuff.

Tonight we were driving around, just killing time until curfew. Alcott found this park that was completely empty, and he pulled out some joints. I don't like to smoke all that much, but I'll do it once in a while. It doesn't do much for me. Just makes me cloudy and spacey, I guess.

It makes Alcott all quiet. We were lying across this picnic table next to each other, looking up at the sky. It was clear and warm and the stars looked brighter to me than they usually do.

"Emmitt," Alcott said, "can I kiss you?"

I didn't even think about it. "Sure," I said. So he did. He rolled over and kissed me. For a long time.

To be honest, I don't remember it all that well. My brain still felt fuzzy from the weed, but my heart was beating faster than it does when I run. Weird. Mostly I was just concentrating on trying not to bite Alcott's tongue or throw up in his mouth.

Then Alcott pulled away. "Don't tell anyone, okay?" he said.

"Of course not," I told him.

We didn't talk at all the whole way back to the dorm. Now I'm in my twin bed, writing and listening to Henny snore, and thinking about Alcott.

I wonder if he's thinking about me.

—Emmitt LaPoint, age 15

FIVE O'CLOCK comes, and I've got the letter ready to go.

It took me forever to write. Way longer than something this short should have taken. But I went through a lot of drafts before I finally figured out what I wanted to say.

Before I knew what I *needed* to say.

I'm not sure it's going to be enough. But I have to try.

I throw on my backpack and leave the library with a nod to one of the librarians. I've been here for hours now trying to make this thing perfect. Who knows what she thinks I've been doing over in the corner, swearing and crumpling up pieces of paper into tiny balls.

I'm rounding the corner to the hallway where Dusty's locker is when I hear it: Dusty's voice. *Shit.* He's not gone yet. I freeze.

"Look, I told you," Dusty's saying. "There isn't any more money. Jack caught me. I can't get any more, and he wants to know where everything I took went."

"I hope you were smart enough not to tell him" is the response.

Every muscle in my body tenses up. I know that voice.

That's Rick. Rick Snyder.

Rick Snyder's been a lot of things in my and Dusty's worlds, and none of them are good. He's hated me since he got kicked off the hockey

97

team and I took his starting spot, and he's hated Dusty since he figured out Dusty is the nephew of the guy who kicked him off the hockey team. He's the one who started the fight at the party last year that ended with me and Dusty getting arrested. Rick's sort of the quintessential hockey goon: tall, built, and wide. His voice is lower than any high school senior's voice should be, and I recognize it right away.

"I didn't tell him," Dusty says. "But he's still asking. What am I supposed to say?"

"You tell him whatever you need to tell him," Rick snarls, "if you don't want this video all over my Facebook page by tomorrow night. And you've got until this Saturday to come up with another hundred bucks."

"A hundred bucks?" Dusty sounds desperate now. Scared. Which makes me want to run around the wall and jump between him and Rick. Protect him in any way I can.

"A hundred bucks. And I don't care how you get it; just get it. Or everyone in the school's gonna see this by Monday. I'll meet you at the hockey rink before the game on Saturday."

There's the sound of footsteps, and then the sound of a locker opening and closing. Then more footsteps.

Forget this letter I just spent hours writing. I need to know what's going on. I need to find Casey.

Luckily for me, he's not far. He's on our couch at home, doing homework with some skateboarding video on in the background.

"Hey." I step in front of the TV and flip it off.

"I was watching that!"

"Really? 'Cause I thought you were doing algebra homework."

"I was doing both," he says stubbornly.

"Whatever. Listen, you wanna tell me again why I needed to bring that letter to Dusty's locker at exactly five o'clock today?"

Casey sits up a little straighter and puts his textbook down. "Why? Anything interesting happen?"

I cross my arms. "I don't know. Did you expect something interesting to happen?"

We stare each other down.

Finally I give in. I don't have *time* for this crap. "Fine. You know what I saw—or heard, I guess. I heard Dusty talking to Rick. They were saying something about Rick wanting money or he was going to show everyone a video. What do you know about this, Casey? You didn't send me to that locker at five o'clock by accident."

Casey shakes his head slowly. "Nope. Here's the thing, Emmitt. You may be my brother, but Dusty is my friend. And sometimes friends make promises that they won't tell certain secrets. So. I may not be able to *tell* you more about what's going on here. But you can make statements about what you think is going on, and I *can* say whether those statements are true or false."

I roll my eyes. This is going to take forever. But I need to know what's going on... so I'll play the game.

"Okay," I say. I do some minor pacing in front of the television. "So. Rick has some video Dusty doesn't want people to see."

"True." Casey nods hard. "Good job. You're doing good."

"Shut up." I glare at him. "Okay... so, Rick's been blackmailing Dusty for money. I didn't even know that asshole was out of juvie."

"He's going to the alternative high school. That's not a secret; lots of people know that."

"Okay. Anyway. This has been going on for...." I try to remember when Dusty started to act strange around me. There was that weird phone call a few weeks ago; that was probably Rick. And that game he missed a while ago. I'm starting to think that wasn't for a class project. "Maybe three weeks or a month."

"Close enough. True."

"What could he have a video of?" I rub my temples; my brain hurts from trying to figure this out. "Dusty doesn't do anything bad. He usually follows all the school rules. He doesn't even drink much at parties. What could Rick have a video of that Dusty wouldn't want people to see?"

Casey just stares at me.

And then it clicks. The one and only thing Dusty has to hide.

Me. Us.

"Crap," I whisper. "Rick has a video of me and Dusty together."

"True! True! True!" Casey jumps off the couch and pumps a fist. "*Yes.* Emmitt, you have no idea how long I've been waiting for you to figure this out. This secret's been killing me!"

"It's been killing *you*?" I don't even try to hide how angry I am. "My boyfriend was keeping a huge secret from me—about me! And you knew! And you didn't tell me!"

"Sorry, Emmitt." Casey shrugs. "Friend code."

"Holy shit." I flop onto the couch next to him. "No wonder Dusty's been acting so weird."

Casey nods. "I only found out because he finally broke down one day. He made me swear I wouldn't tell you and Coach. I tried to help him, Emmitt. You gotta believe me. I tried to tell him keeping this a secret was a bad idea."

"I don't get why he wouldn't tell us. Did he think he could just keep paying Rick off forever?"

"No." Casey sighs. "Emmitt, Dusty figured he'd only have to pay Rick off until you decided you were ready for people to find out. Then you'd tell people on your own and…."

"The video wouldn't matter anymore." I groan. "Only I kept stringing him along about telling people." Everything about our breakup makes a lot more sense now.

"Yeah." Casey shrugs. "He thought he'd take a little money from Coach and pay it off before he and Mrs. Morton noticed it was missing— you know, with odd jobs and stuff. But Rick kept asking for more money. And you were starting to make it sound like you might never tell people. Things got out of hand."

They sure did.

"What do I do, Casey?" I finally ask.

"Well." He frowns. "You didn't leave the note in the locker tonight, did you?"

"No. Kind of got distracted. Didn't you send me there to see Dusty and Rick talking, anyway?"

He shrugs. "I was hoping you'd be able to do both. Anyway, I still think you should ask Dusty to go to the dance with you."

"I've got to do more than that," I tell him quietly. "First I've got to fix this."

He nods. Slowly. "Yeah, you do. How?"

Which is an excellent question.

THE PROBLEM is where to start.

I think about talking to Coach. Dusty probably considered the same idea at some point.

And I come to the same conclusion Dusty probably did: Coach can't do much. He can talk to Rick and tell him to leave Dusty alone, but all Rick has to do is deny the video exists and deny he's been asking Dusty for money. Then he can do whatever he wants with the video.

At this point it doesn't even matter to me whether Rick sends out the video. I've already made up my mind about what I need to do: I need to make this right with Dusty, and making this right is going to mean I stop hiding from everyone. But that doesn't mean I want Rick to be the one who tells everyone about us. I don't want to give him that kind of power.

So going to Coach isn't going to help.

I could try to talk to Dusty. I could tell him we'll figure this out together and ask for his help. But I'm betting he won't listen to me at this point; I wouldn't listen to me. I need to prove to him that he can depend on me.

So the first thing I need to do is take some of Rick's power back. And I'm pretty sure I know the group of people I need to come clean with first if I'm going to make that happen.

I decide to start with Eric. He may not be my biggest fan this year, but he's always been there for me in the past. And hell, Mel's almost gotten him to join the Gay-Straight Alliance. At least I have a shot.

Eric lives on a hill overlooking Colby where the ritzier houses are; his mom's a doctor. I park in their enormous driveway and try not to twitch while I wait for someone to answer the door.

"Oh. It's you." Eric doesn't look thrilled to see me, but he doesn't look unhappy either. His face is blank; there's no expression in sight.

"Hi." I'm probably squirming like a five-year-old. "Uh, can we talk?"

He studies me for a minute before he shrugs. "I guess. C'mon in."

The house is empty, and he leads me back to his bedroom. "Where's your mom?" I ask. The last thing I need is for Eric to throw me out of his house with Dr. Perry watching.

"She's on call." Eric sinks into the leather couch in one corner of his room. His bedroom is bigger than our living room and twice as decked out—huge couch, big-screen TV, every video gaming system known to man.

"Yeah." I sit on the edge of his bed. Half sit. Just in case I'm not staying long. "I'm sorry, man, about what happened on Saturday. Really sorry."

He shrugs, but there's a hint of a scowl peeking out from that blank expression now. "Yeah. Well. You aren't the only person on the team, Emmitt. We all lost that game."

"I know. But I didn't pull my weight, and I know that too. Getting kicked out like that...." I shake my head. "I can't even believe I let that happen."

"Whatever." Eric stretches his hands above his head. "I wouldn't worry too much, LaPoint. I'm sure Coach and everyone else still think you're the golden boy of the team."

He's sure not making this easy. "Eric, don't say shit like that. I'm *not* the golden boy. I just like to play hockey. Same as you."

"Whatever, man." He picks up the remote and aims it toward the TV. "That all you came to say?"

It's go time, I guess. It's not like he's going to listen to me otherwise. "No. It isn't. Listen, Eric... the reason I fucked up on Saturday.... I was upset about something. I was upset because I'd just broken up with someone. My boyfriend."

The statement definitely takes some air out of the room. Eric drops the remote and looks at me. "You're telling me you have a boyfriend," he finally says.

"Yeah. I did. And it was... um. Dusty."

"Dusty," Eric repeats.

"Yeah. We'd only been going out for a few months. But I like him a lot. And he ended it on Friday. Partly, at least... because I wouldn't tell anyone. Because I've been all about keeping it a secret." I shrug. "I decided I don't want to do that anymore. So I'm telling you."

Eric just shakes his head. "Why the hell didn't you tell me sooner?"

I swallow. "Um...."

"I mean, I get being worried about what some of the guys on the team might think. Especially assholes like O'Sher. But Emmitt, you know me. Did you really think I'd care?"

I'm not even sure how to answer that. "I didn't… I didn't know, Eric. I mean, the NHL and college hockey players keep making videos about how they don't care, but none of them are exactly coming out of the closet either, and all of the gay people at our high school seem to be in the drama club and shit like that, and Patrick goes around calling everyone fags…."

Eric nods. "I get that. I guess. But Emmitt, listen up, okay? I don't give a shit who you date. Doug's not going to care either, and neither are most of the guys on the team who matter."

"Are you sure?" I try to keep eye contact with him and ignore the fact that my voice is unsteady. "You're not gonna get freaked out in the locker room if I look your way or something? Or when we're doing checking drills?"

Eric starts laughing. "Emmitt, I've been pretty sure you weren't straight since last summer."

My mouth drops. "What?"

He shrugs. "Hockey camp. You were spending all that time hanging out with Alcott Moreau, and the two of you kept disappearing together at night. I was hearing rumors that Alcott's into guys. So I started to wonder."

My mouth probably stays open. Alcott. My first kiss. First guy I ever fooled around with. "Oh."

"So? What are you going to do? Are you gonna tell the rest of the guys?"

I scrub my forehead. In all Eric's weird acceptance, I'd almost forgotten why I really came here. "I… sort of need help, Eric. Someone found out, and they're about to blow my cover. I think I'm okay with that, but I want to do it on my terms. Dusty's terms. I think I need help."

Eric shrugs. "Sure. Who am I to say no to Colby's golden boy?"

But he's smiling.

CHAPTER
TWELVE

Dear Mr. LeClair,

Today: first day of high school hockey practice. VARSITY high school practice.

Yeah, did I tell you I made varsity? AS A FRESHMAN. I know lots of people said I would, but I never got my hopes up. I keep waiting for someone to tell me they've made a terrible mistake and I should head back to the freshman squad now. Or at least JV.

Things didn't start off so well, though. I got into the locker room and this goon was all over me right away, saying stuff like "Oh, here's the little boy they let on the team!" and "I hope Coach told you to pack your own diapers!" Yeah, super intelligent stuff.

Whatever. I spent an entire summer getting chirped because someone thought "Pointy" would be a great nickname for me. I don't even hear that crap anymore.

By the way, why do hockey players call trash talk "chirping?" I've always wondered that. I should probably Google it. And why are hockey players so into giving each other nicknames? I know some guys like Henny are into theirs, but Pointy was fucking stupid. I'm so glad I got rid of it.

Anyway, then this other guy chucked a towel in the ape's face. "Shut up, Rick," he said. Then he nodded at me. "Good job, making the team as a freshman."

I just shrugged.

The guy's name is Eric Perry. We didn't go to the same elementary or middle school, but I remember him from hockey camps and from playing against him when we were younger. I think he remembers me too. I think he remembers I'm good.

During practice, the goon named Rick tried to mess with me a few times. You know—checking me too hard, crap like that. Only Eric and a few of the other guys started to get after him for it quickly. The coach didn't even have to say anything.

I think I'm going to like the coach. He seems cool. He's quiet, but he definitely knows how to shout when he needs to. It's the right kind of shouting, you know? The kind that makes you want to listen to him instead of ignore him.

I think I'm going to like varsity. And playing for Coach Morton. And Eric Perry.

And Rick? Who cares. Goons are everywhere.

—Emmitt LaPoint, age 14

IT'S ERIC'S idea to tell all the guys at once. That way I can get the whole thing over with. Rip the Band-Aid off, I guess. And I'll know right away if O'Sher or anyone else goes apoplectic over the news.

So Eric does something I don't think a team captain has ever done before: he calls an unofficial team meeting for right before school the next day. One quick text message and things are in motion: *Team meeting in room 104 at 7:30 tomorrow morning. B there dickheads.*

"O'Sheridan's gonna lose his shit," I tell Eric as I'm walking out his front door.

"If he does, you know I'll have your back. And Dougie probably will. And a lot of other guys. You should have given us a chance, Emmitt."

We'll see about that. But one thing's for sure: I definitely should have given Eric a chance. "Eric," I tell him, "I don't know how to say this, but...."

He just shakes his head. "Don't say it, man. You don't need to."

So I just give him an awkward fist bump and think about how lucky I was to end up with Eric as my hockey mentor three years ago.

Back home, Mom's sitting at the counter eating a late dinner. "Casey filled me in on a few things," she says, tapping the seat next to her. I sink into it; I'm so damn tired. "You okay, kiddo?"

"Who knows," I mumble into the laminate countertop. "I just told Eric. Everything."

"Wow." Mom pats my back. "I'm so proud of you! How'd it go?"

"He was… great." I sit up again. "We're gonna tell the team tomorrow. Start there, I guess. I don't think everyone will be as cool with me as Eric is, but at least then they'll know."

She nods slowly. "Emmitt, you're not planning to take on Rick, are you? The last time you tried that, things didn't end well. I'd prefer not to pick you up at the police station again."

Ah yes. The infamous night when Casey, Dusty, and I got arrested at that house party for fighting with Rick and his friends. Also the first time Dusty and I kissed. "Honestly, Mom, I'm not sure exactly what I'm planning right now. All I know is I want people to find out from me, not some stupid video Rick has. So I'm starting there."

She nods and smiles at me, almost wistfully. "I just wish… that I could do more for you, Emmitt. That I could somehow make this all easier for you."

"Thanks, Mom," I tell her. "I know you do. But maybe it's good that you can't, you know? I've got to learn how to handle this for myself. How to stop hiding behind you and Casey and Coach."

She shakes her head. "It's like your first day of preschool all over again."

"Huh?"

"You were so excited—you couldn't wait to go to school and learn new things and meet new people. I was terrified. You were always this sweet, kind child who wanted to please people, and I was so scared that kids in school would take advantage of that. Change you.

"I was dropping you off at school, and I was so nervous I couldn't even let go of your hand. I was shaking. And you looked up at me and said, 'Don't be scared, Mama. I know where we go.'"

I have to smile at that. It sounds like something I'd say.

She gets up to put her dishes in the sink and kisses me on the way back around the counter. "Emmitt, honey. I love you. You know that, right? I love that the world has never changed you. You never stopped being that kind, sweet child who always saw the good in people first. And I've been your mom long enough now to know nobody can change that about you. You'll get through all this; I know you will. But if you need backup... you know I'll be there in a second."

I do know that; it's why I can't imagine having a better mom. We hug for a long moment before she whispers into my hair, "Your dad loves you too, you know."

I jolt away from her. "Where did that come from?"

She sighs. "I might not always get along with him, and he's not always the best at showing it. But he's always loved you boys, Emmitt. And he's always wanted what's best for you.

"I'm going to bed. Good luck tomorrow, sweetheart."

THE NEXT morning I'm pacing room 104 by 7:15. I didn't get the best night's sleep, but at least there was something resembling sleep in there. Doug drifts into the room, yawning. "Hey, man. You know what this is about?"

I just shrug noncommittally. My heart's pounding too hard for me to do anything else.

Eric shows up in the middle of a stream of the other guys and slaps my shoulder. A few more players trickle in, and then it's 7:30. If there's one thing Coach has drilled into us, it's punctuality.

"Everyone, thanks for coming." Eric sits on a desk at the front of the room. "Sorry about how early it is. Listen, I called this meeting—just us, no coaches—because one of our own is in trouble. And we know we protect one of our own."

I'd forgotten how dramatic Eric can be.

"Rick Snyder's back at the alternative school here in Colby." One of the linemen growls when Eric says that, and I have to stifle a laugh.

"Yeah, John," says Eric. "My thoughts exactly. Anyway, he's got this video of Emmitt." All the heads in the room swivel toward me. "Emmitt and I are working on a plan to get the video back. But in the meantime, there's always a chance he'll leak that shit everywhere whenever he feels like it. We all know what an ass Rick is. So Emmitt wanted to tell you all what's on it first, just in case that happens."

Every eye in the room is on me now.

Deep breath, Emmitt. You can do this.

"Yeah. Um, thanks for coming, everyone. So, the video. Well...." I can't spit it out. Eric catches my eye and gives me an encouraging nod.

"I'm gay," I finally blurt out. "Rick has a video of me making out with a guy." Silence.

Dead silence. For a lot of minutes.

Doug finally breaks it. "Oh," he says. "That's not.... I mean, I don't give a shit, Emmitt. Date whoever the hell you want. Just stop getting kicked out of games, okay?"

"Yeah," adds Tommy Wilson, a sophomore I don't know very well. "It doesn't matter to me. Does Coach know?"

"He knows," I say. I decide not to tell them exactly why Coach knows; I don't want to drag Dusty into this. Not without him knowing about it. "He's cool with it."

A few other voices chime in. Things like *It's cool, We don't care, Whatever, dude, No one cares about that shit anymore.* A few of the guys are still silent, just staring at me.

Then O'Sher speaks up.

"You're all okay with this? He's supposed to be the next LeClair! LeClair isn't a faggot!"

And we're back to silence.

"What the fuck is wrong with you assholes? He just told us he's a fudgepacker!" Patrick gestures vaguely toward me. "Go join the sewing club or something. This is hockey." And on that enlightened note, he storms out of the room.

Great.

A few other guys follow O'Sheridan out without looking at me. But a lot of them stay.

Henny comes up to me to say he thinks it's great I'm telling people. "My uncles are gay, man," he says. Then Carl DeVies tells me his cousin's a lesbian.

Maybe it's, like, a thing to spout off a list of all the gay people you already know when you meet another gay person. I dunno. All I know is I'm glad people are still talking to me.

The bell rings, and everyone who's left drifts out of the room as other people start coming in for class. I let out a breath I didn't realize I was holding. "That was… intense," I tell Eric.

He claps me on the shoulder. "You did good, Emmitt."

"How do you think practice is going to be tonight?"

He gives me a weird smile. "If you were ever going to bring your A-game, Emmitt, tonight's probably the night. Be that asshole golden boy I know you can be."

Yeah. I guess I can do that.

I'm not ready to face everyone at lunch. For one thing, it's just going to be awkward, with everyone trying to figure out what they should and shouldn't say to me. For another thing, Dusty's probably in that cafeteria somewhere, and I don't feel like seeing him just yet. Not before I know how to fix what I broke.

Casey and I are walking to the library to spend lunch there when Eric and Mel stop us. "Emmitt!" Mel puts her hand up for a high five. "Eric told me what you did this morning. That's some balls, man."

I glare at Eric. "I thought we were just telling the team."

He's not apologetic. "I thought she might have an idea about how to get the video out of Rick's hands. And I was right; she does. She's kind of badass, you know."

Mel shoves Eric, but she's blushing.

We keep heading to the library, because where else do you hatch a plan to take down an evil villain?

We're one step into the doorway when I immediately stop. Because sitting there, in the corner by the biographies, is Dusty.

We stare at each other for a long moment before Dusty picks up his bag and starts packing his stuff.

"Hang on, guys." Casey jogs over to talk to Dusty, and Mel and Eric both look uncomfortably at me.

"Have you talked to him since…?" Eric trails off.

I shake my head. "No. He's not talking to either of us."

Sure enough, across the room Dusty is shaking his head and concentrating on packing his bag, even though it looks like Casey is jabbering away at him.

Screw this. I can't let Dusty sit alone in the library, worrying about where he's going to get more money for Rick on Saturday and thinking he doesn't have anyone on his side. I go charging over to his table. Casey's saying something, but I interrupt him.

"Dusty," I say, and it's kind of disturbing how desperate my voice sounds. "Look, I know you're pissed at me, but I'm fixing this, okay? I told the hockey team today. They know."

"Yeah, Casey told me," Dusty says drily. "What's next? You taking out an ad in the school newspaper?"

"Maybe. Look, Dusty, I promise you don't have to worry about keeping this secret for me anymore. I don't care who knows. At all."

Dusty gives Casey a side glare. "What have you been telling him?"

Casey throws his hands up in mock surrender. "I didn't tell him anything. I swear."

"Dusty, please—" I'm ready to start begging again, but Dusty interrupts me.

"Congratulations on telling the team, I guess," he says. "But don't tell anyone else for me, Emmitt. I already told you. I don't want to be the reason you lose everything you've worked for." He slings his bag over his shoulder and leaves.

"That is one stubborn motherfucker," Casey whispers.

Yeah. What else would you expect from someone who basically raised his younger brother and sister while he was still in junior high?

I've got to get this video away from Rick before I tell anyone else. I've got to make sure Dusty knows I'm not telling people for his sake alone—that I'm doing it for me just as much as for him.

Mel and Eric have scored us a table in the other corner of the room. Mel gives me a pat on the shoulder when Casey and I sit down. "Didn't go well?"

"Nope. Guys, I need to get that video away from Rick. Now."

Eric and Mel glance at each other. "Mel has an idea," says Eric.

Mel clears her throat loudly. "So here's the thing," she says. "It's not like we're going to get Rick to just *give* us the video. He's probably made copies anyway. So what we need is something bigger on him. Something we can use against him to keep him from ever posting that video up somewhere."

Now *that's* a good idea. "You know something about him?" I ask excitedly.

Mel shakes her head. "Not yet. But here's the thing, Emmitt: you'd be surprised what two girls can get out of a homophobic asshole."

I'm not following. At all. It must show in my face, because Mel just sighs.

"I'm still friends with my ex, Samantha Trowing. And she *hates* homophobes."

"Wow, you used to date Samantha Trowing?" Casey interrupts. "She's hot." He's right. Samantha's kind of the quintessential blonde bombshell goddess—hair down to there and legs up to here.

"She is," Mel says. "Which is exactly what we're going to use against Rick. There's a big party down at someone's lake house on Friday... the kind he always goes to. Samantha and I are going to go too. And we're going to... offer to do certain things for Rick, if he does some things for us in return. And we're just going to happen to have a video camera on us at the time."

Holy *shit*. This girl is an evil genius. I tell her so.

"I know," she says.

It's going to work. It *has* to work. Rick's not exactly the brightest bulb in the package, and once we have video of him doing things he doesn't want anyone else to see? Then we're free and clear.

"Are you sure you don't mind doing this?" I ask Mel. "And that Samantha won't mind? It sorta feels like I'm using you both or something."

"She hates homophobes; I told you that," says Mel. "She'll consider it a public service. And I'm doing it because Eric and I made a deal. Well, that and Rick's an asshole."

"What's the deal?" Casey asks.

"My mom's not too cool with the girl-on-not-guy side of my life right now," Mel tells us. "So Eric's going to take me to the dance. It'll make her happy."

Eric doesn't exactly look upset about this arrangement, so I don't think this is too big of a concession on his part. Still, I give him a nod. "Thanks, man."

"Don't thank me," he says. "Just be a badass at hockey practice this afternoon, okay? We can't lose Saturday, Emmitt."

Don't I know it.

CHAPTER
THIRTEEN

DEAR MR. LeClair,

Today was the last day of hockey camp. It's back to school soon.

It's been a great few weeks. Amazing, actually. Alcott and I have been hanging out a lot. Mostly we just eat, go to that park together. Alcott smokes most nights. Sometimes I smoke with him, and sometimes I don't.

Last night we went to the park again. One last time, I guess, since today Alcott's back in Bennington and I'm back in Colby.

"Emmitt," Alcott asked, "do you ever wonder what the point of all this is?"

We were lying on the picnic table again. The sky was cloudy this time, and most of the light in the park was coming from dim lamps overlooking the swing sets a few hundred yards away.

I thought about it. Not for the first time. "I'm not sure," I finally told him. "Sometimes... I think it's just the ride. Just the experience."

He took a hit from the joint in his hand. "I hope you're wrong, E. But if you're not, you should know I have enjoyed the ride with you these past two weeks." He passed the joint to me. "I assume you can keep this to yourself?"

He hadn't said anything like that since the first night we kissed. He hadn't needed to. We've both got the same things riding on this secret. I took a hit. "Of course." I passed the joint back.

Alcott took a deep drag and covered his eyes with his arms. "My dad," he said all quietly, "is the biggest fucking homophobe on the planet."

112

I didn't know what to say to that. I still don't. So I didn't say anything at all.

—Emmitt LaPoint, age 15

THE WEIRDNESS starts in the locker room.

I'm pulling pads on, the way you normally do before a hockey practice, but things aren't going on as usual around me. A few guys are giving me weird glances. A few others are sort of stalling with getting their own pads, like they're waiting for me to leave the room or something.

"Assholes, I'm not checking any of you out," I finally shout. "None of you fuckheads are good enough for me." That gets laughs out of a few of the guys, and most of them seem to relax a little bit.

Then O'Sheridan comes in, with a few of the other players at his side. Mostly sheep sophomores who probably don't know better than to hang out with him. "No fags in the locker room," he sneers.

"Good thing I'm not a *fag*, then," I tell him calmly, even though my heart is racing. "Just a gay dude." I grab my hockey stick and head out of the room before he can say anything else.

"You okay?" Coach asks as I storm up to the bench.

"Fucking fantastic," I snap.

He eyes me. "Is this Enforcer Emmitt returning? 'Cause I have to tell you, I wasn't too fond of him on Saturday."

That knocks some sense into me. I can't let Patrick control my play this afternoon—or ever. I've got to go back to letting hockey be the place where I escape from everything else. Where I focus on the game and not all the other noise in my life.

"No, Coach," I sigh. "I'm getting rid of Enforcer Emmitt."

"You do that." The rest of the team is gathering around, so he calls us together for another pep talk about how important Saturday's game is and how we have to put everything we have into practice this week.

We hit the ice for warm-up drills, and I do my best to focus on the details of my play: my skating, puck control. I'm doing okay until we get to 1-on-1 drills.

The first one goes okay. Me against Henny; no big deal. I beat him by a mile. Whistle blows and Luis skates to the back of the line.

Next in line is Patrick O'Sheridan.

Whistle blows again, and I go for the puck. Only Patrick doesn't. He just stands there, like he missed the whistle blowing, while I take off with the puck....

Coach Lewis blows the whistle hard. "O'Sher! What's wrong with you? Get your head in the game! He blew by you!"

Patrick just shrugs and goes to the back of the line. Eric's next up. He catches my eye and shakes his head.

The rest of practice goes a lot like that. O'Sher and a few others don't come near me. They don't pass to me, they don't check me, and they don't go after the puck when I have it. There aren't enough of them for any of the coaching staff to notice; everyone just seems to think they're off their game. At one point I see Coach Lewis having an intense discussion with Patrick over by the boards, but he just keeps shrugging.

Practice ends, and Coach gives us another speech about how some of us aren't being aggressive enough, and we need to keep up our discipline without losing our fire. Maybe he thinks some of the guys are backing off because of the way I got thrown out of the game on Saturday.

I briefly think about saying something to him—letting him know I told the team, and that's why a few of them are acting this way. But I decide not to. I don't want to make a bigger deal of all this, and in the end it's O'Sheridan's choice not to play at his full speed. If he keeps it up, he'll just get himself pulled before Saturday. And that'll be his choice, not mine.

Still, I don't feel like dealing with him in the locker room, so I hang out in the rink for a few minutes after everyone else goes in. Skate around a little; do some shooting. When I finally head into the locker room, Coach is sitting on the bench.

"Looking good," he tells me. "And you looked good in practice today. I'm proud of you, Emmitt. You're gonna get through this."

Maybe I will. But surviving isn't the goal anymore. "Maybe," I tell him. "Listen. Tell Dusty... tell him I miss him, okay?"

Coach nods. "Of course I will, Emmitt."

PRACTICES THE rest of the week go pretty much the same way. A few of the scrub sophomores following O'Sheridan's lead end up getting themselves benched because Coach thinks they aren't playing at full speed—which they're not, at least not when I'm around. I'm back to my form from before last Saturday's disaster, and I know I'm playing like I have something to prove. Because I do.

Patrick keeps his spot, though. Coach lectures him a lot, and there are a few times when I think he wants to ask me if I know what's going on with O'Sher, but he doesn't. Maybe he doesn't want to wreck whatever careful balance I've got going.

Friday night after practice, though, my mind isn't on Patrick anymore. I know if he can't make the plays in the game tomorrow, he's the one who's going to get pulled. Now my mind's on Mel and Samantha, who are down at the bay trying to salvage my dignity. And Dusty's.

Eric, Casey, and I are playing video games and trying not to talk about the mission Mel and Samantha are on. Dusty hasn't talked to Casey or me since the library incident on Tuesday; he's ignored about twenty-five texts from Casey. This plan has to work, or I don't know what I'm going to do next.

"You think they'll pull it off?" I finally ask Eric as I flip my car over in the racing game we're playing. My attention is definitely a little off tonight.

"If anyone can pull something like this off, it's Mel," he says. "She gets what she wants."

"Yeah?" asks Casey as he comes over with sodas. "'Cause I think the next thing she might want is you."

Eric never blushes, but right then some red creeps up his cheeks. "Nah. She's into this girl Tonya who's in our science class. Too bad Tonya's straight."

"Then you still have a chance," I say as I crash my Corvette into a tunnel wall. "Damn."

"I dunno," says Eric. "I'm not sure I'm that into her anyway. She's not...."

"A bimbo? An idiot? All makeup and no brains?" I ask.

"Shut up. I date girls with brains."

"Sure," I tell him. "That's exactly what Tiffany Louton's best quality was. Her SAT scores."

He scowls at me and pulls his Viper across the finish line. "Beat you, asshole."

"Whatever. As long as you're not thinking of blowing Mel off because she's president of the GSA."

Eric doesn't answer me.

We get through two more games—I lose both—before someone knocks on the door. It's Samantha. She's wearing her hair up in a tight, long ponytail, and a skirt that's so short *I'm* a little turned on. Mel's right behind her in tight pants and a flowing shirt.

"Shit," Casey says. "This plan *has* to have worked. You two are crazy hot together."

"Thanks!" says Samantha. "I always thought so." She grabs Mel's face and pulls her in for a kiss.

Eric almost drops his glass.

Mel laughs and pushes her away. "Why'd you break up with me, then?"

Samantha shrugs. "After tonight, I might just have to give us another try. That was *fun*."

"What happened?" There are more important things on my mind right now than the hot girls making out in my living room.

Mel holds up her phone triumphantly. "We've got the goods. But… they're not exactly what we thought they were going to be."

I gesture for them to come in and sit down, and I bring over some glasses and more soda. Least I can do. "What happened? What did you get?" I haven't been this excited since Valentine's Day.

"So," says Samantha. She clasps her hands together and quickly glances at each of us to make sure she has our full attention. I'm starting to see why this girl's in the drama club. "We get to the party, right? And they let us in no problem because *hi*, our clothes. Men are such pigs." She shakes her head. "Anyway, so we find Rick. And we're pleasantly surprised to see he's already a few beers in, because that's definitely going to make everything easier. Mel gets all close to him and giggly, and I get him another drink."

116

I try to imagine Mel giggly, but it's not coming. Mel must sense what I'm thinking. "I can be giggly," she insists.

"Anyway," says Samantha. "So Mel and I get all up in Rick's space and get him a few more drinks and shoo away anyone else who's interested. And then we make out with him a little and tell him he's hot… and we'd like to see him in a bedroom if he's interested."

Next to me, Eric's body is so tensed up I'm a little afraid he's going to break if someone touches him. I can't tell if he's completely turned on or pissed off about the idea of Mel making out with Rick.

"So we get him into a bedroom, right? And here's the plan: we're going to tell him that we'll put on a little show for him, but for everything we do, he has to say something for us… and we're planning to make him say things about how he'd kiss a guy if he could or stuff like that, basically whatever we can get out of his mouth that would be embarrassing for a homophobic nutwad like him."

Nutwad is probably my new favorite word of all time.

"So we get him on the bed, right? And he's kind of trashed at this point. Mel tells him he's a nice guy, and she misses watching him play hockey… and the guy loses it."

"Loses it?" Casey asks. Mel nods.

"Loses it," she says. "Here. We'll show you. Sam got the whole thing on tape."

She unlocks her phone and finds the video. And there's Rick Snyder, in all his assholish glory, lying on the bed next to Mel.

"I used to come to your hockey games," Mel says to him. "You were great. I loved watching you play." She strokes a finger down his arm.

Rick gulps a little. "You… useta come to my games?" he asks her.

"I sure did," she tells him. "We both did." She gestures around her, probably at Sam.

"I miss hockey," says Rick. "I miss it a lot." Then, suddenly, he gets up off the bed and starts pacing. "I used to be so good at hockey," he says. "That's why ya liked watching me play, 'cause I was good at hockey. I was so good at the hockey. And then I ruined it. I always… ruin… I ruin… everything." He sits down on the edge of the bed and buries his head in his hands.

I couldn't be more shocked if John LeClair knocked on the door and told us he just dropped by to introduce himself.

"What happened?" Mel's asking Rick in the video. Rick raises his head and moans—*the dude actually moans.*

"After my parents got divorced, I… I fucked up. I didn't care anymorrrre. Morrrre." His drunken slurring would be hilarious if his words didn't hit so close to home. My stomach tightens up. "And I partied more and I didn't go to practice all the time and I did other shit. Bad shit. And then I got kicked off the team." Now Rick's crying. Openly crying, and Mel is patting his shoulder. "I didn't mean it! I miss playing," he whines. "I screwed up. But now they won't let me play anymore." He shakes his head. "I miss skating and games, and I should be playing this season and going to the playoff this year, but I'm not because of fuckhead Coach Morton." He's bawling harder now. "I fucked it all up." He turns around and buries his head in Mel's shoulder. "You understand, right? You know I didn't mean it?"

Samantha stops the video. "There's more, but it's basically just him sobbing. Eventually we got him calmed down and took him home," she adds cheerfully. "If I didn't know what an utter dick that guy's been, I'd almost feel sorry for him."

Yeah. Me too.

"Think that'll be enough?" Casey asks. "I mean, it is just him crying."

"Oh, it'll be enough," I tell him. "Rick's got way too much wrapped up in his badass image. Once he sobers up and realizes that video exists, he'll do anything to make sure it never gets out."

"But Mel's in the video too," Eric says a little anxiously. "I don't want you to… you know…. I don't want people to think you guys are dating or something…."

Mel smirks. "What do you care? Anyway, it's no big deal. My brother's good with video editing. We'll get him to block out my face and cut some things." She gives me a high five. "I'll send you the edited video first thing tomorrow morning, Emmitt. What are you going to do with it? Confront Rick before the game?"

I want to. There's nothing I'd like to do more than put that asshole in his place. Stare him down and tell him he's not going to bother me or Dusty anymore.

But something seems off about that solution. "I'm not exactly sure yet," I tell her. "I'll figure it out. Before he meets with Dusty tomorrow."

"Aww, I hope you get back together." Samantha leans over and kisses my cheek. "He *has* to forgive you so you can go to the dance together. I'll just *swoon*!"

I don't exactly know how to respond to that.

"Now I remember why we broke up," Mel says drily.

"What, because you have no emotional soul?" answers Samantha. "C'mon. Let's get this video to your brother. The day isn't saved yet!"

"Thanks, guys," I said. "Seriously. You don't know how much this means to me. What can I do to make it up to you?"

"I meant what I said," Samantha tells me. "Go to the dance with Dusty. Be out and have a good life with your boyfriend. That'll be more than enough thanks for me."

"Me too," says Mel. "Good luck, Emmitt."

"I'll go with you guys," says Eric. "Emmitt, see you tomorrow. Let me know what you end up doing with that video." We fist-bump and then he follows the girls. Casey closes the door behind them.

"Wow. I can't believe Rick has a soul."

I nod. We both sink into the couch and just sit for a moment, staring at the paused video game on the TV. Not saying what we're both thinking: that I could have just as easily been Rick. That things could have gone the other way.

"It never would have been you," Casey finally says.

I don't think I'll ever get tired of these kinds of conversations. The kind where we both just know what the other is thinking.

"Yeah? How can you be sure?"

"Because we're what we do, you know? And doing what Rick did after our parents split… that was never gonna be you, Emmitt. You've never been that person. You've never been Rick."

"Makes it a little harder to hate him."

"Yeah. But hopefully after tomorrow you won't need to anyway."

"Yeah." I know what I need to do with that video. It's not mine to do anything with.

It's Dusty's.

CHAPTER
FOURTEEN

DEAR MR. LeClair,

Big day yesterday. I told my mother I'm gay.
It went... better than I ever imagined it would.
Our family had Thanksgiving dinner with Dusty's family. Dusty was out of control nervous. I hadn't thought much about it, but the only time he's ever met my mom so far was when she picked Casey and I up at the police station the night we got in the fight with Rick. So he was trying to be all polite and gentlemanly; he was even calling her "ma'am" at first. I told him to relax, and after that he switched to Mrs. LaPoint.

Anyway, dinner was good and my mom definitely liked Dusty, Matt, and Julia. Dusty told her a little bit about why they're living in Vermont now—just the basics, not the details—and I could tell Mom was impressed that he'd taken care of Matt and Julia so well without his parents all those years. During dessert Casey took Matt and Julia into the living room to watch a movie, and Dusty and I told Mom we had something to tell her.

Coach and Mrs. Morton were sitting there, which made the whole thing a little less scary. "Mom," I said, "I need to tell you something." I grabbed Dusty's hand.

She raised an eyebrow, but she didn't say anything.

"I'm dating Dusty," I said. "I like guys."

She just stared at us for a long minute. Finally she said, "Oh."

I didn't know how to respond to that. Neither did anyone else at the table, I guess, since everything went silent.

I don't think I've ever been that scared in my entire life. Not the day Dad moved out. Not the day Casey got lost in the mall and we couldn't find him for two hours. Not even the day Dusty ran away and I wasn't sure if I'd ever see him again.

Then Mom started nodding. "So is this how you explain your obsession with West Side Story*?"*

Mrs. Morton burst out laughing so hard she actually snorted water up her nose. "You like West Side Story*?" Dusty asked me incredulously.*

"It's got great music," I told him.

After that, the five of us talked. Mom hugged me and said she was glad I'd told her and that she never wanted me to think I had to keep secrets from her. She told Dusty that he seems like a very nice young man. She said she was worried about what this meant for us—worried that keeping up our secret would be incredibly difficult, and worried that telling people would be even more difficult. Mrs. Morton and Coach said they worried about the same thing for us.

"No one ever wishes for their child's life to be hard in any way," Mom told me. "But I just want to make sure you know... I will always love you. No matter what. No matter what your grades are, or how many hockey games, or who you date. I will always be proud to be your mother."

At times like this I don't even care that my dad isn't around. Not at all. Mom and Casey are all I need.

—Emmitt LaPoint, age 16

THE NEXT morning, Mel sends me the edited video with a text: *Use it for good, not evil.*

Fair enough.

I eat breakfast while I compose the text I need to send to Dusty. I try out eight different versions before I end up with one that works.

Thanks for what you did for me. Show Rick this, and you won't need to protect me anymore.

It takes me ten minutes to get up the courage to hit Send.

I've already taken a shower and gone through some warm-up stretches in the living room before he finally answers. *Thanks.*

That's all. But it's enough. Now it's time to play some hockey.

Burlington's good. Not as good as we are, but they're good. They're not in the quarterfinals for nothing. At the end of the first period, the score is tied. We should be up by one, but O'Sher refused to pass me the puck when I was wide open on a 2-on-1 with him. He tried to dangle around the defenseman himself, and they stole the puck from him.

The buzzer sounds, and Coach circles us up. "We're outplaying them," he reminds us. "The problem is that we're not outscoring them. We've gotta think like a team, men. You're a unit. Know where your teammates are at all times. Have all of them in your vision." He points at Patrick. "We had that goal on your 2-on-1 if you'd just passed it to Emmitt instead of trying to score yourself. Team sport, everyone. Make sure you all act like it."

Patrick scowls.

I'm having a great start to the second period. The Burlington players just can't keep up with my speed, and I'm beating them on every play. Too bad we're not capitalizing on opportunities because Patrick still isn't passing me the puck.

We blow another scoring chance when Patrick passes to Eric instead of me. Eric immediately turns the puck over, and Burlington comes back our way and almost scores on an odd-man rush. Coach quickly calls for a time-out.

"What is wrong with you?" he yells at Patrick. "Emmitt was wide open!" Coach is usually better than this at keeping his cool, but we are in the playoffs.

O'Sher throws down his helmet. "Coach, he told us he's a fag! I'm not playing with no fag!"

There's a brief glint of pride in Coach's eyes—so brief I'm sure no one else notices. "Yeah? Well, I don't care, and no one else seems to care except you. And you're about to become a *duster*, O'Sheridan."

"Duster" means someone who sits on the bench. Collecting dust.

"Sit down and get your head together," Coach tells him. Patrick slams over to the bench, and the buzzer sounds. The rest of us head out to the ice, and Eric pulls us into another quick huddle.

122

"No one else has a problem with Emmitt, right?" There's a round of shaking heads. "Good. Because we're not giving up this game. And we either take it together, or we lose it together. No individuals here. Don't forget that."

After that it's like I'm unstoppable. I'm ahead of the Burlington players at every play, and I'm out from under their checks before they even know I'm gone. I score once in the beginning of the second period and again off an assist from Eric at the beginning of the third. They get a power play goal when one of our guys gets sent to the penalty box for slashing and they've got the one-man advantage.

So we're up by only one goal when Coach sends O'Sher back into the game, but there's also only two minutes left.

Whatever I might think about Patrick, he's good at drawing penalties. Which makes sense; he's an asshole who likes to goad people. So he quickly gets one guy for high-sticking and another for hooking. And suddenly we've got a two-man advantage.

What happens next should be right out of the movies. We begin to set up the 5-on-3 and I slide into position along the hash mark. O'Sher reluctantly passes the puck my way and we begin to get their defense out of position. Soon Patrick's slipped his defenseman and moved into an open position in front of the net—only he doesn't tap the ice to signal me for the puck. He doesn't do anything.

I pass it to him anyway. And he sends a howitzer straight into the goal.

The light goes off and the siren sounds and the rink goes nuts, because that goal should seal it. It's going to be crazy hard for Burlington to tie things up now. Most of the team skates over to congratulate Patrick, but I stay on my side of the ice.

He gives me a quick nod, and I give him one back. This is a team sport. No way was I not going to pass it to him.

At least he knows that now. One step at a time, I guess.

We win, which just means now we've got one week until the semifinals. While we're changing, Coach Lewis comes in with news: Rice beat St. Johnsbury. We're playing them again in the semifinals.

"We'll get 'em this time," he tells us. But his eyes definitely linger on me for a moment when he says that.

I'm heading out of the building when Coach calls me into his office.

"Nice game today," he says from his desk as I settle into the chair across from him. "So… I gather you told everyone."

"Just the team so far," I tell him. "But I'm not keeping it a secret anymore. It'll get out to a lot more people soon, probably. I don't know how the scouts will feel about that."

Coach smiles. "The ones you want to be playing for won't care."

I hope he's right.

"I'm proud of you, Emmitt. Coming out to the team like that…. I can't even imagine how hard that was for you." He shakes his head. "You impressed me the first day I saw you at freshman tryouts. You haven't let me down since."

That's definitely not true, but it is nice to hear. Even if he doesn't know the biggest way I've let him down.

"Coach," I say hesitantly. "Has Dusty told you anything about why he took that money?"

His face darkens a little. "Not yet, no. He's still not saying much to us at all. He's not talking to you or Casey either?"

I shake my head. It's on the tip of my tongue to tell him everything I know—why Dusty took the money and what I sent to him this morning. But those aren't my secrets to tell. Dusty kept my secrets for me when I needed him to, and I have to return that favor.

"Not yet," I tell him. "But I'm hoping that will change soon."

Coach smiles. "Me too, Emmitt. Me too."

MONDAY MORNING is full of congratulations from everyone who was at the game. We're only two away now from winning the state championship, which doesn't happen every day. And despite what I told Coach, the news about me being gay hasn't been spreading at school. I'm not sure exactly why. The guys on the team aren't telling anyone. However Patrick and his goons might act around me, at least they're respecting my right to tell people on my own time. So that's cool.

Or maybe they just don't want to admit they've been playing hockey with a fag all this time.

I don't see Dusty during lunch; he must be hiding out in the library again. I keep hoping he'll send me some kind of message about how things went with Rick on Saturday. Text, e-mail, carrier pigeon… I'll take anything at this point. Nothing.

So toward the end of lunch, I hang around his locker, just to see if he'll talk to me.

He shows up carrying an armful of books. "Hey," I say hesitantly.

He nods and starts spinning his combination. "Hey."

Silence.

"Umm. Things go okay on Saturday?" I finally ask.

He shrugs. "How'd you know something was happening on Saturday, anyway?"

Might as well come clean. "I kind of heard you and Rick talking after school last week."

Dusty scowls. "Fucking Casey."

"Hey." I'm instantly defensive. "He was just trying to help, Dusty. So what happened? Did Rick back off?"

Dusty slams his locker shut. "You don't have to worry, Emmitt. Your precious secret is safe. Rick's not leaking that video anytime soon."

"No, that's not what I meant." I follow him as he starts walking down the empty hallway. "I meant… are you okay? Is he going to leave you alone now?"

"Yeah, Emmitt, it's fine. You saved the day again, okay? Big bad Rick is going to leave me alone, and you don't have to worry about anyone besides the hockey team finding out about you."

Shit. Suddenly the hockey team's silence is backfiring on me. "Dusty, people are going to find out," I tell him. "And I'm okay with that now. I swear."

The bell rings, and the hallways start filling up with people. Dusty disappears into a crowd of freshmen coming out of the band room.

"TIME FOR a grand gesture," Casey tells me when I get home from hockey practice that night. "Did you save the letter you wrote to him?"

I did. So the next day I put it in Dusty's locker before school starts.

Total radio silence. I text him, asking if he got the letter. I leave him a voice mail when he doesn't pick up his phone. Nothing. By Thursday morning I'm becoming convinced Dusty's never going to talk to me again.

"What am I supposed to do?" I ask Casey on the way to school.

"I don't know." Casey seems just as baffled by this whole thing as I am; Dusty still isn't talking to him either. "Maybe he thinks you aren't serious about telling everyone."

"I put a letter in his locker asking him to come to the dance with me! Doesn't he think people are going to notice that?"

"Stop shrieking. You sound like Julia."

"I wasn't shrieking!" I lower my voice as far as it will go for that retort.

"Maybe Dusty doesn't believe you. Maybe he thinks the invite to the dance is just a ploy to get him back or something, that you're not actually going to do it."

"So much for the grand gesture," I grumble as I pull into the school parking lot.

"*Never* underestimate the grand gesture!" Casey shakes his finger at me as we get out of the truck. "Maybe you just need something a little grander."

I wince. "Do I want to know what you have in mind?"

IT'S THE stupidest idea he's ever had.

I'm not going to do it. I may finally be okay with telling my entire school I like dudes, but that doesn't mean I need to make an ass out of myself. I'm just going to have to think of something else to get Dusty to give me another chance.

Eric and I go into the cafeteria for lunch, and I'm surprised to see Dusty there, sitting over by the soda machines with a bunch of people I don't know. Looks like he's over boycotting the cafeteria.

"I'll, ah, come find you in a minute," I tell Eric.

He sees where I'm looking and nods. "Yeah. Sure, man."

I walk over to Dusty's table, trying to look as casual as I can, and sit down across from him.

"Hey."

He doesn't look up from his food. "Hey. What are you doing here?"

There's conversation going on all around us, but for me he might as well be the only person at that table. "So, I, uh, left you a letter in your locker."

"Yeah. I got it." He takes a bite of his sandwich.

"Oh. Well, what do you think? About what I said?" I'm not going to be this nervous at the state championships, if we make it. Dusty, somehow, looks completely calm.

He shrugs. "I think… nothing. It's a nice idea, Emmitt. But we both know it's not happening. We're not going to the"—he stops and glances around—"*that place.*"

"Sure we are. You're going with me." I sound a lot more confident than I feel.

"Emmitt, shut up." Dusty takes another bite. "I know what you're trying to do. You're trying to be the upstanding guy you always are and do the right thing and fix this. But you can't fix this, Emmitt. You're a hockey player, and you're going to lose everything you've worked for if we… well, if, you know."

"You don't know that." I practically growl the words at him.

"Yeah, I do. Listen, Emmitt…. What you put in that letter. I'd love if it were possible. I can't imagine anything better. But it's not. So just go back to your table, okay? Go back to the hockey team." The last two words are loaded with vitriol.

I'm out of my seat before I even realize I'm standing, and then I head around to his side of the table. Sure, Casey's idea is stupid. And it's going to make me look like a total douche bag. But it's definitely a grand gesture, and it's pretty clear right now that I need a grand gesture. Nothing else is going to work.

I get to the other side of the table and do this wolf whistle my dad taught me when I was a kid. Most of the tables around us go silent—that whistle is *loud.* "Hey, everyone? I have an announcement to make. You know the dance that's coming up? I'm going—"

Before I can finish, someone shoves me over. Normally I'm pretty good at taking impacts—hours of experience being checked against boards—but I'm not expecting this hit, and I slam hard into the cafeteria floor. "What the hell?" I grunt.

I hear Dusty's voice above me. "He's going to make sure Colby wins the state championship that day, and we're all gonna celebrate," he says lamely. Great. Now I just sound like an egomaniac.

Never underestimate school spirit, though—half the cafeteria erupts into cheers and screaming.

"Go Colby!" Dusty adds loudly before he leans over. "What are you thinking?" he hisses at me.

"You're not listening to me!"

"Get up." He pulls me up with one hand and grabs his books before he takes off for the cafeteria doorway. I'm just a few steps behind him.

He stalks quickly down the hallway before he pulls me into an empty classroom and closes the door behind us. "What the hell were you thinking?"

I'll never forget the first day I saw Dusty. He had a giant chip on his shoulder back then—didn't want to be in Vermont, didn't want to be living with Coach, didn't want to be at our high school. He scowled the entire time Coach was introducing us.

I liked him right away; I can't explain exactly why. It was like I could see there was so much more buried under that expression—as if I could see the hope, the kindness and goodness sitting under the anger in his eyes.

He's got that same exact expression now that he had the morning we met. Dark. Brooding. Arms crossed. Miles away from any kind of happiness.

I grab his face and lift it, pulling him into me as I press my mouth against his. Hard. It's the same instant chemistry Dusty and I have always had but somehow more intense. It's been long enough that I've almost forgotten what kissing him feels like.

At first I feel like he might be pulling away from me, but then he seems to relax into the kiss. Soon his tongue's there with mine, and he's wrapping his arms around my shoulders, and I'm wrapping mine around his.

This kiss isn't *like* the first goal I ever scored in hockey. It's better. Infinitely better.

Eventually we pull away from each other. Slightly, like neither of us is really willing to let go. "What were you thinking?" he asks again. A lot more quietly than the last time.

"I dunno," I say. "Casey said I needed a grand gesture. He said I needed to do something publicly to show you I'm serious about us being together. For real this time. But you didn't believe me when I invited you to the dance in that letter, so he said I should ask you in front of everyone. I thought it was a stupid idea… but you were just sitting there at the table, not talking to me… and Dusty, I fucking miss the hell out of you."

This time he kisses me.

When we pull apart again, he shakes his head. "I wanted to stop hiding our relationship, asshole. Not have it plastered all across Facebook."

I smile. "Hey, it worked, didn't it? Maybe let's don't tell Casey, though. He'll never stop talking about what a genius he is."

"Nah, this wasn't Casey." Dusty pulls a rumpled piece of paper from his pocket, and I recognize it. It's the letter I left in his locker. "I… it sounds stupid, but I keep carrying it around." He opens it up and smiles as he says the words on the paper out loud. Not that he needs to. I've got them memorized—all thirteen of them.

Dusty,

I'm sorry.

I love you.

Come to the dance with me?

Emmitt

"Well? Will you? I promise not to get down on one knee and ask you to dance in front of everyone."

He laughs. "I think we're going to make a scene no matter what, Emmitt, if we're going to the dance together."

"Sure we will. Who cares?" I pull him into me for a hug. "I mean that, Dusty. I don't care anymore. Scouts, my dad, whatever—this isn't 1996. I can be a hockey player and be your boyfriend; I know that now.

And even if I couldn't have both…. Dusty, you have no idea how much I've missed you. I think I'd pick being your boyfriend."

He shakes his head. "That wouldn't be fair to you, Emmitt."

"Getting what I want isn't fair to me?" I shake my head. "I don't think you should get to decide that anymore."

He carefully folds up the letter and places it back in his pocket. "Maybe we should decide together from now on."

We make out until the bell rings. Surrounded by whiteboards and desks and textbooks.

And some hope.

CHAPTER
FIFTEEN

DEAR MR. LeClair,

Dusty and I kissed tonight. Then we got arrested together.

Yeah. So THAT was an eventful few hours.

The kiss was great. Excellent. Amazing. I know I said I'd never try anything like that, that it was too risky, even if I have thought for a while that Dusty might feel the same way about me that I do about him. But honestly? In the moment, this didn't feel risky at all. He was looking at me the exact same way I was looking at him. It was like we both just knew what was about to happen.

And then it did. And it was amazing. Perfect. Everything I thought it was going to be. More.

Only then we got into a fight with Rick Snyder and a bunch of other guys, and we got arrested, and now I'm freaking out. I keep thinking about Alcott and how scared he was to tell anyone that he likes guys. Partly because of his dad, but also because he's so worried that no one will treat him the same way anymore. I keep thinking about how much hockey and the NHL mean to me.

You get that, right? Coach is always saying that people make a lot of sacrifices to play this game. You must have made a ton of sacrifices to get as far as you did. So you get it, I bet. I bet you'd understand.

Tomorrow I'll tell Dusty that we can't do this. That we can't... be anything.

131

I hope he'll understand this isn't what I want. It's just how things have to be.

—Emmitt LaPoint, age 16

WE DECIDE we'll tell Coach and Mrs. Morton everything that night.

It seems like the right thing to do. They deserve to know all the ways we both screwed up. Plus Dusty's grounded indefinitely right now, and we're both hoping that coming clean will get him a reduced sentence.

Coach knows something's better the second I get to practice. "You're smiling," he says as I lace up my skates.

"Yeah." I can't stop, actually. "Um, Dusty and I are back together."

"No way!" Coach slaps me on the back so hard I almost fall over. "Emmitt, this is… fantastic. Do you know what happened with him and the money?"

I can't look him in the eye. "Um, yeah. Listen, I kind of want to be there when Dusty tells you about that. Okay if I come over tonight? After practice?"

"Of course. Just as long as you don't lose focus now that my hormone-filled nephew is back in your life." Coach fakes a shudder.

"Whatever." I roll my eyes and proceed to have a killer practice.

For a while hockey was what I did to take my mind off Dusty. Now it's something I can do to make him proud again, I guess.

When I get to the Morton/Porter house that night, Mrs. Morton's in the kitchen cooking. "C'mon in, Emmitt!" she calls out. "We're making fried chicken."

"Yum." The kitchen's filled with combating and combining smells. "I guess you heard?"

"Yes." She comes over and kisses me gently on the cheek. "It's nice to have you back, Emmitt."

"Emmitt!" Matt runs into the room and launches himself at me. I grab him for a hug. "I missed you! You haven't been here in a while. Is Casey here?"

So much for my adoring fans. "Not tonight, Matty. But soon, I'm sure." Casey, it turns out, was on the other side of the cafeteria when

I tried to make my "announcement" and Dusty dragged me out of the room. Right afterward he texted me to say *Told u it would work. GRAND GESTURE!! U guys are together again, right?*

He's never going to stop talking about how he's the reason Dusty and I got back together. At least not for the next five years or so.

"Hey." Dusty comes into the room and smiles. I know he feels the same pull I do—to cross the room and just *touch* each other again and make up for all that lost time. But Matt's here, so we just give each other a quick fist bump.

Matt rolls his eyes at us. "I'm *nine* now," he tell us. "I know you guys get all kissy and stuff. It's okay."

Dusty almost chokes. "Excuse me?"

"You like each other, right? And Dusty, you've been all sad when Emmitt hasn't been here lately. You can kiss him. I won't throw up or anything. Even though kissing is pretty gross. Did you know that Darla Farris tried to kiss me on the playground? She got in trouble, and then she had to stay in for the next recess. So I guess you can't just try to kiss people everywhere. But you can kiss each other in front of me. It's okay."

Mrs. Morton just keeps frying chicken, but she looks like she's trying not to burst out laughing all over the hot oil.

Dusty ruffles Matt's hair as he leans over to softly brush his lips against mine. A quick jolt of electricity shoots through me.

"Darla, huh?" Dusty asks Matt. Matt just rolls his eyes again.

Dinner's good. Dusty jokes that fried chicken is what the Mortons make when they want everyone to forget what they're upset about; it's what they made Dusty, Matt, and Julia on their first night in Vermont. I hope it helps the two of *them* forget what they're upset about when Dusty and I tell them what happened with Rick.

It doesn't.

We all sit together in Coach's den after he gets Matt and Julia settled down with their homework. "You ready to tell us what happened, Dustin?" he asks.

Dusty hesitates, just for a moment. I squeeze his hand, and I can hear him draw in a deep breath. And he tells the story.

I interrupt to explain how it's my fault that Dusty thought he had to keep Rick from telling people. But mostly I just let him talk.

"I'm sorry," he finally finishes up. "I know you're going to tell me I should have come to you both. But I couldn't. You would have had to say something to someone, and then Rick would've gotten pissed off and posted the video…. I couldn't let that happen. And Emmitt, if I told you, you would have tried to help me by coming out to everyone right away or something. Because that's what you do—you help people. And I couldn't let you wreck everything you've worked so hard for. So I had to take the money."

Coach shakes his head. "Dustin, when Rick came back from juvie, you *promised* me you would come to me if he bothered you again. After all that time he spent harassing you last year and that fight he got into with you and the rest of the hockey team…."

"I know," Dusty says quietly. "I'm sorry, Jack. But Rick was threatening to share that video everywhere…. I couldn't take the chance."

"*Dustin.*" Coach leans forward, waiting for Dusty to meet his eyes. "Do you really think I'd let Rick hurt Emmitt like that?"

"Of course not! I just couldn't think of anything you could do!"

Coach smiles. "We would have figured it out. Together. You need to start trusting me and Beth to help you with your problems."

"And me," I murmur.

"I know." Dusty drops his head into his hands. "I screwed up, okay? I just didn't see any way out other than giving him the money."

Coach pats Dusty's shoulder. "Well, he's giving it all back. I'm paying Rick's school a visit tomorrow to have a chat with him. He's definitely not keeping all that cash."

Dusty shrugs. "If you want. He's never gonna share that video around now. Not with the one we have of him now."

"Yes, what's on this video?" Mrs. Morton cocks her head at us. "You both failed to mention that."

"It's nothing illegal," I tell her quickly. "Just… something Rick isn't going to want people to see." Coach raises an eyebrow at that, but he doesn't ask any more questions.

"So how long am I grounded for?" Dusty asks them.

Coach and Mrs. Morton look at each other and do that thing where they communicate without talking. It's creepy.

"You're not," Mrs. Morton finally says.

"What?" Dusty and I both reply at the same time.

Mrs. Morton shakes her head. "Dustin, what you went through all those weeks… terrified to tell us or Emmitt what was going on… I can only imagine how horrible that was. Hopefully that experience will be enough to remind you we are all here for you. No matter how terrible or unfixable a problem seems, you can always come to us. We'll find a way to fix it."

A smile slowly spreads its way across Dusty's face. "Thanks, Aunt Beth," he finally says. His voice cracks on the end of the words, and she comes over to pull him into a hug.

"I love you," she whispers. "I will walk across hot coals to fix your problems. Don't forget that again."

Dusty hugs her back. Hard.

Later on we're in his room, making up for lost time. "So you ready for Saturday?" Dusty asks when we both come up for some air.

"A lot more ready now," I tell him. "I play better when you're in the stands."

"Of course you do."

I elbow him in the ribs. "So… how should we tell people?"

"No more announcements in the cafeteria?" he jokes.

"You didn't seem to like that idea today. Seriously, Dusty, everyone on the team knows. And they're fine with it… well, mostly. Everyone else? I don't care how they find out."

Dusty leans on his elbow. "Maybe… then maybe let's not worry about it."

"What do you mean?"

"The stressful thing before was always *not* telling people. Always having to be so careful to keep it a secret. But if you don't care anymore, and I don't care, then let's just not worry about it. We don't have to advertise it and start making out in the hallways between classes. We can just… be us. Do what we want to do. People will find out when they find out. Or they'll find out at the dance, right? If you still want to go with me." He says that last part with a hint of hesitation.

"Hell, yeah. That sounds good."

"Good." He grins. "You're going to crush Rice on Saturday."

Yeah, we are. And Dusty's going to be there, watching us.

"I have to tell you something." He leans farther over and moves his elbow until his head is resting on my shoulder. He's never done that

135

before. It feels… right. Like he's supposed to be there. "That video Rick had? He showed it to me. And I don't think he's the one who took it."

"Huh?" I'd sit up straight with surprise if Dusty wasn't basically lying across me right now.

"I know when it was taken. It was from when we kissed in your truck for the first time after I came back from New York. You know, the day you were teaching me to skate." Yeah, I remember that day. I'll probably never forget it. It was the day Dusty and I officially became… us.

"Anyway, the video was grainy, but not that grainy, so it was taken pretty close to your truck. And it definitely couldn't have been Rick who took it, because—"

"He was in juvie then," I murmur. "Shit. Did you ask him where he got it?"

"Course. He just kept saying I didn't need to worry about anyone having it except for him."

"Damn."

"Yeah. I mean, maybe we don't have to worry, you know? Whoever took that video… well, if they were going to do something with it, wouldn't they have done it by now?"

"Maybe. I mean, I guess. Even so, there's nothing we can really do about it now. Probably no point in worrying about it. Didn't we just agree we weren't going to worry about how or when people found out?" I'm surprised by how much I mean those words.

"Yeah. I guess we did." I can feel Dusty relax against me again. "It's just weird, you know? Who would take a video of us like that and just pass it off to Rick Snyder?"

It's a good question. But Dusty's lying on my shoulder, and I'm two days away from playing in the Vermont Division I hockey semifinals, and my team finally knows the one thing I always wished I could tell them.

Life's too good right now. I'll worry about details later.

FRIDAY'S GONE in a mess of pop quizzes and kicking Dusty's foot under the lunch table and hockey practice. And a pretty intense lecture from Coach right afterward.

"Look, men," he says, "I'm not going to lie: getting Rice in the semifinals wasn't an exciting draw for me either. They're the only team this entire year that outplayed us. The team we let ruin our perfect season.

"But that's also why they're the perfect opponent for this matchup. We have more to prove to them than anyone else in this division. More to prove to ourselves. We need to show them what we really play like; who we can really be. We need to show them they can't destroy us twice."

"So tomorrow we're going to do what we didn't do the first time. We're going to play together. You're going to know where everyone else is on that ice at every single moment of play. You're going to be disciplined. No stupid penalties. No letting them into your heads."

I definitely wince at that statement.

"You're going to show them the kind of men you really are. *Men.* Not boys. Last time you played like boys. This time? There won't be any boys on that ice. Just men taking back what belongs to them."

He finishes the speech with a round of yelling "Who are we?" with us screaming "Colby!" at him over and over again. It feels like being on this team used to feel, before they knew about me. It feels like we all belong together, like we're all one unit again. Even O'Sher's stopped glaring at me or refusing to enter the locker room when I'm changing there. He's definitely not eating lunch at my table again or anything like that, but it's like he's accepted that I'm part of the team, and that he needs me if we're going to win. I'll take it.

"You nervous?" Dusty asks me on the phone that night.

"Yeah. Of course. The playoffs are always a big deal."

"Just keep it together," Dusty reminds me. "I may have missed the last time you played Rice, but I heard all about it from Jack. I don't think I'd like Enforcer Emmitt too much."

I laugh. "Nah. He's not exactly your type."

"Nope. So just be Emmitt. Not John LeClair, and not Enforcer Emmitt. Just you. Hey… I just realized I never asked you something. What about the scout who was watching that game? What happened with him?" He sounds hesitant, and I'm betting he already knows the answer to that question.

It's going to be painful saying that answer out loud. I got an e-mail from Dad about that a few days after he left, but I've been so caught up in fixing things with Dusty and telling the team and getting through the last game that it's been surprisingly easy to ignore the possible destruction of my future as a hockey player. "I guess he told Dad they're still interested, but they want to keep an eye on me for a while longer before they make any decisions. In other words, I fucked up that game, so now there's a good chance they'll never glance at me again."

"Shit." Dusty sighs. "This is all my fault, isn't it? Emmitt, I'm so—"

"Stop it," I tell him. "This is actually why I was hoping you'd never ask about that guy. Dusty, the way I played in that game is all on me. Yeah, shit sucks sometimes. But I'm not giving up yet. We're in the playoffs, and as far as I'm concerned, I've still got the chance to impress some scouts. I was never planning on going to the national team anyway, remember? That was never supposed to be in the cards. It popped up as a possibility, it didn't happen, it's over. But hockey isn't over, and all my other chances aren't over." It's an easy speech to deliver, because it's the one I've been giving myself in my head periodically whenever the words in Dad's e-mail start to haunt me.

"Yeah?" Dusty asks.

"Yeah," I tell him. And I'm 90 percent sure I mean it.

It's so good to have Dusty back. That one fact alone gets me through a lot of the nerves leading up to the next game. It carries me through breakfast, with Mom and Casey going on and on about how excited they are and how much they can't wait for the game. It gets me through driving to the rink, blasting "Tangerine" because it's Dusty's favorite song and it's somehow become mine too. It gets me through the locker room, where I keep my headphones on to avoid losing the solid focus I've got going. It gets me through warm-ups and another one of Coach's pump-up speeches.

Then we're lining up on the ice, and I'm across from the only guy who's ever gotten me kicked out of a hockey game. "Look who's here," he says with a smirk. "Gonna make it through the second period this time? Or you gonna get your panties up in a wad again?"

I can tell already there's going to be a lot of chirping in this game. But this time I think I know how to chirp back. I wink at him. "You better hope I play more than two periods," I tell him. "Since a bender like you needs to be learning from someone who can actually skate." *Bender* is one of the worst insults you can make about a hockey player's skating, since it's supposed to mean their ankles are hitting the ice. My opponent's scowl darkens, but he doesn't have time to say anything.

Because the puck drops.

The first period is mostly both of our teams feeling each other out. We're evenly matched. Rice is more aggressive, but thanks to Coach hounding us, we're playing more disciplined hockey than we were in our last game against them. Rice takes several penalties, and eventually Eric manages to score on the one-man advantage.

The crowd's going crazy at the start of the second period. This is already the tightest game either of our teams has played all season, and everyone knows it. They also know both our teams probably deserve to be playing in the state championship, and only one of us can.

So it's probably inevitable that the period starts off rowdy.

First I get an offensive zone face-off with my arch nemesis, which I dominate. I get the puck over to Eric, but Henny gets overexcited and ends up tripping the Rice player he's tangled up with. Even before the ref calls the penalty, the Rice player has gotten up and shoved Luis into the boards, so then he gets called too. And things unravel from there into a sloppy period with lots of penalties… and us getting just as many as Rice. I manage to keep myself out of the penalty box; Enforcer Emmitt is long gone. But it's hard to stay on your game when your team is falling apart around you. After I send a beautiful saucer pass—being humble is important and all, but sometimes you have to call something what it is— to Alvis Ankers, and he misses it because he's checking someone into the boards unnecessarily, Coach calls for a time-out.

Coach doesn't even get to say one word before I pull off my helmet. "We're playing their game!" I yell. "Not ours! They're *not* better than us. As good as us, maybe, but not better than us. And they want us to play like this because this is the way they know how to beat us. They can beat us if we're sitting in the penalty box more than they are. They can beat us if we get frustrated and forget to look for each other on the ice. That's how they know they can beat us, and they're doing it *right now!* Look, I've done it before. I let one of their players get me kicked out of our last game, and I'm not letting it happen again. I'm not playing to his level anymore, and the rest of you can't either, or we're not going to the championship next week!"

I stop, realizing I've probably completely taken over Coach's time. But he's smiling at me. "Couldn't have said it better, Emmitt," he calls out. "All of you! *Play as a team!* You're not a bunch of pissed-off little boys. You're men. You play together!"

Eric takes the next face-off and wins it. He sends me a long, cross-ice pass, and I streak down the far-side boards. I wind up for the shot without breaking my skating stride, and I rip off a slap shot.

It beats the goalie on his glove side. Straight into the net. The rink goes nuts, and I give everyone on our side a nod.

That's the kind of hockey we need to play.

It's not like that seals the game for us or anything, though. They score on us once at the end of the period, leaving us tied again. Then they open the third period with an offensive rally and a lot of shots on net, and Doug lets one by. Score is 3-2, and there's not much hockey left.

Luckily their aggression gets the better of them eventually. Two of their guys get called for penalties halfway through the period, and O'Sher scores while they're down.

Tied again, and less than seven minutes left to go in the game.

The hockey's prettier now, but it's still intense. We're too cautious—defensive when we should be offensive. Eric catches my eye at one point and shakes his head. He knows we can't play that style if we want to avoid overtime.

It feels like it takes until the last minute of the game for us to get back to our regular speed again. Then, with only fifty-eight seconds left, it happens. We've got the puck, and Luis drops it back to Eric, who lobs it over to me on the left side of the ice. I move up fast across the center ice, and I'm about to take the shot on goal, and this is it: I can feel it. I've got their goaltender beat; he's come out too aggressively, and his angle is bad. There's no one else around to stop this shot. As long as I'm accurate, I'm about to score this goal.

And then we win.

I'm going for the shot when my favorite Rice player slashes my stick from behind with his, and it goes flying.

Shards of hockey stick fly across the ice as half the rink cheers and the other half groans. The ref's whistle is loud and heavy across the ice.

His voice sounds foggy in my brain.

Penalty shot, number thirteen.

Thirteen. That's me.

If my brain wasn't washed out with adrenaline, that would have been obvious. I had a clear shot on the goal and would have scored if that asshole hadn't taken out my stick. So of course I get a penalty shot.

In the last minute of play. For the game.

"I'll enjoy watching you fuck this up, faggot," says Rice Boy as he skates by me toward the boards.

I just smile at him.

The referee leaves the puck at center ice, and I skate toward it. Still smiling. Because I already know I have this.

In spite of what everyone else thinks, I'm not Colby's golden boy. I'm not perfect, and I'm never going to be. I may not even be the next John LeClair. But if there's one thing I am, it's observant. I've been watching this goalie for three periods now, and I know what he may not know: if you fake him to the left, he opens up his five-hole wide enough for you to slide the puck in along the ice.

I take off at full speed with the puck, fake to the left, and slide the puck between his legs before he even knows what's coming.

Lights and sirens, and I can't stop myself from throwing my stick into the air. *Goal.*

The rest of the team skates back on, yelling and screaming and slapping me and shoving me in their excitement. "Still forty seconds left to play!" I remind them above the noise. "Don't lose it now!"

We play the next thirty seconds guarded, careful. Defensive. Because we can be now.

With ten seconds left, they get the puck deep into our zone and end up passing it behind the goal. Before any of us can get back to the puck, one of the Rice players is taking a shot on goal.

I see the time ticking down on the clock at the exact same time I see the puck flying toward the goal.

Five… four… three… two… one….

Doug falls on the puck just before it crosses the line. And the buzzer sounds.

The rink is madness. Everyone's rushing down from the stands, and everyone from our team is skating into each other in celebration, and all I hear is senseless noise echoing off my eardrums. I fight through the mass of bodies to the boards, trying to find Dusty. This is the *moment*. The one I've been waiting for. We took Rice down, finally, and I got the winning goal. We're going to the state championships, and Dusty's going there with me.

I finally find him standing by our benches with Matt and Julia and Casey and Mrs. Morton and Mom. So many of the people in the world who mean something to me. O'Sher's standing next to them, kissing his girlfriend, Jean. Coach sees his family at the same time I do and grabs Mrs. Morton up in a lifting hug, giving her a quick kiss before he sets her down again.

I don't even think. I should, probably, but I don't. I skate up to the board and throw off my helmet, and Dusty's standing there. The one person I care about impressing more than anyone else in this rink.

I throw my arms around him and press my lips into his.

If this were a movie, the whole rink would probably come to a standstill while everyone stared at us. Luckily this isn't a movie, and the celebration goes on. But there are definitely some camera flashes next to me, and it's a particularly bright one in my eyes that has me suddenly pulling away.

"Wow," I say. "I'm…."

Dusty shakes his head. "You're going to the championships," he tells me. Beaming.

Now I'm doing plenty of thinking, and I don't care about any of it.

So I kiss him again. There's no going back now.

CHAPTER
SIXTEEN

Dear Mr. LeClair,

You wer in the newspaper today! Did you see the artikal? The reporter said thing all about the teams you played for and what you do now. It was so cool!

I cant wait to be a famous hockey player like you so that I can be in a newspaper to. That is going to be amazeing!

—Emmitt LaPoint, age 7

A LOT of what happens right after I kiss Dusty is blurry.

I know at some point Coach tugs me gently away from Dusty, shoves me into the middle of a group of my teammates, and tells us all to get to the locker room. I know there are people trying to ask me questions from the periphery of the group. *"Emmitt, can we talk to you?" "Emmitt, great goal!"* But the guys from the team keep me between them, and we walk as one to the locker room without saying much. There's a lot of high-fiving, and relieved sighs, and the occasional cheer. But not much talking.

We get to the locker room, and Eric drops his helmet on the floor and shakes his head at me. "Guys," he announces to the room, "tonight we all did something amazing. And we did it together." He picks up his helmet and raises it in the air. "Men, we're going to the championship!" The cheering is so loud they can probably hear it back in the rink.

"And," Eric adds loudly, "whatever you think about what just happened at the end of this game, remember: we may have tied Rice as a team, but one person was on the ice when we put that last goal on the board." He points his helmet at me. "Emmitt LaPoint, you may not be the next John LeClair. But I know one thing. I'm fucking glad you're Emmitt LaPoint." No one's more surprised when he hugs me.

The rest of the team is cheering again and patting me on the back. Sure, a few people—O'Sher included—are hanging back on the periphery just watching the action. But they're watching, not glaring. And at some point, everyone starts cheering together again.

Things go blurry once more after that. I know Coach comes in and give us another speech about how proud of us he is and how excited he is to take our group to the state championship game next week. How there isn't any other team he'd rather take. At some point he pulls me off to the side and tells me he's proud of me no matter what. Then he also tells me he's having Casey bring my truck around back to pick me up, because there are a lot of local reporters who want to talk to me right now, and he doesn't think I'm in the best frame of mind for that.

Definitely not.

Casey and Dusty pick me up at the back of the rink, and Dusty and I hold hands most of the way to Coach's house, where we eat pizza and ice cream with Mom and Mrs. Morton and Matt and Julia and… well, celebrate.

And we don't talk about what Dusty and I did. No one even mentions it until it's finally time for me, Casey, and Mom to leave. Mom and Casey take off first, and then Dusty walks me out to my truck. "You doing okay?" he asks.

"Yeah," I tell him. "I'm… great."

He grabs two belt loops of my jeans and pulls our hips together. "You didn't have to do that today," he tells me.

Time to be honest. "Actually," I tell him. "I wasn't planning it or anything. It just… happened."

He pushes our lips together briefly. "Well, whatever happens next—no matter how weird things get—you can feel free to do that anytime you want."

"Totally worth it," I murmur.

And I think I mean it.

THE NEXT morning, when I wake up, things have finally sunk in.

I'm going to the state championship.

And I kissed my boyfriend in front of most of the Vermont high school hockey community.

Breakfast is on the table when I leave my room, which is weird. Mom was supposed to be working the morning shift today. "What's going on?" I ask.

She smiles. "I took the day off. Jack called. His phone's been ringing off the hook. We both think we're going to need to make a plan for how you want to communicate with people about what happened after the game." She never stops smiling the entire time she's talking, which seems weird for someone who's basically launching an unwanted PR campaign with her not-quite-seventeen-year-old son.

"Why are you so happy?" I ask her suspiciously.

She comes around the side of the counter and kisses me on the cheek. "Because I've never been prouder of you," she says. "I don't know whether you planned to do that last night—"

"I didn't," I interrupt.

"But I do know I've never been more impressed by you. And you've spent a lot of your life impressing me, Emmitt."

I don't know what to say to that. So I just go with "Thanks, Mom."

She goes back to the stove to put together a plate of french toast and bacon for me. When she comes around the counter to hand it to me, she sits down and says, "We need to talk about one other thing. Your father called this morning."

I groan. "He already heard? The local newspapers don't even go out on Sunday."

"Well, Uncle Dave was at the game. And even if he hadn't been… honey, you're on the Yahoo! home page right now."

I cough so hard I lose my bite of toast. "Excuse me?"

She nods and goes over to the kitchen table to pick up her laptop and bring it to me. And there, on the front page of the Yahoo! line of sliding stories, is the picture I knew existed but still hadn't seen. The

145

picture of Dusty and me, surrounded by celebrating bodies, with me in my uniform and my helmet off.

Kissing.

"Holy shit," I whisper.

High School Hockey Player Comes Out of the Closet
to Celebrate Playoff Victory

High school hockey is getting ahead of at least one professional league. While the NHL has yet to have a current or retired player come out, the rising stars of the field are proving they're not afraid to show off their sexual orientation.

On Saturday sixteen-year-old Emmitt LaPoint, star of his highly successful high school hockey team in Colby, VT, celebrated his team's semifinals victory over a rival school by very publicly kissing another boy about his age. The boy is rumored to be LaPoint's boyfriend and his coach's nephew.

According to local sources who first released the photo, LaPoint has been out to his team for some time but has not, prior to this scene, been out to the rest of the community.

The NHL and the LGBTQ community have a strange history. It was hockey players and executives who first launched the You Can Play ad campaign, which aims to address the importance of equality in sports. The NHL was the first professional league to have members from every team participate in that campaign. Despite these advances, NHL players have remained silent on the subject of their sexual orientations, even as NBA and NFL players have come out. Caitlin Cahow, a former member of the US women's hockey team, traveled to the Russian games as part of a delegation of openly gay players and has widely discussed the struggles female and male hockey players face where the topic of sexual orientation is concerned. Both male and female professional hockey players have come out while playing for various leagues around the world, but the NHL has yet to see a current or retired player do so.

LaPoint certainly isn't the first teen athlete to come out to his team or his community; many other teen LGBTQ athletes have chronicled their own experiences in this process. But the talented LaPoint has been on the radar of a variety of college and elite junior hockey programs, and his very public celebration on Saturday will certainly raise more questions within the hockey community about just how open and accepting the sport is.

"Holy shit," I say again.

"Have you checked your phone?" she asks.

I shake my head. "I turned it off before the game. I haven't turned it back on yet. I'm kind of... afraid to."

"Good. Not that you're afraid of it—just good that you haven't turned it on yet. Who knows how many people have probably been calling or texting you? I've never been so glad we got rid of the house phone after you boys got cell phones; at least we're not easy to track down these days. Listen, Jack's coming over with Dusty in an hour so we can make some plans. Is that okay with you?"

I take another bite of french toast, and I'm surprised to find I'm still hungry. "Sure." At least no matter what comes next, Dusty's going to be there.

While we're waiting for them, I make the mistake of going on Facebook. My page has been lit up with people sharing the Yahoo! article and a few others that are going around. Most of what people have to say is actually encouraging—stuff about how it doesn't matter who I like as long as I keep winning Colby games. There are a few ugly comments here and there. Things like how obvious it's always been that I'm a fag and shit like that. Nothing I can't handle.

Then I make the mistake of reading the comments under the Yahoo! article.

Casey comes out of his room while Mom's in the shower. I'm about halfway through the comments. My eyes are glued to the screen, and my stomach's down somewhere around my knees.

"Yeah, I was just reading that," Casey tells me when he glances at the screen. "You've gone national. Kinda cool, huh?" Then he notices what section of the article I'm in. "Emmitt, don't read those!" He slams the laptop closed and smashes my thumb in the process.

"Ow! What the hell?"

"Why were you reading the comments on that? Are you crazy?"

I pile my head in my hands. "Dude, that was… intense. Everybody hates me. Unless they love me. Unless they think the whole thing was a publicity stunt to get onto an elite team. Unless they think I'm never gonna get onto an elite team now because no one will want me. Unless they think I'm going to hell anyway so it doesn't matter. Unless they think I'm the bravest and most amazing person ever."

Casey pats me on the shoulder. "Never read the comments. Never."

Lesson learned, I guess.

The bell rings and I get up to answer it. I'm still in the sweats I slept in, but Dusty isn't going to care, and neither is Coach.

"Hey." Dusty steps in and gives me a side hug before he fist-bumps Casey. "Did you see that Yahoo! article?" I can hear him murmuring to Casey.

"Emmitt read the comments," Casey whispers back. "Dumbass."

"How are you doing?" Coach asks me.

I shrug. "Just making national news. As per usual. Hey," I add, "I'm sorry I got Dusty messed up in this."

Coach shakes his head. "He's not. And neither am I. Emmitt, Dusty and I will tell you if you need to start worrying about us in all of this. For now, just concentrate on worrying about yourself. You're the one who's going to get the lion's share of attention here."

"Yeah," Dusty says. "Anyway, man, something good already came out of this for me."

"Like what?" Casey asks.

"You guys know how I've never told Race about me and Emmitt, right? I saw that article, and I figured it was time to suck it up. I didn't want him to find out one of his best friends is gay from Yahoo! news. So I called him."

That is good news. Not telling Race has been eating Dusty up for way too long now. "Dusty, that's killer," I tell him. "How'd he take it?" I mentally cross my fingers that Race was half as cool as Eric was.

"Okay." Dusty shrugs. "It was still way early out there, and I think he was half-asleep still. He was surprised, for sure. But I think it's gonna be good."

Coach claps Dusty on the back. "I'm proud of you, kid." Dusty just smiles.

Mom comes into the living room, still poking at her wet hair. "Thanks for coming over, Jack. I didn't know what to do when I saw the news story this morning and my phone started buzzing incessantly."

Coach laughs. "No worries. We'll figure this out."

Mom ushers us all over to sit in the living room, where Coach starts right into the conversation. "Emmitt, here's the thing. A lot of people want to talk to you right now."

"As long as they leave Dusty alone," I say.

Dusty rolls his eyes. "I'm not a wilting flower. And they don't care about me, anyway. I'm not the outed hockey player."

"Anyway," says Coach, "I think the best odds at controlling this and keeping your—and the team's—focus on the game this Saturday is for us to get out in front of things. I'm friends with the sports editor at the *Colby Courier*, and he was calling me the second you left the ice yesterday. If you do an interview with him, he'll be respectful and not too intrusive. From there we can deflect any interest from national outlets by asking them to go to him and use his interview."

"And then they'll leave me alone?" I ask.

He smiles. "No guarantees, Emmitt. But you still are just a high school kid, and only a junior at that. I think we can hope this burst of interest in you will be relatively short. I don't imagine paparazzi will be stalking you at school or anything."

For the first time since he got to the house, Dusty looks nervous. "What if they do? What can we do about it?"

"We'll make sure they don't," Casey says with a lot more enthusiasm than I feel. "Ya know, the hockey team and the skateboarding team. We gotcha covered."

Coach looks like he's trying not to smile at Casey's conviction. "Sure you will, Casey. And your mother and I will also make sure school security is on the lookout for anything strange. Essentially, this is the plan: you give the people what they want just once. Then you go underground until the game next week while we wait for this to blow over."

That sounds good to me. Except…. "What about Dad? When's he coming? You know he's going to have his own ideas about what I should do."

Casey snorts.

Mom pats my knee. "Don't worry about your father. He can't come out until Wednesday, anyway. I'll talk to him before that and make sure he knows how we're handling this. He'll stick to the plan."

"Because that's such a skill of his," Casey mutters.

"And what about scouts?" I ask. "That article said I'm on people's radar right now. What were they talking about? Did they mean that guy from the national team? I thought he wasn't interested anymore. Or were they talking about specific colleges? Am I supposed to contact them or not worry about it? Or will they contact me if they want to talk to me? Or will—"

Everyone starts laughing, and Coach holds up his hand to cut me off. "I just want to make sure I handle all that right," I growl.

"Listen," says Coach. "Don't worry about scouts right now. Just play your heart out in the state championship on Saturday. You do well there and none of this matters."

I'm not sure I believe him. But I want to, so I go with it.

FOUR HOURS later I'm dressed and sitting in Coach's living room, doing an interview with Scott Carter, the sports editor of the *Colby Courier*. He wanted to come to my house, but that felt strange to me—letting a reporter into the space that's been mine and Mom's and Casey's for so long. Coach said he didn't mind if we used his house, so here we are.

"First of all," says Scott, "that was quite a game on Saturday. Congratulations."

"Thanks," I tell him.

"It was such a turnaround from your first game against Rice. Can you tell me what was different about this matchup?"

I relax the instant he starts asking about hockey. Maybe Coach told him to go there first.

"The last time we played them, we weren't playing as a unit," I tell him. "We were there with individual goals and game plans, myself included. I had a rough day, and I wasn't focused on where my teammates were on the ice. So Rice was able to get between us.

"They were able to do that to us again for a few minutes on Saturday, but this time we caught what was happening and refocused ourselves. We were disciplined, so we won."

Scott smiles. "You're well-spoken for someone of only sixteen. Many of your teammates call you the leader of the team, even though you're only a junior. How do you think you've developed such maturity so young?"

"I'll be seventeen in March," I tell him first, just to set the record straight. "I'm not that mature all the time. I make mistakes just like every other high school junior. I say dumb stuff and do things without thinking. You know, because our prefrontal cortexes aren't fully developed yet," I add, suddenly glad I paid attention in biology freshman year. "But with hockey, I've always loved it so much… maybe my prefrontal cortex developed faster or something so I could keep getting better faster. I love to play. It's always been the thing that made me happier than doing anything else. So I've always done whatever I had to do to get better at it." I feel like I'm rambling a lot in that answer. Hopefully he won't print the whole thing.

He just smiles at me. "I'm told you'd already come out to your team before the game on Saturday. Is that accurate?"

Ah. Now we're getting to the big stuff.

I nod. "Yeah. I told them… right after the last game of the season, actually. The one we lost to Rice."

"Any reason you told them then?"

My heart speeds up slightly. Now we're going for the personal jugular. "It was time. Part of the reason I wasn't focused during that game was because my mind was on other things. Things that had to do with my… not telling people I was dating a guy. I decided it was time."

"Interesting. So until hiding hurt your playing, you were okay with keeping your sexual orientation to yourself?"

I shake my head. "I wasn't ever okay with it. It just seemed to be what I had to do. And hiding didn't just hurt my game; it also ended up hurting someone I care about. Even if my playing wasn't suffering, I couldn't have kept hiding this much longer. So I decided it was time to tell the people who know me best. My teammates."

Scott nods. "This person you ended up hurting… would that happen to be the same person you kissed after the game on Saturday?"

"We're not talking about him," I say, more harshly than I meant to. "This interview is about me, okay? Not him." I'm sure lots of other reporters wouldn't let me get away with that, but Coach must've warned Mr. Carter that the topic is off-limits for me—or he just knows we're both talking about his friend's nephew—and he decides not to push. Either way, he changes the subject.

"Were you surprised to see your face on national Internet headlines this morning?"

"Yeah. For one thing, that happened *crazy* fast. For another, I'm not even playing in any of the big junior hockey leagues. But I guess, in some ways, I'm not that surprised. There's a reason I haven't been out all this time, you know? I've worked hard all my life. All I ever wanted was to be a hockey player. But there aren't any gay hockey players in the NHL, or even former NHL players who've come out, so I started to think I couldn't have both. That I couldn't be a successful hockey player and still be gay. I don't know exactly how my picture got to the national news, but people are probably interested for the same reason I kept this hidden for so long—it's not *normal* yet to be a hockey player who's gay." I hate that I have to use the word *normal* in that sentence, but it seems to be the only thing that fits.

"A lot of people—particularly hockey players—have been trying to get the word out through campaigns like the You Can Play project that it should be normal, and perfectly okay, to be any sexual orientation and still be an athlete. Do you think things are changing? Is that part of what prompted you to come out publicly?"

I shake my head. "I haven't seen a lot of the hockey world yet. I made the decision a few years ago to stay in Colby and play hockey here. There are a lot of people who I'm sure would say that's a stupid decision, but it's been the right one for me, and I don't regret it. Because of that choice, though, I don't know much about how my hockey world fits into the rest of the hockey world. I play for a small town in Vermont, and all the hockey camps I've been to were in New England. I've only been to a few NHL games in my entire life, and they've all been Habs games. Go Canadiens, by the way. Sure, I read about stuff like the You Can Play project, and I think things might be changing out there. But here? Things have sort of been the same the entire time I've been alive. It's always been fine to be gay at my high school. We have a GSA, and people support them, and they do a lot for our school. I think most people would say Colby High School is a safe place to be a gay kid. But a gay *hockey* kid? I just never knew. Because no one was. So I played it safe, until I didn't anymore."

"How did your team accept you? When you came out to them?"

That's a question that makes me smile. "They made me wish I'd trusted them a lot sooner. Most of them have been supportive. Some of them… it's taking time. The majority, though, didn't care at all. Maybe that's the problem, you know? You've gotta have faith in your teammates, to believe they're going to be better than the world's making you think they are. You gotta believe in the people who know you best instead of worrying about the rest of the world, even though the world seems a lot bigger and more powerful. I guess NHL players are going to have to start doing what I did and have more faith in the people around them. But then, they have a lot more eyes on them than I did. A lot more people to worry about. I think I get why they aren't coming out."

Scott shuts off the recording device he's been using. "That's plenty, Emmitt. You did well." He stands up to shake my hand, which I realize is trembling.

"Yeah?" I ask. "Can you not print anything from when I started rambling? I do that sometimes, when I'm nervous. Ramble."

"You weren't rambling. Well, not much, anyway. Listen, this story will go in tomorrow's edition. After that, national outlets will be able to pick it up if they wish. Jack tells me you're not planning to talk with anyone else?"

"Nope. Consider this a… what do they call it? Exclusive?"

He chuckles. "Good luck, Emmitt. With everything. If anyone deserves success, it's you."

I don't know what I deserve anymore. You should only deserve what you work for, but that doesn't seem to be how the world operates.

CHAPTER
SEVENTEEN

Dear Mr. LeClair,

Today I was playing around on the Internet, and I found this thing called the You Can Play project. Have you ever heard of it? It's interesting. I guess hockey players on college and NHL teams and whatever talk about how anyone should be able to play hockey, whether they're gay or a different race or whatever.

It's a cool idea, and I'm happy they're doing it. I read somewhere that it started because this hockey exec had a gay son who died, so this is basically in his memory. Cool.

For a few minutes it made me feel better about... stuff. If all these teams and coaches were saying they didn't care if players were gay, maybe I could stop worrying so much about being gay. Then I thought about it: if people are making all these videos, why aren't more players telling everyone they're gay? If it's so safe to be gay in hockey... why isn't anyone? There have to be gay people in the NHL, right? It would be statistically impossible for there not to be. But they're not saying anything.

It's bullshit. It's like when your people tell you that you can be anything you want when you grow up, but they actually mean you can be anything you want except for the stuff that's super hard to become.

Fuck this shit. I'd never say that to you in person, by the way. But it's what I feel right now. If this is how things are, with everyone saying they don't care if I'm gay and nobody meaning it, then I'm never telling anyone about what I might be. I'll start asking girls out or whatever. It's just safer.

Fuck this shit.

—Emmitt LaPoint, age 14

THE NEXT morning, Dusty's at my house at six thirty. And Dusty's not exactly a morning person. "What are you doing here?" I ask as I open the door and rub the sleep out of my eyes.

"Jack had to go into school early to get some work done, so I asked if he could drop me off here. You know, so you could drive me."

After the interview yesterday, Dusty, Casey, and I spent hours on his living room couch with Matt and Julia playing games and watching movies. Somehow it still feels like it's been days since I've seen him. "That sounds great," I tell him. I hug him, because I haven't brushed my teeth, and there's no need for him to find out how disgusting my morning breath is.

Casey and I get ready while Dusty watches morning television. "You're not on national morning shows yet, at least," he calls over the living room couch.

"Give it time," Casey calls back. "And don't you mean 'we'?"

"Pretty sure I'm just the unidentified guy in the background right now," Dusty says. "And I'm more than fine with that."

Casey pours a bowl of cereal and sits down next to Dusty with his phone in one hand and a spoon in the other, just like every other morning. It's so normal I forget for a minute that in just over an hour, we're walking into the hallways of the one place that has the power to rip me to shreds: high school.

The forgetting thing only lasts until Casey opens his mouth. "Hey," he says, "um, you should probably know that the guy who runs the You Can Play project is tweeting about you."

I drop my toast and speed to the couch. "What are you talking about? And what are you doing on Twitter? I thought you said Twitter was stupid."

"Twitter is stupid, but I'm still on it. And a bunch of people from the skateboarding club are on it, and one of them just retweeted this." He passes the phone to me.

Emmitt LaPoint is the future of hockey in this country.

"Holy shit," I breathe. There's got to be a record for how many times you can say that over three days.

"Yeah," Casey says. "I think a bunch of other hockey people are tweeting about you too. The captain of the Canadiens just said you're brave. Oh, and he's glad you're a Habs fan. There was some stuff in French too, but my French sucks."

"Holy shit."

"And a bunch of players from the Avalanche are talking about you. And some guys from the Rangers and the Penguins. And Sidney Crosby told ESPN that you—"

"Stop." Dusty pulls the phone away from him. "Casey, you're freaking him out. Look." He points at my face, and Casey squints. "That thing about Sidney Crosby pushed him over the edge. Who the hell is Sidney Crosby, by the way?"

"*Really?*" Casey and I say in, like, perfect unison. Dusty shrugs.

"He's basically the best player in modern hockey," I tell Dusty. "Think of him as the new Gretzky."

To Dusty's credit, he doesn't ask who Gretzky is.

"*Sidney Crosby* is talking about me." I'm not sure what I'm supposed to do with that piece of information.

Dusty rolls his eyes and hops over the back of the couch. "Yeah, he is. But you know what? This doesn't change anything, Emmitt. Calm down. You're still Emmitt, and we still have to go to school, and you still have a state championship to play in on Saturday. If you get caught up in this other crap, you're going to forget all the things that actually matter."

That snaps me out of it. Mostly. I mean, he's right. Sidney Crosby using my name? I don't even know what he said yet, and it's still one of the most amazing things that's happened in my life. But it's not going to mean anything if I can't back it up with a solid game this weekend.

Which means I need a solid and focused week going into it.

Which means I need to get through today.

Which means I absolutely cannot look at the ESPN article and find out what Crosby said exactly.

We get to Colby High at the usual time. Usually the first thing I do when I get to school is leave Casey at his locker and head to mine. Today the three of us leave the truck and just stand there for a minute. Like we're all trying to figure out where to go next.

Mel comes running up to us. "Emmitt! Oh my God! You're amazing! You're an idol to little LGBTQ athletes everywhere!" She grabs me in a hug I never saw coming. "When I saw you look at Dusty like that on Saturday, I thought, *no way is he actually going to do what I think he's going to do.* And then you did it! Just like that! It was… epic!"

This is too many exclamation points for my morning. "Thanks, Mel," I say weakly. "Uh, have you seen Eric?" I haven't talked to him since he made his speech in the locker room on Saturday. I owe him a thank-you.

"No, but he's probably at his locker." She frowns. "Are you worried about going inside?"

"No. Of course not. It's just… well…."

"It's weird," Casey finishes lamely.

"Super weird," Dusty adds. Super lamely.

She shrugs. "It's only weird as long as you let it be weird."

"Or it could be weird because people pour blood on my head," I remind her.

"This isn't 1996. Or the plot of a Stephen King book."

"Why does everyone keep bringing up 1996?" I ask.

"I told you," Casey butts in, "that's when—"

"The Defense of Marriage Act was passed," Mel finishes with him.

Dusty just shakes his head, like he's trying to shake out the confusion.

Mel grabs my arm. "People will be weird. And maybe even a little shitty. They still are sometimes with me. And you'll get over it," she tells me. Then she marches me through the side entrance of Colby High School.

The entire hallway doesn't stop and stare. A few people look up, and there's some whispering. But there's also some fist-bumping and the occasional "great game this weekend!"

We get to Casey's locker. All the way there. And not one person has tried to dump blood on my head.

"See? You're going to be fine. I have to go to science. I'll tell Eric you're looking for him!" Mel rushes off, and Casey, Dusty, and I just stand there. Eventually Casey opens his locker to get his stuff, but Dusty and I don't move.

"I think that's him," some girl whispers from a few lockers away. "You know, the one who made out with a guy after the game on Saturday."

"Isn't that the guy he made out with?" her friend asks. "They must be together! That's so cute!"

Casey frowns. "Your biggest problem might be the females in this school all fetishizing you," he tells us.

Dusty gapes at him. "Where are you learning these words?" he finally asks.

The rest of the morning is a lot like that. *Whisper whisper.* Sometimes a comment to my face about how amazing I am. I catch some dirty or creeped-out looks from the corner of my eye—nothing to my face, though. Dusty reports similar news when I see him just before lunch.

"Are we up for the cafeteria?" I ask him.

"Gotta face it sometime," he reminds me.

We get to the cafeteria early, so there aren't many people there yet. Mel and Eric are sitting together at the same table where Casey and I first brought the skateboarders and hockey team together. Maybe now the GSA is joining too; Patrick's head is going to explode. We grab chicken burgers—because hey, comfort food—and sit across from them.

"Your interview's in the paper," Eric says, not looking up from where he's scrolling through something on his phone. Probably the article.

"Great," I mutter. "How much of an asshole do I sound like?"

He smirks. "Only in one or two lines, I swear. The stuff you say about how awesome your team is… good stuff."

I glare at him.

"Steven Crosby is talking about him on ESPN," Dusty announces. Eric looks confused.

"Sidney Crosby," I correct him.

Now Dusty looks confused, and Eric looks shocked. "What? *Sidney Crosby* knows who you are?"

"I guess. I decided not to read the article. Too many distractions, you know?"

Eric shakes his head slowly. "Only you could have Sidney Crosby talk about you and decide to ignore it because you need to keep your focus."

Dusty kicks me softly under the table. He's smiling.

Mel waves over some of her friends from the GSA, and soon Samantha and her friend Grace and this guy named Garrett, who I remember from National Honor Society, are all sitting with us. The hockey team starts filling in around us, and Casey and Dusty's friends show up too. I'm hoping we can get through the rest of lunch pretending nothing happened on Saturday except for us winning an epic hockey game, but no such luck. Doug plops down in a seat and announces, "Like, everybody on the planet is talking about Emmitt. This is crazy shit, man."

Eric rolls his eyes. "Emmitt's not thinking about any of it. He has to *focus*, you know."

Doug points a roll at me. "You better think about it. This is an amazing opportunity for all of us. What if someone famous decides to come to our championship game or something?"

"Doug, I don't think—"

"This is getting national attention, man! You have to get on Twitter and tweet some shit and tell people—"

He gets interrupted when a roll hits me in the back of the head. "Faggot!" someone calls out.

The cafeteria doesn't exactly go silent, but it does get an awful lot quieter. "Who did that?" Doug gets up and yells. "Stand up, shithead, if you're such a badass!"

No one's standing up. I look around frantically, expecting some adult to appear out of nowhere and grind this scene to a screeching halt, but all I see around me is a sea of high schoolers. This could go *Lord of the Flies* awfully fast.

Only it doesn't.

"Yeah? That's what I thought," Doug calls out. "Brave enough to throw a roll, but not brave enough to stand up and own what you do. Grow the hell up!" He sits back down.

Samantha's gazing at him with admiration. "That was baller," she says.

He shrugs. "You know. Can't have homophobes running Colby." I glance around to see if O'Sheridan or his buddies are somewhere, but they don't seem to be.

Dusty kicks me under the table again. "You okay?" he mouths. I brush the crumbs off the back of my head and shrug.

It's better than a bucket of blood. And Doug standing up so fast like that—that didn't suck.

After that, the day just moves… forward. No more rolls. No more people openly calling me a faggot. Just more stares and the occasional glare. Until last period, when I get to precalc early and discover my class gathered around the window, staring down into the street.

I walk over to where Henny is standing. "What's going—" I look down.

And quickly wish I hadn't.

Below me is a small row of people standing in front of our high school, holding signs. *GOD HATES FAGS* in bright red is the one that stands out more brightly than all the others. Nearby, another small row of reporters flash pictures of the group.

I scoop up my books before Mrs. Limely can get to the room, and I take off.

I head back to my locker. I'm getting my keys and going out the back, and I'm getting the hell out of here.

Only Dusty's sitting there, waiting for me at my locker. Shit. How did I forget that Dusty would have also seen this by now?

He puts up a hand so I can grab it and pull him up. "C'mon," he tells me. "I told Jack we were leaving."

"He gave us permission to skip school?"

Dusty holds up his phone to show me a text. *Text me if you need me and I'll get someone to cover my class. If you and E need to get out of here, do it either out the back or wait for dismissal so no reporter catches up with you. Tell E I'll see him at practice.*

We end up in the Burger King parking lot. There aren't a lot of places to go in Colby on a Monday afternoon when you're a high schooler who's supposed to be in school. Especially not when you're easily recognizable to most of the town.

We take turns dipping french fries into shakes. "Dusty, I'm so sorry," I tell him.

He shakes his head. "For what? For doing what I wanted you to do all along?"

I bang my head against the steering wheel. "This is exactly what I was afraid was going to happen!"

"It is?" Dusty asks lightly. He takes another bite of ice-cream covered fry; it's an underrated combination. "I always thought you were afraid of the team rejecting you. Of not getting to play hockey anymore. Or of scouts rejecting you because you're gay."

Huh. I guess that is what I used to be afraid of.

"Which didn't happen," Dusty adds. "Doug stood up for you today and threatened to take down someone over throwing a roll. And famous hockey players are tweeting about you, so I don't think that's a bad thing for your career. So some crazy zealots are pissed that there's a picture of you kissing a guy on the Internet and that you're getting a lot of attention. I didn't exactly see the rest of the school rushing out to wave signs with them."

I groan. "How do you always do that?" I ask him.

"Do what?" He looks at me innocently.

"Make me realize I'm being a total ass."

"You're not being a total ass. Other stuff happened. Stuff we didn't expect."

"That's for sure." I cover one of my own fries in ice cream. "I didn't even think about how... public this could be. I didn't imagine a scenario where random people stood outside our school to yell about how much they hate us. Or one where people stared at us all day long. Or talked about how cute we are."

Dusty laughs. "We're fucking adorable, I bet."

I lean over and stick my fry into his mouth. "Straight out of the movies. Coming soon to a Facebook page near you."

He swallows the fry and leans over to kiss me. "Movie of the week coming soon."

I put my shake on the dashboard so I can pull him closer to me. "ESPN 30 for 30."

He stops and raises an eyebrow. "What's that?"

"Never mind." I press our lips back together and forget everything else. Forget everyone tweeting about us, or yelling hateful things about us, or talking about how fucking adorable we are. We just kiss. In my truck, on a Monday afternoon in the Burger King parking lot.

And I think about how maybe we can do more of that from now on.

161

CHAPTER
EIGHTEEN

DEAR MR. LeClair,

Today Dusty and I had our first date. Sort of. I mean, it was on my hockey coach's living room couch, and Dusty's little brother and sister were there. So maybe that doesn't count? I'm not sure anymore. All I know is that we hung out together and we had a lot of fun, and it felt like a date.

Last week I kissed Dusty in my truck. Did I tell you that? I know I said I wasn't going to... that hockey had to come first. But he took off for Colorado, you know? And I was scared. I was so scared I'd never see him again. Scared I'd never get to hang out with him again or get to kiss him again. Things with Dusty just don't feel the same way they felt with Alcott. When camp ended, and I knew I'd probably never make out with Alcott again, I was sort of okay with it. I knew I'd miss the company, and I'd miss having someone around who could see that side of me. But actually... I didn't miss Alcott himself that much.

With Dusty, I didn't just miss the way he sees this other side of me. I missed him. Every part of him. His weird facial expressions and his snarky remarks and the way he only half smiles when he's actually incredibly happy about something. I guess I also missed the way he gets all the sides of me. Not just the side that likes guys or the side that likes hockey or is good at school. He gets the side that's a big brother, and the side that hates his dad but doesn't want to, and the side that feel insecure all the time. The side that is terrified of failing.

He gets all of it. So we kissed again, in my truck. Now he's my boyfriend.

Tonight we watched some cartoon movie with Matt and Julia, and then we went up to his room. We fooled around on his bed—nothing big to report; Coach was home and it would weird me out to do too much knowing he was in the same house while Dusty and I did anything... well, you know—and then we just lay there, talking.

"Does it suck for you—having to keep this a secret?" I asked him.

He smiled. "Sometimes. But I've kept bigger secrets before, remember?"

Sometimes I forget that Dusty successfully hid his parents' disappearances for a lot of years before he got caught. I frown. "I don't want you to think of me the way you think of... your parents."

"Hey, I don't," he told me. "Emmitt, I didn't hide what my parents were doing all those years for them. *I did it for Matt and Julia. To keep them safe, and to keep us together." His face went softer, and then he did that half-smile thing. "To keep us together."*

I think it's going to be a good year.

—Emmitt LaPoint, age 16

PRACTICE THAT night goes surprisingly well. Coach pulls me aside before it starts to tell me I don't need to worry about seeing that hate group again. "Principal Wahalla was furious," he says, smiling. "She's made sure they'll never be within a thousand yards of our property—or your property—again. I haven't seen her that angry since someone painted a penis on the statue in front of the school." I don't ask him exactly who the group was, and he doesn't ask me if I want to know.

I go into Tuesday expecting some other brand-new shoe to drop, but the day is surprisingly calm. Not exactly normal—I think it's going to be a while before school feels normal for me again. There's still a lot of staring and sly pointing and whispering, and Dusty and I eat lunch in the library because I just don't have the energy for the cafeteria. But no one throws shit at us or writes crap on our lockers or anything, and that guy Garrett even asks me if he can work with Luis and me on this precalc project that gets assigned. Coach grinds us into the ice at practice; he's convinced the best way to keep us focused on the championship and not on the frenzy surrounding us is to make us skate our asses off. And I think it actually works. By Wednesday everyone on the team has stopped mentioning Sidney Crosby to me. They're all too exhausted.

I'm just starting to think normal might be closer than I'd imagined it could be. And then Dad shows up.

I'm still ignoring my phone as much as possible, so I don't even see the warning text Casey tries to send me. I do find it later, though: *The asshole has landed.*

I get home from practice tired and sweaty and ready for a shower. And there's Dad, sitting alone at our kitchen table.

He stands up quickly. "Your mother had to work," he says. "I hope you don't mind that I waited for you."

I throw down my hockey bag. "Where's Casey?"

Dad nods toward the closed bedroom doors. "Doing his homework."
Which means ignoring you.

"Back again, Dad? You couldn't take off fast enough after I told you I was gay. Nice e-mail, by the way, ignoring all that and letting me know the national team was through with me. Way to communicate effectively—too bad you didn't have time for a phone call."

Dad winces. "Emmitt, about all that…."

"What do you want, Dad?" I grab a Gatorade out of the fridge and stand by the counter. It seems safer to be a few feet away from him. "Come back to tell me I've ruined my career and I'll never play hockey again? 'Cause some people have been cool about this. Even NHL players."

Dad sighs. "Emmitt, I just want to talk to you. Will you sit down?"

I don't want to. But he *is* my father, and he did come all the way back here. I make my way slowly to the table.

"Listen," says Dad, "I know I upset you with what I said after you got kicked out of the season-ender. But Emmitt, I need you to understand that I wasn't asking you to take the easiest way out. I never thought that you keeping this to yourself was going to be easy. I was asking you to do what I thought would be best for your future. I'm sorry you felt like I wasn't supporting you."

I roll my eyes. "You've never supported me, Dad. Not for years. You left, remember? You haven't been around in years."

He nods intently. "I know that, Emmitt. And I was trying to make up for that and be here for you. I'm sorry I botched it. I should have supported you. I should have called you after you told me about your—uh, boyfriend. I should have given you the news from the scout in person or over the phone. I just didn't know how to talk to you, Emmitt. I haven't known how to talk to you in years."

"Maybe that's because you don't try." I can't keep the edge out of my voice.

"I'm sure it is," he says quietly. "And that's on me. I know that. Listen… I heard from that national team scout again. He wanted to make sure we knew that your coming out won't affect any decision they make about you, and that you're still on their radar. They're still keeping an eye on your playoff run."

"For real?" I can't keep the surprise out of my voice. I'd effectively written off all hope of ever seeing that scout again.

"For real. It sounds like they were watching your run anyway—that one bad game didn't put them off you completely—but I'm sure making the national news kept you in the forefront of their minds."

"Huh. So being gay may actually do something positive for my hockey career."

Dad chuckles. "Well, in some way. Listen, I think you need to ride this positivity right now. This is your chance to get the national team back in your good graces and get other programs and colleges watching you more closely. So I contacted *Hockey News*, and they want to interview you."

My fists are clenching underneath the table. "Dad… *why the hell* would you do that? Didn't Mom tell you the interview with the *Courier* was the only one I was going to do?"

He nods quickly and holds up his hands like he's surrendering or something. "I know, I know. She did. But that's a mistake, Emmitt. People are waiting to see how you handle this. You need to prove to them that you can keep up with the media on this without letting it distract you. You need to show them how mature you are. People might make videos talking about how everyone can play, but not everyone means it,. You have to show them that—"

My ears are ringing, and my head feels like it's about to explode. I've never been this angry at anyone, not even Rick Snyder or that

Rice player who came after me. "What is wrong with you?" I yell, leaping to my feet. "Why can't you ever just listen to me? Or anyone? You always think you know what's best, and you *don't ask*! You take off to Ohio without asking, and you tell me to keep secrets without asking me what I want, and you call scouts without asking me, and now you're standing here in the kitchen telling me you booked an interview I don't want!"

I'm not sure who's more surprised—him or me. I've never yelled at him like that before. Not when I was little, not when he told me he was leaving us, not when he told me he was getting remarried and having another kid. I step back quickly. "Shit, Dad. I didn't mean… I just meant…."

"I should go," Dad murmurs. He pulls his jacket off the back of the chair. "Emmitt, I…." He doesn't seem to know how to finish the sentence. "I'll see you soon."

Then he leaves.

I notice Casey staring at me from the bedroom doorway.

"Wow," he says.

"Pretty much."

Casey comes over and sits down at the table. "Sorry, Emmitt."

"What are you sorry for?"

He shrugs. "You okay?"

I shrug back. "Will be."

"He had that coming, you know."

Did he? I'm not sure he did. But I'm not sure of much these days. Casey ends up turning the TV on to some stupid cop show, and we spend most of the next hour watching it. We don't say another word to each other about our father.

I'M ALL set to spend Thursday morning obsessing over what happened with Dad the night before, but Aleks Krysjevski changes those plans.

I'm still eating breakfast when Casey finishes up and flops down on the couch to watch TV. Lately we've been avoiding the sports channels— just in case—but he starts to flip past one and flips right back to it.

"Emmitt!" he calls hoarsely.

I get up and head over to the couch, where this headline is scrolling across the screen: *Vancouver Canucks player Aleks Krysjevski announces he's bisexual… says he was inspired to come out by teen hockey player….*

The anchors are talking about some football player who got arrested for DUI, so Casey starts flipping through the other channels, looking for someone else with more information. It only takes him three tries.

The reporter's already halfway through the story, but at least we catch some of it. "Krysjevski cited teenager Emmitt LaPoint, the sixteen-year-old boy who kissed his boyfriend very publicly after winning a state semifinal hockey game last week, as a primary reason he's finally decided to come out to the hockey community." They flash a statement from Krysjevski on the screen while the reporter reads it aloud. "Mr. LaPoint and other young people like him have been leading the charge on making the sports world realize how close-minded we can be. I've finally realized that a sixteen-year-old shouldn't have to be my role model; I should be a role model to the sixteen-year-olds in the world. What Emmitt LaPoint said in his interview about never having seen a gay hockey player got to me. How else will our youth know that it's okay for them to be themselves if we don't show them it is okay? He had incredible bravery when he chose to trust his team. We all need to have that same bravery. We need to believe others will be better at accepting us than we are at accepting ourselves. My team was amazing when I told them of my bisexuality, and I'm proud to be a Canuck."

"Holy shit," I whisper. Again.

Casey just blinks at the TV. "It sure isn't 1996 anymore," he says.

That should set me up to have an excellent day. I helped inspire the first NHL player in history to come out of the closet.

But I still arrive at Colby High in a crappy mood.

For one thing, Dusty texts me that he and Coach are running late, and I shouldn't wait for him to do our locker routine. This shouldn't bother me as much as it does; I'll have plenty of time to talk to him at lunch. But I wanted to talk to Dusty about what happened with Dad last night, and I'm not going to do that surrounded by our lunch crowd.

Then I get to English class and our teacher, Mr. Postelly, comes up and slaps me on the back in front of everyone while the class is filling up.

"Emmitt, you saw the news?" he practically shouts. "This is incredible! The first openly LGTBQ player in the NHL—and all because of you!" A few people clap and look impressed or ask what happened, but the whole situation is mostly just embarrassing.

Then, between English and AP history, I check my e-mail on my phone. Tons of junk from more news outlets who want to talk to me— and nothing from any scouts.

Until Dad mentioned the scout last night, I hadn't thought much about how none of them have contacted me. I guess I figured if people like Sidney Crosby were talking about me, then I didn't have to worry about the scouting thing right now—that I just needed to play my best hockey and show them what I could do. If those big NHL players don't care that I'm gay, why would any scouts?

But what if Dad's right? What if they're waiting to see how I handle this? What if they want to see me tweeting and doing interviews and winning the state championship, just to prove that I'll never let media attention get to me?

What if I should have taken Dad up on that interview instead of screaming at him?

After AP history is a free period. I'm in the library staring down at some math problems that are swimming in front of me when Mel and Eric plop down next to me.

"Hey!" says Mel. "Did you see the news this morning?"

I glare at her. "Even if I hadn't, my English teacher decided to announce the news in front of our whole class."

"So?" She pulls some textbooks out of her bag. "Emmitt, do you have any idea how big this is? *The first bi player in the NHL!* And *you* made it happen! You should be dancing right now!"

"I don't dance," I tell her grouchily.

"What's up with you?" asks Eric as he pulls a tablet out of his bag. "Are reporters stalking you about this or something?"

I shrug. "Yeah, I guess they are. It's more like who's not stalking me. My dad dropped by last night... reminded me that there haven't exactly been a lot of scouts in touch with me."

Eric rolls his eyes. "Emmitt, calm down. Half the hockey world is in love with you right now. Stop worrying about scouts."

"Easy for you to say. You didn't just come out to the entire country," I murmur.

"Yeah, well, I also didn't have Alex Krysjevski talking about me on national television this morning," Eric says, a little loudly. Some girl a table away looks up from her laptop to shush us.

"Boys, boys," Mel interrupts—quietly. "Both of you, chill out. Emmitt, stop freaking yourself out about this. Eric's right, there's nothing to worry about. And Eric, don't be an asshole."

"I'm not an asshole," Eric tells her. He's trying to keep his voice down, but he's not doing a very good job. "He always does this! Takes up the entire spotlight and then manages to get pissed off about it."

"I do not!" I hiss at him. "I thought you were on my side."

"I'm trying to be!" he hisses back. "But you make it pretty hard when all you do is complain."

"You think this is easy?" Now my hiss has definitely risen to more of a low growl. "I didn't want any of this. I just want to play hockey. I don't want to have to be different, or be a poster child, or worry about whether scouts are going to love me or hate me because I'm into guys. I just want to *play hockey*."

"And you can and you are," Mel adds. "Listen, Emmitt, take a moment to be grateful for that, will you? Ten years ago if someone had done what you did after the semifinals… well, it probably wouldn't have gotten tweets from NHL players, you know? You owe the fact that you're still playing hockey right now to a lot of people who stood up for themselves, and for you, before you ever did what you did the other night. And Eric, you *are* being an asshole. You have no idea what it's like to wonder every day if people are going to accept you. To be terrified to say certain things out loud."

That speech gets me off my high horse fast, and it seems to take Eric down at the same time. We frown at each other.

"I'm sorry," I finally say. "You're right. I need to stop freaking out and just… take things as they come. And be grateful. I sort of wigged out and yelled at my dad last night."

"Yeah, I'm sorry too," says Eric. "What happened with your dad?"

"He set up this interview for me with *Hockey News* and I didn't want it."

Mel and Eric both gape at me. Mel keeps laughing, and Laptop Girl shushes us again.

"Only you," Eric finally says, "could get pissed off at someone for getting you an interview with the best hockey magazine in the country."

It's not a bad point.

I manage to get some math problems done after that, and by the time study hall is over, I feel slightly better. Eric and I are walking to lunch together, because Mel had to go talk to her photography teacher, when he stops me just a few feet outside of the library. "Can I talk to you?" he asks.

"Sure." I'm wary. Is he going to give me more crap for what I said?

"Listen." He's fidgeting and shifting his backpack a lot, which isn't like him at all. "I did something bad. Really bad. I've been afraid to tell you... but I have to. What you said earlier, about never being sure if people accept you or not... I screwed up once. I did something I'm not proud of. I have to tell you. It's killing me not to tell you."

I don't know what to say to *any* of that. So finally I just nod. "Uh. Tell me."

"You know that video Rick had?"

My stomach lining starts to coil slightly. I have a horrible feeling I know what he's about to say.

"I took it. I'm the one who gave it to Rick."

I step back from him like he just told me he has the bubonic plague.

"Emmitt," he says, and his voice has a pleading note in it I've never heard from him before, "you have to understand. I didn't plan it or anything. I was at the rink, and I saw you and Dusty that day, and it—it shocked me or whatever. I didn't even think about it; I just pulled out my phone."

"You always automatically pull out your phone when you see someone kissing?" My voice doesn't even sound angry. Just... hollow.

"No! No. The whole thing was just... surprising. I took the video without even thinking about it. Maybe I thought you'd deny it if I tried to talk to you about it? Honestly, dude, I don't even know what I was doing."

That brings up a whole slew of questions. "But you didn't talk to me," I say hoarsely. "You gave the video to Rick."

He shifts his weight awkwardly again. "That was an accident too. I didn't know how to talk to you. Or if I should. So I just kept not talking to you, and not saying anything to anyone, and in the meantime you were getting all this attention I wanted to be getting. I was more and more pissed off at you every day. I even convinced myself for a while that Coach was giving you more ice time than me because you were dating Dusty. That's crazy, I know. Coach would never do that, and you earn your ice time. But I was mad.

"And then I saw Rick at this party right after he got out of juvie. I was pissed off and drunk, and you'd just pulled off that hat trick in the game against Missisquoi. I started talking to Rick, and he got me going about what a dick you are.... Emmitt, I don't even remember sending him anything. I didn't even know I did. But when you told me he had a video of you and Dusty, I knew where it must have come from."

"But you still didn't tell me." Somehow I'm still not shouting. Or even raising my voice.

"No." He shakes his head. "I couldn't. I couldn't admit I'd pulled such an asshole move. And maybe the worst part of the whole thing? I know now that the entire time you were going through all this—keeping everything a secret, and you and Dusty breaking up, and both of you having to tell everyone—I could have helped you a lot sooner. I could have been there for you. I was just too busy being pissed off."

"Yeah." I shake my head. "I guess so."

"You think... can you ever let it go? I am so sorry, man. For everything."

I believe him. But I'm not sure it's enough.

"Can you sit somewhere else at lunch today?" I finally ask him. "I need some space from you."

He nods. "Yeah. I can do that." He turns and starts to walk away before he turns back quickly. "I can't even explain how sorry I am, Emmitt. Especially for what happened to Dusty. Tell him I'm sorry, when you tell him about this. Okay?"

I just nod again.

Then watch him walk away.

CHAPTER
NINETEEN

Dear Mr. LeClair,

Have I told you how weird Casey has been acting lately? Ever since Dad moved out. Well, it's gotten even worse since he left for good and went to Ohio. At least before he was at Uncle Dave's house and we still saw him once in a while.

First Casey quit hockey. Just stopped going to practice one day. I thought his coach was going to cry. And he wouldn't say why either. He just kept saying that hockey is lame.

Then he asked Mom to buy him a skateboard. We don't have a lot of money right now, but she did it anyway. Prolly she was just so happy he was finally going to leave the couch. He has been watching lots of TV since Dad left.

Then he started hanging out with these kids at school who are crazy weird. They all dress in these way-tight jeans and shirts and some of them wear makeup. Like eyeliner and stuff. Some of them skateboard and stuff too. Casey has been hanging out with them at the park near our school all the time.

Yesterday he came out of his bedroom, and he was wearing all black with these crazy tight pants. They looked hella stupid on him.

Mom wasn't home, and I didnt know if I should say something. I'm in charge in the mornings, so I thought maybe I should.

Then I thought about how Casey never tried to tell me to quit hockey just because he did. And someday, maybe I'll want to tell Casey about how weird I am. That I don't want to go to the movies with Mary this weekend. And if I ever tell Casey that stuff, I don't want him to tell me I have to be like everyone else is.

"Interesting look," I told him. "It... it looks decent on you."

He smiled all big. It was prolly the first time Casey smiled since Dad left.

—Emmitt LaPoint, age 13

"You're kidding. It was all Eric's fault? The whole thing?"

Dusty and I are walking to my truck after practice—which Eric didn't come to. Coach said something about him not feeling well, but he definitely looked my way when he said it. So I'm assuming Eric spilled to Coach after he talked to me. I didn't want to tell Dusty the story at lunch, with everyone else sitting there, so I asked him to wait for me during practice and come over to my place afterward.

"Yup. He kept apologizing, and he wanted to make sure I told you he said he was sorry. At least he knows he put you through a bunch of crap."

We hop into the cab, and Dusty starts playing with the radio stations the second I've turned over the engine. It's always the first thing he does whenever he gets into my truck, I've noticed. "What do we do?" he asks.

"I don't know." I've been trying to figure that out all day. "I mean, he's still my teammate. And he was my friend. And he's the one who helped me tell the team, and helped get Rick off our backs—"

"That was mostly Mel and Samantha," Dusty interjects.

"But he asked them for help. And he was there for us after I kissed you that day." I shake my head again. "But all that time, he knew. And he never said anything. And he gave a video of us to Rick."

"Which he says he doesn't remember doing."

"I guess." I decide the truck's probably warmed up enough for us to leave, and I steer us out of the parking lot as Dusty keeps flipping through stations. Eventually he settles on that old song about being with Julio down by a schoolyard.

"Your taste in music is crazy," I tell him.

"Whatever. I've always liked this song. Mom used to play it... it always made me feel better about how I wasn't like everyone else."

"Huh?" I've definitely never paid that much attention to this song.

"The lines about being taken away. How what the mama saw was against the law. I used to think maybe it was about someone who was gay too."

Huh. We listen to the song together in silence as I pull the truck up into my driveway and park. The song ends, and Dusty flips off the radio.

"Maybe what Eric did wasn't so bad," he says.

"What do you mean?" I ask incredulously. "Because of him, Rick blackmailed you for months. We broke up, remember?"

Dusty's looking at the window. "Yeah… and then because all of that happened, we ended up being able to tell people." Dusty finally turns and looks at me. "I know you don't love being all over the news and Facebook, and you're freaked by what your dad said about scouts… but Emmitt, look at all the *good* things that have happened. You and I getting back together and not having to hide anymore. Doug yelling at the person who threw that roll at you. NHL players talking about you. An NHL player *coming out* because of you."

"And because of you," I remind him.

"And because of Eric. Kind of," he adds hastily when he sees the look on my face. "None of this would have happened if it wasn't for him."

"Maybe you're right. But when I think about everything you went through with Rick…." My hands tighten on the steering wheel just imagining Rick contacting Dusty. Threatening him. Laughing at him.

Dusty laughs. "Don't get me wrong—this whole protective vibe you have going is pretty hot. But don't waste it on me, Emmitt. Eric's your friend, and he's saved the day just as much as he's fucked it up. Forgive him or forget on your own terms, not mine."

That's something to think about.

I'm about to push the truck's door open when I notice something: sitting in the driveway, next to my mother's car, is a silver Chevy Volt. "That's Dad's rental car," I tell Dusty. "Crap. Want to go to your house?"

"Emmitt, you're going to have to talk to him eventually."

"I don't feel like talking to him right now. Seriously, let's go to your house." I start the engine back up.

"Um, Emmitt…." Dusty points out the window. My father is walking toward the car.

"Great." I turn the engine off again as he knocks on the window.

I go against my better judgment and roll it down for him. "Uh, hi, Dad. Dusty and I were just about to go to his house."

"Oh." Dad frowns. "And you decided that right after seeing my car, I assume." He looks across the seat to Dusty. "It's nice to finally meet you."

Dusty nods at him warily. "You too, Mr. LaPoint."

Dad turns back to me. "Listen, can we talk, Emmitt?"

"What do you want to talk about?" I'm trying to keep any frustration out of my voice. The guy *did* get me an interview with *Hockey News*. It may not have been what I wanted him to do, but I probably shouldn't keep classifying it like an international crime.

"I want to apologize. And talk through all this. Can I take you out to dinner?"

"Is Casey coming?"

Dad shakes his head. "He's... not exactly talking to me."

I think about that for a minute. Maybe it's time we all buried the hatchet around a few things. But if I'm going to give Dad another chance, it's going to be on my terms this time. "I'll go to dinner with you, Dad. But only if Dusty can come too. And I'll get Casey to come."

Dad's eyes skip past me and back to Dusty. He suddenly looks slightly apprehensive. I guess it's one thing to know your son's gay; taking his boyfriend out to dinner is probably something different entirely. But those are the terms I'm sticking to.

"Okay," he says, and I'm surprised how little hesitation there is in his voice.

"Dusty? You up for dinner?" I ask, because I just realized I never even included him in this conversation.

But he's smiling slightly. "Course, Emmitt."

I text Casey. *Get ur ass out here. We're going to dinner with Dad. I need you.*

It takes him less than thirty seconds to text back. *We?*

Dusty's coming. Please? Need u there.

The next text back takes a little longer. Finally I get a *Fine. U owe me.*

"Casey's coming," I tell Dad and Dusty. Dusty's shoulders sag with relief.

"Great!" Dad beams. "We'll take my car."

We end up at Nino's, a pizza place that serves high-end pasta and pizza. It's Casey's favorite place to eat, and none of us are complaining.

We get through the car ride, sitting down in the restaurant, and the ordering phase with a whole lot of small talk and mumbled answers from Casey. *It's so nice to be having dinner with you boys. Dusty, I understand you're on the skateboarding team with Casey? And that Coach Morton is your uncle?* It's actually amazing how much my father has retained from the short and sporadic phone conversations we've had with him over the past few months.

We're waiting for the pizza when Dad starts edging us toward the subject we're all not talking about. "Emmitt," he says, "I'm glad we all came out to dinner together. Dusty, I'm glad I finally got to meet you."

Dusty nods back respectfully, even though he's not exactly smiling. "Me too, sir."

"You could have met him anytime you wanted, Dad," Casey interjects, and his facial expression is definitely closer to a scowl than a smile. "You never asked. You took off the day after you found out they were dating."

I glance around quickly to make sure no one's hearing this—Colby already knows enough about my private life, thank you very much. Luckily the restaurant isn't that full, and most people are busy with their food.

"I know." Dad nods again. "I should have made more of an effort, Emmitt, to stay involved after that last game of the season. But I did have to get back to work. Leaving wasn't exactly my choice."

"It was your choice to move to Ohio," Casey mutters. "It was your choice to marry some other chick after you left Mom."

I almost tell him to stop being a dick, but I don't. Why shouldn't he get to say exactly what's on his mind? This is his father too.

"Yes, it was," Dad says. "And I'm sorry that was hard on you boys. I'm sorry you both seem to feel I haven't been involved enough over the years. I've tried—"

"You didn't try, Dad," I interrupt. "That's why Casey's pissed. Sure, you called. You sent stuff from time to time. You helped out with the truck. But you never visited, and you never asked us to visit you. It was like… one day we were your kids, and the next day we weren't. Like you suddenly had this new wife and this new family, and we didn't matter anymore."

Under the table, Dusty grabs my hand and squeezes it.

Dad shakes his head. "I can see how things feel that way to both of you. But you need to understand… I always wanted you to be my boys. You *are* my boys. Emmitt, what you said to me in the locker room that day—about me always taking the easy way out—you're right; I was doing what I thought was easiest. But not for me. I thought what I was doing was the easiest thing for *you*. I honestly thought it would be easier for you both if you didn't have to get to know a whole new family, or see me and your mom fight every time I visit. I thought I was making the break cleaner, somehow. It appears I had that wrong."

Casey looks skeptical. "You honestly thought it would be easier for us if you basically stopped showing up?"

Dad's clearly uncomfortable. "Yes. I honestly did. And I need you to both believe me when I say it wasn't easy for me. I've missed you so much over the years. I've missed being there for you so many times." He sighs heavily. "I want to be here for you now, Emmitt. That's all I was doing when I tried to set up that interview; I promise. I was just trying to be there for you."

Eric's words are on repeat in my head. *Only you could get pissed at someone for getting you an interview with the best hockey magazine in the country.*

"Did you cancel it?" I ask him.

He nods. "I did. Only now that Krysjevski's come out, they're even more interested."

I snort. "Yeah. That figures."

"It does," Dad says. "It's huge, Emmitt, as I'm sure you know. The first NHL player to come out—this is a historical moment. And it's all happening because of you. I'm proud of you, Emmitt. You have more courage than I could ever imagine having."

I don't even know what to say to that. Under the table, Dusty squeezes my hand again.

"Does that mean you're not worried about scouts losing interest in him?" Casey asks. There's still an edge to his voice, but the malice that was there before seems to be gone now.

"I'll always worry," Dad tells him. "About both of you. Because you're my kids. Even if I don't always act like it. But I'm ready to change that if you're ready to let me. The invite to Ohio this summer still stands. It will always stand."

The waitress arrives with the pizza, and for a few minutes we all concentrate on choosing slices and passing them around. Dusty's spending a lot of time staring at his pizza, and I have a feeling he's thinking about his dad. Who didn't even bother to show up when Julia was in the hospital.

"I'll come to Ohio," I tell Dad. "After hockey camp."

"You will?" A slow smile spreads its way across Dad's face. Casey looks up, surprised.

"People make mistakes," I tell him. "But… if we're gonna get to know each other again, I want you to get to know the real me. So I want to bring Dusty to Ohio with me."

Casey chokes on his pizza.

"Uh, Emmitt—" Dusty says.

"No, no," Dad says, putting up his hand. He draws in a breath and smiles at Dusty. It's forced, but not as forced as I expected it to be. "Dusty, I'd love to have you visit this summer. If your uncle's okay with it, of course."

"Well… okay. Thanks," Dusty says quietly.

Casey rolls his eyes. "Fine, I'll go too," he says loudly. We all turn to stare at him. "What? It's… Ohio. What the hell's in Ohio? You two won't even know what to do without me."

I smirk at him. "I'm sure we'd figure out something."

Dad's face suddenly reddens. "You'll be staying in separate bedrooms, of course," he adds quickly.

Then *I* turn red.

Dusty takes a bite of pizza. "I'm excited for this trip," he tells us all calmly. Not a hint of sarcasm in sight.

Dad smiles at him. "Me too," he says. "Me too."

I DRIVE Dusty back to his house after dinner. We're almost in his driveway before he brings up the Eric thing again.

"So after that touching reconciliation scene with your father," he says, "you going to have one with Eric too?"

I glare at him. "You're hilarious. I dunno, Dusty. It's like… there aren't a lot of people I've trusted in the past few years. Maybe in my whole life. Mom, Casey, you. Eric. Knowing he did what he did is… well, what am I supposed to do with that?"

Dusty nods. "I guess I get that." He pauses. "Hey, do you still write letters to John LeClair? You know, the ones you said you used to write?"

I have no idea where he's going with this. "Yeah. Not recently, I guess, but yeah."

He nods. "I know you never send any of them or anything, but does it ever feel like you know him? Like he knows you?"

I pull the truck into the driveway. "If I say yes, don't I sound crazy?"

Dusty laughs. "No. That's actually the point I was trying to make. You probably trust John LeClair more than almost anyone on the planet, and I bet he has no memory of ever even meeting you. Probably would have no idea who you were if it wasn't for the news. Who knows if he's even okay with you being gay? But that isn't what matters, you know? What matters is he was the person you talked to when you needed someone to talk to. Even if he didn't know it."

I never thought about that. "I guess you're right. But I still don't get where you're going with this."

He shrugs. "I'm just saying… not everyone is going to be everything you've built them up to be in your head. Not everyone's going to live up to your expectations."

"Just like I can't always live up to everyone else's expectations?" I smile at him wryly.

He leans over and kisses me. "I'll see you tomorrow, okay?"

WHEN I get home that night, I text Eric.

It's okay, I tell him. *Shit happens. I'm over it.*

Five minutes later he texts back. *That was fast.*

Truth.

Game's Saturday. No time for grudges.

U really over it? he wants to know.

Maybe I'm not. But I'm at least close.

If I'm not, will b.

He doesn't answer for a while. Finally, he sends back this: *we r going to kick ass Saturday.*

Yeah. We are.

CHAPTER
TWENTY

Dear Mr. LeClair,

You probably don't remember me, because I bet you meet a lot of hockey fans. But we met when I was seven.

You've been, like, a hero to me ever since. Before you, I didn't think people like me from small towns in Vermont got to play in the NHL. Ever since I met you and realized I could have that, it's all I've ever wanted. For years I've worked as hard as I could. Hockey camps, extra practices, Saturday and Sunday workouts. Whatever it took.

I'm a junior now, and this Saturday my team is playing in the state championship. There are some colleges and other hockey programs looking at me, or at least I think there still are. There were.

Then something happened. About a week ago, I kissed my boyfriend after our team won the semifinals. And now the whole world knows I'm gay.

Here's the weird thing, Mr. LeClair. You don't know this, but I've actually been writing letters to you since I was seven. I never sent any of them. I just kept writing to you. About hockey and my life. About things that made me happy and things that stressed me out. You've been listening to me for almost ten years, and you don't even know it.

The world's been a weird and scary place this past week, but I think I'm doing okay, all things considered. I'm excited to play some hockey this Saturday. I'm excited to go on real dates with my boyfriend instead of just hiding in his uncle's living room. I'm excited to finally send you a letter telling you who I am. Who I really am.

Thanks a lot, John LeClair. I don't mean that in the sarcastic way some people do when they say it. I'm being sincere. Thanks for being someone I've always looked up to, and for being the person I wanted to become. Thanks for listening to me for all these years, even if you didn't know you were.

Who knows what you'll think of me once you read this letter. Who knows if you'll even read it. Either way, I wanted to write it. I wanted to send it. I've been saving the e-mail address you gave me for over nine years.

Thanks a lot. For everything.

—Emmitt LaPoint, age 16

I SEND a letter to John LeClair for the first time on Friday. The day before the state championship.

Dusty's sitting at the foot of my locker when I get to school. He's reading a book. "Hey," I say, kicking him gently in the ankle. "Whatcha reading?"

He stretches out and shows me the cover. *The Hockey Guidebook.* "I figured I should finally understand everything that happens during one of your games."

I slide down the lockers so I'm sitting next to him. His hair is all tousled and sticking up around his head, and he's wearing these old jeans that are so ratty they look like they're going to fall off at any second, and I just want to kiss him right then and there. Then I realize something: I can. It doesn't matter that there's people all around us. All of them know.

"You're fucking hot when you read about hockey," I whisper, and I lean over just long enough to brush my lips against his. Dusty looks surprised for exactly one second, and then he just looks happy.

I don't look around to see what expression anyone else in the hallway is wearing. It doesn't matter.

"That was so *adorable!*" I hear a voice whisper from somewhere nearby. "I totally bet they make out again if we win tomorrow."

Dusty and I just look at each other.

"We're being fetishized," I murmur. "Gross."

"Yeah," Dusty agrees. "But I can think of worse things for people to say about us."

I guess that's true. At least no one's chucking bread rolls at our heads.

And I get through the day without any real weirdness or further bread roll incidents. Eric and I are a little awkward around each other during lunch, but it's not so bad that it will affect our playing. We'll get over it.

Mostly the day is just a lot of pats on the back and people telling me good luck. Not *that* different from any other Friday before a game.

Until we get to practice.

It starts the same way they always do: warm-ups, drills. We're in the middle of a scrimmage when Coach calls out, "Henner! Go in for Emmitt!"

Play goes on as I skate to the boards. Coach beckons me over to where he's standing next to some stranger wearing a Canucks jacket.

I make the awkward walk on skates over to them, and the stranger turns around.

My mouth goes dry. It's *Aleks Krysjevski*.

Coach is smiling widely. "Emmitt, you know who this is?"

"Uh, yeah." That seems to be all I'm capable of saying. I pull my right hand out of my glove while I get myself together. "I mean, of course. Mr. Krysjevski, it's... it's nice to meet you. Really nice to meet you. Amazing, actually."

He shakes my hand. Hard. Seriously—this guy's got a dangerous grip. "Mr. LaPoint. It is good to meet you." He's got a thick accent. Eastern European, I think, but I can't remember exactly where he's originally from. "I have a game in Montreal this Sunday. I decided to stop here first and meet the person who has been such an inspiration for me."

I pull my helmet off. "No, sir. You're the inspiration. What you did... wow. It's amazing."

Jack's looking back and forth between us and the ice, where one of the assistant coaches is whistling a play dead. "I should check on things out there. Why don't you two go back to my office for a few minutes? Then Aleks can meet the team when we're done with practice?"

"It would be my honor," says Aleks. The *NHL player*.

I put on my skate guards and follow him.

"I hope you don't mind that I have stopped by without warning," Aleks tells me when we're sitting across from each other in the small room.

"Are you kidding?" I blurt out. "You can come to our hockey practices anytime!"

He laughs. "Thank you. You are an impressive person, Emmitt. Impressive athlete, courageous. You'll go far."

My face must fall slightly when he says that, because he asks me, "You do not think so?"

I shrug. "A lot of people think that about me. It's…." I can't quite figure out how to put it.

"Difficult to live up to," Aleks says. "Yes, I understand what you mean. I have felt that way before. As though so many people were resting their hopes on me. That is one reason I kept my secret for so long."

"Me too, I guess," I tell him.

"Ah! Then you see." He shrugs his shoulders. "You have nothing to worry about. You are the one of us who was brave enough to stop worrying what they thought."

"I don't think it was bravery," I tell him. "More like… I didn't have a choice left."

He shakes his head. "I know that is not true. There is always a choice." He nods appreciatively. "And you made a hard one. This is impressive."

I don't know exactly what to say to that. "Thanks," I finally go with.

"Your coach tells me you are concerned you will not play hockey anymore after high school."

Looks like Dusty and Coach have been talking. I'm not surprised. "I just… I worry, you know?"

He waves a hand dismissively. "All you need to worry about is your playing, Emmitt. These… sorts of things… will bother some coaches, and they will not bother others."

That does make sense. The NTDP scout sure wasn't upset about me coming out.

"Yeah?" I ask him. "I mean, I worry about that, and I worry that I'm not good enough. I just want to play hockey. For as long as I can."

"I am certain you will play hockey, as long as you keep up your hard work and level of play."

"No pressure," I jokingly say.

"Of course there is always pressure," he tells me seriously, and I realize he missed my joke. "That is what makes it fun."

Maybe he's right.

"I still can't believe you're here," I tell him.

"I am glad I got to meet you, Emmitt," Aleks tells me. "I am glad you made me realize it was time professional hockey changed. I look forward to playing with you one day. By then, I think, we will look back and be surprised at how things were now."

"You think so?" And I mean both parts—us playing together, and us playing in a world where none of this matters.

"I'm sure of it." He smiles and stands up. "I look forward to meeting your team. The way they supported you is also very impressive."

"Yeah," I tell him. "It is."

He claps me on the back. "Don't be too nervous tomorrow. You will do fine."

I follow him out of the office. Dusty and Casey are standing at the side of the rink—I almost forgot they were waiting to get a ride home after practice. Dusty gestures widely at Aleks. *He came to see you!* he mouths at me.

Captain Obvious in the house. *I know*, I mouth back. Even Casey looks impressed.

I'll definitely be nervous tomorrow. But I think I'll be okay.

I've got a lot of amazing people on my side.

SO THERE I am, staring down a player from Middlebury for the opening face-off. His eyes are narrow behind his face mask, and he's not taking his eyes off me.

Because this is the state fucking championship.

"Emmitt, you can do it!" There's Mom.

"You've got this, Emmitt!" That's Casey.

"Play hard, son!" And that's… Dad. Cheering for me. From the stands.

Time to block out the crowd noise and work up some serious concentration. But first I look up into the stands. There's one more face I need to see. Sitting next to my biological family is my other family: Mrs. Morton, Julia, and Matt.

And Dusty.

He's cheering loudly along with everyone else. When he sees me looking, he pulls something out from under his jacket and holds it up.

It's the medal. The one I gave to him on Valentine's Day. The one he gave back to me the day I thought I'd lost him forever.

The one I returned to him this morning, just before we left to drive to the game together.

Next week is the spring dance, which we'll probably go to. And it will be weird at first, being at a dance with another guy. Weird for us, and probably weird for other people too. But Dusty and I will be together, and everyone else will get over it.

And someday soon I'll hopefully have big decisions to make. Maybe about whether to leave Colby and spend the rest of high school in a place like Michigan, or maybe about which college program to go play for. Maybe someday even what NHL jersey to wear. I'll be incredibly lucky to have to make any of those choices.

But wherever I end up, it won't change how I feel about Dusty, or how he feels about me. I don't know what the future will be for us, but I know one thing: he'll always be the kid in the dirty jeans who made being the real me worth all the trouble.

The ref blows the whistle, and the puck drops.

Game on.

JOHANNA PARKHURST grew up on a small dairy farm in northern Vermont before relocating to the rocky mountains of Colorado. She spends her days helping teenagers learn to read and write and her evenings writing things she hopes they'll like to read. She strives to share stories of young adults who are as determined, passionate, and complex as the ones she shares classrooms with.

Johanna holds degrees from Albertus Magnus College and Teachers College, Columbia University. She loves traveling, hiking, skiing, and yelling at the TV during football and hockey season.

E-mail: johannawriteson@gmail.com
Twitter: @johannawriteson

Fact: When Zebulon Pike attempted to climb what is now known as Pikes Peak, he got stuck in waist-deep snow and had to turn back.

That's the last thing Dusty Porter learns in his Colorado history class before appendicitis ruins his life. It isn't long before social services figures out that Dusty's parents are more myth than reality, and he and his siblings are shipped off to live in Vermont with an uncle and aunt they've never met.

Dusty's new life is a struggle. His brother and sister don't seem to need him anymore, and he can't stand his aunt and uncle. At school, one hockey player develops a personal vendetta against him, while Emmitt, another hockey player, is making it hard for Dusty to keep pretending he's straight. Problem is, he's pretty sure Emmitt's not gay. Then, just when Dusty thinks things can't get any worse, his mother reappears, looking for a second chance to be a part of his life.

Somehow Zebulon Pike still got the mountain named after him, so Dusty's determined to persevere—but at what point in life do you keep climbing, and when do you give up and turn back?

www.harmonyinkpress.com

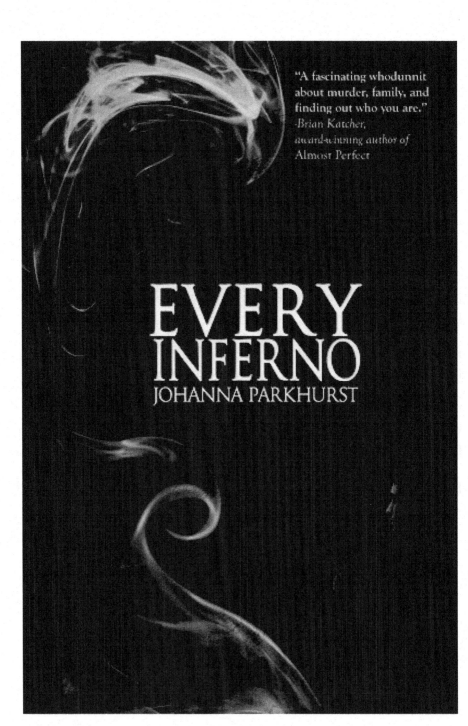

EVERY
INFERNO
JOHANNA PARKHURST

Depressed. Defiant. Possible alcoholic. These are just a few of the terms used to describe fifteen-year-old Jacob Jasper Jones. Lately, though, JJ has a new one to add to the list: detective. He's been having strange dreams about the fire that killed his parents ten years ago, and he thinks he finally has the clue to catching the arsonist who destroyed his family.

A murder investigation isn't the only thing the dreams trigger for JJ. They also lead to secret meetings with his estranged sister, an unlikely connection with a doctor who lost his daughter in the fire, and a confusing friendship with McKinley, a classmate of JJ's who seems determined to help him solve the mystery.

All JJ wants is to shake the problems that have followed him since that fire, and he's convinced he must catch the arsonist to do it. But as JJ struggles to find the culprit, he sees there's more than one mystery in his life he needs to solve.

www.harmonyinkpress.com

Also from Harmony Ink Press

THE ONGOING REFORMATION OF
MICAH JOHNSON

SEAN KENNEDY

www.harmonyinkpress.com

Also from Harmony Ink Press

www.harmonyinkpress.com